A Curious Pebble

The Hollow Earth and Pursuit of the Holy Lance

More Books by the Authors

There's Only One of us Here! A Guide for Aspiring Lightworkers
by David DiPietro Weiss   2012   127 pages $12.95

Impressions from Yonder Soul: Truth & Belief / Choice & Intuition
by David DiPietro Weiss   2015   70 pages $11.95

The Hollow Earth: Revisited
by Danny L. Weiss   2013   320 pages $15.95

Voices From Within

David DiPietro Weiss SoulTalk series   36-44 p. $5.95

1 – *A Contract with your Soul / Rebirthing into Spirit* (2015)

2 – *The Dilemma of the Third Dimension / The Spiritual Laws of Opportunity / Enlightenment* (2016)

3 – *Love, Actually / Possibility Consciousnesss / Astral-Energy Events / The Spirit is Moved by Choice* (2016)

4 – *There is no God! / The Story of Haiku / Haiku poems* (2017)

5 – *Thoughts on Ethical Eating / The Foundation of Spiritual Awakening* (2017)

6 – *Free Will: Truth or Wishful Thinking? / Why Do We Write? / Poems from the Soul* (2017)

7 – *Illusion / Salt of the Earth: A Song for My Father* (2017)

Available from:
www.riversanctuarypublishing.com

A Curious Pebble

The Hollow Earth and Pursuit of the Holy Lance

David DiPietro Weiss

with Danny L. Weiss

Cover Design by Melanie Gendron

Printed in the United States of America

ISBN 978-1-935914-78-5

To order additional copies please visit:

www.riversanctuarypublishing.com

RIVER SANCTUARY PUBLISHING
P.O Box 1561
Felton, CA 95018
www.riversanctuarypublishing.com
Dedicated to the awakening of the New Earth

Contents

PREFACE

Ancient Nordic legend postulates that the structure of the earth developed as it cooled from its molten state during its planetary formation. The rotation of the new planet created a centrifugal force that caused the heavier substances, rocks and metals, to be thrown outward towards its periphery where they established its outer crust, leaving the interior hollow with openings at the poles. The original fiery and incandescent materials remained in the center of the earth as a central sun, much smaller than our sun, but capable of emitting light and supporting animal and plant growth. The Northern lights phenomenon, known as the Aurora Borealis that illuminates the Arctic sky, emanates from the central sun as its rays shine through the polar opening.

The legend tells of Odin, the Sky God and Allfather who lives in Asgarth, the citadel of the Gods in the center of the earth. It is here where the masters live. It is here where the Gods live in paradise. It is here that man is forbidden to enter. It is here, says the philosopher Plato, "where the God who sits in the center, on the navel of the earth, is the interpreter of religion to all mankind."

These legends form the backdrop for this story. The characters, except for those noted as historical figures, are fictional. The story is mostly fictional; however, many of the incidents and depictions are based upon biblical, historical, experiences, spiritual beliefs, and speculations emanating from both legend and fact.

For example, the idea of the Hollow Earth is not a mere fabrication. It is not commonly known that the Smithsonian Museum in

Washington D.C. was established after the U.S. Congress commissioned an expedition to search for the entrance to the hollow earth in 1838. The expedition did not find the entrance, but gathered many objects and artifacts during the trek which ultimately became the first exhibits to inaugurate the national museum. Author David DiPietro Weiss, when he visited the Smithsonian in the 1980s, found an entire room dedicated to this mission including models of a hollow earth along with maps and pertinent artifacts and articles. The room has since been archived as a customary practice of exhibit rotation for the museum.

In addition, the history and significance of the Holy Lance is a dominant theme of the entire book. Its importance dominates the premise of the book. Chapter Seven gives an extensive account of the legends regarding the Lance – the spear of Longinus that was used to pierce Jesus' side as he languished on the cross in order to ascertain if he was still alive.

In 1984 -1986, co-author Danny L. Weiss spent extended time with the *Ritter Von X, (Ritter – Knight)* one of many pseudonyms taken to protect his true identity, (see dedication) in extensive personal interviews and was shown artifacts and writings from the Hartmann Expedition that returned the Lance from Antarctica in 1979. He was shown what the Ritter asserted to be a sampling of artifacts returned from the historic Antarctic journey. Ritter Von X claimed to be a crewman of the U-530 that delivered the Lance to the Nazi stronghold in Antarctica in 1945 before surrendering the ship to Argentine authorities. He, throughout the years, proudly displayed his prominent U-530 belt buckle and wore it regularly.

In 1995, Dan had the privilege of visiting with the extensive kin of Admiral Richard E. Byrd and developed a warm relationship with the family, especially Byrd's daughter, Anne Bolling-Byrd Clark. He attended their family gatherings and conferences while hearing more evidence regarding Byrd's flight into the hollow earth and the alleged diary of the journey written by Admiral Byrd.

Co-author Dan also lived in Reykjavik, Iceland for over a year and gathered a myriad of information and insights on Icelandic history, lore, legends and customs. In many aspects, the central characters of the novel, Garrett and Gugga, are based on Dan's life experiences and friendships.

Under the pseudonym Wilhelm Bernhart, the Captain co-authored the book *Adolf Hitler and the Secrets of the Holy Lance.* Bernhart co-wrote the book with an American Colonel, Howard A. Buechner, who had been contacted by Bernhart after the publication of a book by Buechner documenting his witnessing of the liberation of the Dachau concentration camp, just a few miles outside of Munich. Bernhart disputed some of the text regarding the allied recovery of the Lance and showed Buechner several photos and artifacts, as well as the log by the Hartmann expedition that convinced him that Bernhart was correct in his assertion that the Lance had been brought back from Antarctica by the Hartmann expedition. Buechner stated, after interviewing most of the members of the alleged expedition and others involved, including Hitler Youth Leader Artur Axmann, that he had become convinced that Bernhart's claims were true. (Axmann was reportedly at Hitler's bunker and carried off some of Hitler's ashes and helped to bury and set fire to an anonymous couple's bodies in an attempt to confuse the Russians.)

Neither of these books is still available, but original copies remain in the possession of this book's authors, personally signed and dated by both Bernhart and Buechner.

The Ritter also greeted the return of the Hartmann Expedition in 1979 and was gifted a diary of the journey by Hartmann at his home. Much of the diary's content is included in Chapter Six. Also known as *The Captain*, the Ritter was given the opportunity to hold the Lance before it was taken back to Germany. Dan regularly met or corresponded and spoke on the telephone with the Ritter for over ten years. Dan possesses extensive taped recordings of his interviews.

One of the gifts presented to Dan during the time of these interactions, was a geode stone which the Captain referred to as a *curious pebble* (hence the title of the novel). The Captain challenged anyone to identify or cut and examine the pebble, as he maintained that it was delivered by UFO and originated in the inner earth. Dan still has the pebble in his possession.

The Captain chronicled his visits and travels with an inner earth being known as Thal. His descriptions of Thal and his ship are written into the text of this book.

The Captain formed the *International Society for a Complete Earth (ISCE)* in 1977. The leadership and administration of the organization was formally transferred by the Captain to author Danny L. Weiss in 1992. The organization has been renamed the *Hollow Earth Research Society (HERS)*, focusing upon clarifying legend and fact regarding the existence of a Hollow Earth. Visit: (www.hollowearthresearch.org).

We refer often to MIBs (Men In Black), whose folklore and appearances date well before the popular movies of the same name. MIBs are essentially mysterious biologically engineered robots, perhaps from the inner earth and possibly serving as representatives of the Arianni. More detail on the MIBs is included in the footnotes of Chapter Three.

The *Arianni* are the residents of the Hollow Earth. Their central city is known as Asgard or Agartha. Warmed by an inner central sun, they are a highly developed civilization which has been responsible for many, but not all, of the *flugelrad* (German for winged wheel – flying saucer) sightings reported all over the planet.

This book also alludes to the application of ancient Icelandic Runes, an alphabetic system pre-dating Latin that utilizes symbols inscribed on stone or wood. Details on the history of Runes can be found in the footnotes of Chapter Seven. Many of the persons mentioned in the text are real and are footnoted for those interested. The majority of the photos in the book were gifted to author Dan by the Captain.

The *Knights of the Teutonic Order* or *Teutonic Knights,* featured prominently in this book, is an actual organization formed initially in 1191 by a secret organization of Crusaders at the time of King Leopold, dormant until resurrected in 1834 by the Austrian Empire. It still exists today, although secretly and clandestinely, with members spread around the world. The organization is today formally known as the *Knights of the Holy Order of the Sacred Lance,* or simply, *Knights of the Holy Lance.* Their stated mission remains consistent: dedication to the cause of world peace and the freedom of democracy for all people. The group asserts the cause of righteousness directed by the influence of the Holy Lance which represents the Power of the Nordic Gods. They have expressed the intention to reveal themselves at an appropriate time.

Every effort has been made to credit those authors and sources who are the originators of the material whether it be quotations or thematic writings. In most cases the authors have disappeared, died, or dropped out of sight and for various reasons, cannot be identified or contacted. The overwhelming body of information supporting this novel, however, has been obtained by direct interviews or private writings obtained and retained by the co-authors of this book.

Again, this story is a novel. It is a fictional account based on the reported history of the Holy Lance, Icelandic Nordic legends, the questions of the Hollow Earth, and the actual history of German activity on the mysterious continent of Antarctica. It also documents the historical voyages of the German submarines U-530 and U-977 to Antarctica.

We invite you to enjoy this writing from any perspective that resonates with you.

David DiPietro Weiss
Danny L. Weiss

ACKNOWLEDGEMENTS

Writings don't end up as published works without the assistance and inspiration of several participants. We would like to thank and acknowledge the following people who helped bring this book to publication.

Everlasting gratitude and thanks to *Annie Elizabeth*, spouse of co-author David, whose editing skills, lay-out expertise, and general supervision and critique, brought this work to its final published form. A published author in her own right, Annie was instrumental in the fundamental structure of the story.

The personal support and counsel of co-author Dan's spouse, *Irina Podgornova-Weiss*, allowed us to utilize another set of critical eyes and ears to manage that which is true, fantasy or literary in order to keep the manuscript consistent. Her artistic skills contributed to the overall presentation.

And gracious thoughts to *Adra Ross,* whose dedicated review, proofreading, critique and editing helped define the work in its present form. Adra has served in the same capacity to previous books by the author.

Additional appreciation is extended *to Melanie Gendron*, a noted artist who designed and finalized the cover art. Melanie has produced covers and artwork for numerous publications and patrons. Her signature book on Tarot and her accompanying Tarot Deck has become an industry standard.

Thanks and gratitude to *Elizabeth Walker-Goldkuhl* whose poignant encouragement and interest reconvened my destiny to complete the book which we began in 2002.

Yes, and thank you to Gugga, the Icelandic airline flight attendant, whose loving real life presence enhanced the character featured in the story.

A final tribute is to the memory of *Frederick Arthur Weiss,* elder brother of the two authors, and a brilliant savant who maintained throughout his life that in a past life he was Longinus, the Spearman, the foundational possessor of the Holy Lance.

David DiPietro Weiss
Danny L. Weiss

DEDICATION

This book is dedicated to Ritter Von X, also known as, Captain Wilhelm Bernhart, William Bernard, Willie Schaus, or simply, the Captain. He has always used an anonymous name at his request.

It has been a privilege to have met extensively with him at his home in the State of Missouri, and to have corresponded with him for ten years from 1984 through 1994 until his return to what he called his *Heimatland* (Homeland) within – and never to be seen or heard from again.

His knowledge of the Hollow Earth and direct personal experience with Thal, Commander of a Flugelrad (UFO) squadron within the outer magnetic grids of earth between the Northern and Southern poles, has been essential in understanding events.

Ritter Von X was born in Berlin, Germany, joined the Kriegsmarine (German Navy) in 1943, and was assigned to the Reich Undersea Boat Service, U-Boat Flotilla Group, Danzig. He served aboard the U-530 until 1945 when his ship formally surrendered at Mar del Plata, Argentina.

That year he participated in a voyage to Antarctica and served as an intermediary in the recovery of the Holy Lance — (the spear that pierced the side of Jesus Christ) in 1969. In 1979, he assisted in the planning of the Hartmann Expedition which journeyed to Antarctica to recover Adolf's Hitler's secret treasure. He is a Knight of the Holy Order of Knights of the Sacred Lance. This order has dedicated itself to the course of righteousness directed by the influence of the Holy Lance which represents the power of God. He states that the time will come when the knights will make themselves known to the world. He is the author of *The Return of the Holy Lance – Adolf Hitler and the Secrets of the Holy Lance,* and *Hitler's Ashes.*

Ritter Von X is a citizen of the United States and often frequented Argentina to visit colleagues. His military decorations include the Undersea Boat War badge (comparable to the U.S. Infantry Combat Badge), the Reich Eagle Award, the Iron Cross, and the Knight's Cross.

He is the former director of the I.S.C.E. (International Society for a Complete Earth) and has seen the inner world as the home of the Nordic race or Arianni. In the 1970s, the I.S.C.E. was based in the mid-west. The Society used as its emblem the crest of the Thule Society: a sword in front of a swastika ringed in oak leaves. He said the I.S.C.E.'s goal was to establish contact with the Arianni, the "tall, blond, blue-eyed super race" that rules the inner world. The Arianni, he wrote, spoke "a language very much like German," lived in "cities built of shimmering crystal," and used their saucers called "Flugelrads" (winged wheel) to patrol the skies of the surface world and keep an eye on the outer world.

In 1992, I assumed the directorship of the I.S.C.E. after initiating personal contact with the founding director in 1984 and continued in correspondence with the Ritter for over ten years.

The ISCE, originally founded in 1977 by Ritter Von X, is now known as *The Hollow Earth Research Society (H.E.R.S.) www.hollowearthresearch.org* and carries on the work of examining the efficacy of the existence and culture of a hollow earth. It has been gratifying to have known him — as he has defined, articulated, and validated the experiences of the UFO phenomena and the origin and mission of the inner benevolent beings from the interior of the earth. This book is dedicated to his memory.

Danny L. Weiss, Co-Author

INTRODUCTION

In the waning days of the Second World War, the only remaining sea exit from Germany was the Northern Baltic port of Kiel. During the war, the German nation had launched many submarines from this heavily siloed and protected port into the Atlantic to disrupt Allied shipping. The final non-military mission of U-Boat 530 was now being prepared.

Nazi dictator Adolf Hitler, apparently, was dead, possibly committing suicide in his bunker in Berlin as the Russian army entered the city signaling sure defeat of the Nazi Third Reich. The other allied forces of the United State and Great Britain were rapidly overrunning Germany and defeating the remainder of Germany's armed forces. Meanwhile, a final secret mission was in the process of being carried out, perhaps at the direction of Hitler, but essentially by a small cadre of civilians and a very few select members of Hitler's most brilliant advisors. Their sole purpose was to assure the security of six large brass trunks and transport them out of Germany to a secret location on the continent of Antarctica that the Nazi's had established on the Princess Martha Coast near the Ritscher Upland region in Antarctica in 1938 and 1939. The six plus trunks would be carried by two submarines, the U-530 and the U-977. From a concrete-covered tunnel in the Baltic port of Kiel, the specially equipped submarines would embark on their final mission . . . not one of war, but one of historical purpose and significance to all mankind.

Not until safely at sea were the sealed orders opened by the U-530 Captain, Otto Wermoutt.

> *The U-5301 would proceed to Antarctica and secure the three brass trunks at a secret Nazi cave stronghold inland, snuggled at the base of the mystery continent's nearby mountain range.*

The story begins here.

Chapter Notes:

1. U-Boat: German submarines or Under-Sea boats. Most of the earlier U-Boats were diesel powered but had to surface to recharge their batteries. Those U-Boats, such as the U-530 and the U-977, both of which surrendered in Argentina well after the war ended, were of a later construction. Known as Type XXI and Type XXIII, they were equipped with a "snorkel" that gave them the capability to make the entire passage from Germany to Antarctica submerged, although they usually surfaced at night for recharging. Ten U-Boats were made available based in Oslofjord, Hamburg, and Flensburg for the transport of German officers and scientists. Most officers were members of Himmler's SS and the Kreigsmarine, seeking to escape the vengeance of the Allies. All left their home ports between May 3rd and May 8th, 1945 to proceed to Argentina where they would be welcomed by the friendly regime of Juan Peron. It is highly likely that a companion U-Boat, the U-977, followed the U-530 to Antarctica and Argentina carrying other sealed boxes from the Third Reich. It is probable that both boats brought several high ranking officials from Germany, including Maxmillian Hartmann, to be disembarked to the coast of Argentina by small rubber rafts before the craft was surrendered.

Chapter 1

ANTARCTIC ODYSSEY
1945

*C*aptain Otto Wermoutt, the twenty-five year old Captain, peered through the periscope of the German Kreigsmarine U-530, his steely azure blue eyes fixed upon the sweeping horizon of the Antarctic Sea. To his port side the whitish blue ice flows washed abruptly into the moving sea. His piercing eyes surveyed the land and ice mass in front of the submarine and the rising brackish mountains to the interior. With military preciseness, he turned the scope to visually assure that no other ships or activities were present before he would venture to surface.

His first officer, Lieutenant Kurt Wirth, confirmed the position of the U-Boat as 71 degrees, 30 minutes south by 14 degrees, 51 minutes west.

"We are here," Wermoutt muttered to himself as he confirmed his bearings with the land mass.

"Down periscope! Prepare to surface! " he commanded his first officer.

"Aye, Kapitan! Preparing to surface!"

"Very well. Surface!"

The efficient sea crew went into action as the submarine slowly began its rise to the surface of the thinly covered iced waters. In the forward torpedo room, now empty of any remnants of warheads or munitions, six darkly attired civilian passengers gathered around six medium-sized, hermetically sealed brass boxes, each filled with artifacts known aboard only to them and Captain Wermhoutt. The muffled excitement of the arrival and anticipated mission buoyed the energy of the crew and passengers after a long and tedious undersea trip during the daylight hours – surfacing just long enough in the night hours to charge the batteries of the diesel powered craft for the resumption of their underwater ocean trek. The civilians would accompany the boxes inland until secured safely in the Nazi Germany underground vault near the Mühlig-Hofmann Mountains.[1] It would be a relatively difficult march inland, estimated to take sixteen days with somewhat inelegant sleds laden with the boxes and survival gear. The mission was so critically important that three of the six civilian passengers were charged to accompany the specially trained crew members so they could each accurately verify and assure the mysterious cargo's safe arrival and storage.

As the U-530 burst bow-first through the thin surface ice, it quickly shed its water ballast and leveled on the surface. The crew immediately took positions on the conning tower while the captain asserted commands and secured the surface position, all the while scanning the sea and sky for unlikely but possible unwelcome visitors.

As the designated crewmembers and six mysterious passengers emerged from the U-Boat, they began the process of carefully loading the mysterious brass boxes onto rafts especially designed for the mission. Four persons and two precious brass boxes occupied each of three rafts, the contents of which would be mounted on ice sleds along with two additional rafts with sleds and other equipment necessary to the journey. It was nearly a two kilometer journey to the edge of the ice flow shelf where the group would disembark and begin their trek to the carefully secured vault.

Wermoutt suddenly caught a glimpse of a flying object as it rapidly approached his boat. His binoculars held steady as he watched the saucer-shaped *flugelrad* [2] dart above the boat and linger for a moment. Its silvery, slick form reflected a bright light over the landing crew as they reached the ice-flow banks. The crew, excited and astonished, stared disbelievingly at the craft until one of the mysterious passengers shouted, "Schnell! Schnell!"

Captain Wermhoutt mumbled to himself, while not acknowledging anything to his conning tower crew, "Ahh, so Hess and Haushofer were right!" [3]

Flugelrad viewed from U-530

The well disciplined crew, after the admonition by one of the passengers,[4] quickly went back to work as the strange craft immediately disappeared seemingly as abruptly as it had appeared. The remaining crew on the deck of the U-Boat also returned quickly to the duties at hand, noting that the Captain remained unmoved by the appearance of the strange craft. Quiet astonishment, yet minimal mumbling by the crew were squelched because of the apparent acceptance of the craft's appearance by the Captain and the guest passengers. The offloading continued rapidly as the rest of the equipment was beached and prepared for travel along the ice and then inland with the crew's reverent handling of the obvious prizes, the brass boxes.

As the landing party began to move across the icescape, the U-530 submerged where it would lie in wait until the expedition returned. The young land crew members struggled to encourage the sleds to move over the ice-flow. It would take some time to get used to the task of moving heavy sleds over the ice. At the moment the weather was relatively mild according to Antarctica standards, yet all knew it could rapidly deteriorate at any time. The view from the ice-flow to the interior destination appeared foreboding and weather indicators were not reassuring. The leaders, however, seemed to know exactly where they were going and urged the crew onward without hesitation.

As fortune would have it, the anticipated journey was not smooth. The men pulling the sleds struggled to traverse the unforgiving landscape, and to add to the misery, the map they were following proved faulty and several days were lost. Upon reaching their final destination, the crew heaved a mighty sigh of relief and felt justifiable personal pride at their successful endeavor.

One of the mysterious passengers (none of whom would reveal their identities to any crewmember except by pseudonyms) directed the accompanying munitions expert to set a small explosive charge at a specific spot against the mountain wall. As the party stood aside, the charge was ignited and a cascade of snow and ice exploded off the mountain side revealing a large steel door set against the mountain rock with the familiar Nazi Swastika[5] imbedded on the exterior. Several years earlier, under the direction of Admiral Karl Dönitz, Germany sent men and material to Deutsche Antarctica to carve out a series of natural underground caves wherein the German military would be able to store valuable research findings and artifacts of the Third Reich, thereby keeping such secrets safe until a time they could be successfully recovered.

The door was unlocked by one of the civilian passengers who produced a large key that was strung on heavy beads around his neck, and the brass trunks, still on the sleds, were brought inside a large hollowed cavern. By their seeming familiarity with the process, it was clear the passengers had been here before as they quickly surveyed and inventoried the contents of the vault's steel encased cave. The cavern had other doors in the interior leading to other chambers, but the crew was only allowed to be in the initial steel encased room, and only for as long as necessary to deposit the brass trunks. As quickly as they arrived, their mission now almost complete, the expedition immediately began the return trek to their awaiting submarine.

The trip back was much less challenging without the loaded sleds and certainly quicker than their tedious journey inland. Upon arriving back to the original ice-flow landing spot, they found their tethered rafts still securely fastened to long spikes set in the permafrost. The ice had, in the time of their journey, frozen over the surface water above the submarine. A young crewmember tossed a grenade over the frozen ice signaling the U-530 that they had returned. Within moments, the submarine surfaced, appearing as a frightening icy-steel monster rising from the middle of a large white and lonely wind-swept prairie. Through the broken calm of the frozen wasteland, their sleek underwater sanctuary emerged and cracked its way to the surface. The expedition members were quickly absorbed into the U-Boat as it began its journey to its ultimate and final fate. Captain Wermoutt surveyed once again the final part of the sealed orders. It had read:

> *Upon successful delivery of the special cargo, you are to surrender the U-530 to the Argentine authorities near the port city of Mar del Plata, Argentina.*

He folded the sealed orders and burned them as he continued looking over the stark white horizon with a satisfied feeling of the nearing completion of a well planned mission.

The U-530 surrendered as ordered on July 10, 1945. Each of the crew members, the officers, and the six mysterious passengers disappeared into the populace of Argentina. Their mission was accomplished.

Chapter Notes

1. A mountain range in Antarctica where the alleged Nazi storage cave is located. It is best reached from a Southerly direction from Tierra del Fuego, at the tip of South America.

2. German term for "flying saucer," translates to "winged wheel."

3. Rudolf Hess
   One of the original Nazi party members who allegedly flew to England in 1941 to ostensibly negotiate a peace with that country. He was captured by the British and held captive until the end of the war when he was transferred to Spandau prison in Berlin where he remained, without visitors, for the remainder of his life. It is said that he remained in prison because of what he knew, rather than

for war crimes. He was guarded by the four victorious powers of the war, the United States, Soviet Union, France and Great Britain, in rotating schedules. He died in captivity in 1987.

Karl Haushofer
Known as the "Wizard of Germany." A professor at the University of Munich who was a mysterious influence on the leadership of Nazi Germany. He was reported to be the main resource of the secret of the Holy Lance and shared the knowledge with Reinhold Heydrich, his favored student. He was considered one of the five power leaders, the H's of Nazi Germany: Hitler, Himmler, Hess, Heydrich and Haushofer.

4. Only two of the mysterious passengers have been tentatively identified. One was Martin Bormann, the private secretary of Hitler and the other was SS General Kurt Müeller. Müeller was very significant as he was one of only two people who knew of the Swiss Bank deposit box which held the key to the Lance. Rudolf Hess was the other.

5. The swastika (as a character: 卐 or 卍) is an ancient religious symbol that generally takes the form of an equilateral cross, with its four legs bent at 90 degrees. It was adopted as such most notably by the Nazi Party and Nazi Germany prior to World War II. In many Western countries, the swastika has been highly stigmatized because of its use in and association with Nazism. It is considered to be a sacred and auspicious symbol in Hinduism, Buddhism, and Jainism and dates back to before 2nd century B.C. It continues to be commonly used as a religious symbol in Hinduism and Buddhism. One of the anomalies of the war was that the U.S. Army 45th division, now known as the Thunderbird Division with a Thunderbird figure arm patch, had previously used the swastika as their own division patch. Hitler referred to them mockingly as his special army division.

Chapter 2

OVER ANTARCTICA

*I*t was February, 1947, summertime in the Antarctic, two years after the U-530 surrendered at Mar del Plata on the coast of Argentina. The skies were relatively bright with a breaking overcast that shrouded the continent – a good day to fly. Daylight prevailed almost 20 hours a day and even the short nights were not fully darkened, in contrast to the opposite extreme that ruled during the cold, stark, dark of the winter. Maneuvers by U.S forces during Operation Highjump[1] were able to function for nearly a 24-hour work day. Flying routine missions over vast areas of the continent was becoming habitual, as mapping and surveillance was a primary objective of many nations with operations in Antarctica – including the United States.

The Americans were in Antarctica, working semi-cooperatively with most of the other major international states, to stake a claim for any potential material interest and benefits each might perceive important from the many resources and mysteries of the unexplored continent. Each government, allies during the recent war, had its own Antarctic agenda and cooperation often was overshadowed, at least privately, by competition and suspicion.

International agreements as well as the extreme difficulties maintaining a viable winter base on the Southern continent prevented any one nation from claiming the sub-continent as its own. However, it was also well-known that Nazi Germany had laid claim to areas that were still of major interest to the world nations. Reports of a secret

Nazi base near the Muhlig-Hofmann Mountains spurred the art of spying on one another into a regular and first protocol activity. All were concerned about rumored Nazi secret weapons and inventions that might be contained in the caverns dug out by the Germans during World War II. The defeat of Hitler and the reigning Nazi regime gave all nations, specifically Russia, Great Britain, and the United States preemptive interest in the designs and progress the Germans had made in jet aircraft and rocketry, as well as rumors regarding the development of an atomic weapon. There was also evidence of a craft which the Germans termed a *Flugelrad*, a flying disc that was of great fascination to the competing Allies.

Conflicting reports of a flugelrad crash in Germany in 1938, wherein the Germans salvaged parts of the craft, as well as the survival of one of the occupants, was fast becoming another concern of the Allies. Had the Germans reverse engineered the workings of such a craft to help them develop a working clone of the saucer? Were German research scientists now in Antarctica furthering such development?

Such were the post-war concerns of the former Allies, now in competition not only with their international coalition of friends, but also with unfolding political realities regarding the aims and goals of the Soviet Union.

****

The dual engine U.S. Navy R-4D[2] soared over the Antarctic prairies at an altitude of 2000 feet, low enough and slow enough to give the pilot and co-pilot a good look at the terrain, yet high enough to maintain instrument calculations and readings, avoiding any possibility of a *white out*.[3] The laborious roar of the R-4D engines could drown out any easy conversations aboard the craft, but the two occupants were used to flying with one another and had become accustomed to the strained level of communication above the engine noise.

After an hour or so of essential flight conversation, the pilot looked over at his passenger and said,

"Well Lieutenant Hill, you and I have flown quite a bit together these past few months, haven't we?"

Hill glanced back at Admiral Richard E. Byrd, the commander of the American forces in Antarctica, again noticing the familiar patch on his shirtsleeve with the not-so-common moniker of Admiral over the left chest of his flight jacket. Lieutenant Oliver K. Hill had been Admiral Byrd's chief aide and flight partner over the past months and had grown to admire the Admiral immensely. There seemed to be a personal rapport between the two that transcended the usual military protocol, although Hill would never think to call his military superior anything but Admiral. They regularly flew missions three to five times a week, sometimes more, depending on the whim of Byrd, who had an uncanny knowledge and curiosity about the permafrost covered continent.

Hill replied, "Over seven months, sir. It has been an honor and a pleasure."

"As it has been for me," Byrd replied. "You've been a loyal and trusted aide. I often think of you as a son."

Byrd checked their position. Compass readings are relatively inefficient at the poles. As a longtime navy captain, he was an expert in utilizing a sextant and always knew where he was in flight. He meticulously pre-planned each flight and mapped out each area he would visit.

He dipped the plane slightly to port and headed towards the interior mountains, away from the coast. He continued to watch the horizon and scan the skies above him as if he were looking for something. Lieutenant Hill didn't pay much attention to the Admiral's apparent preoccupation with his scanning as he knew, as a pilot himself, that keeping a close eye utilizing visual flight rules at all times was absolutely necessary, even if they were flying over an area deemed desolate and void of air traffic.

"You know Ollie, Operation Highjump is rapidly coming to a close. While our mission here may never be termed complete, we are being called back to the States. It's time to consolidate what we know and prepare for the next mission."

"Will there be a next mission here on the continent?" Hill inquired.

"There's always a next mission," Byrd chuckled.

Young Ollie Hill, a very competent and loyal naval officer, was shocked that Admiral Byrd called him by his first name and surprised by the Admiral's sharing Operation Highjump information with him. But he recognized that Byrd was showing his human side and was confiding in him due to the relationship they had developed after spending so much quality time together, and was demonstrating his personal bond with him. Often the admiral would ask Ollie personal and intimate questions about his family, his background, and his philosophy of life. At times Byrd would share tidbits about his own life. Having the famous Admiral Byrd say that he felt toward him as a son further swelled Ollie's pride, loyalty, and admiration for this wondrous man.

"Don't be so shocked!" Byrd asserted. "I call all my trusted friends by their first names. Don't you?"

"Well, yes sir . . . but you're the . . ."

"Admiral?"

"Yes, sir. I don't think I can call you anything else."

Admiral Richard E. Byrd

The Admiral patted Ollie's knee gently, smiled amiably and said, "That's O.K. son, you can call me whatever feels comfortable for you. But we'll be leaving for the States soon and I've come to regard you as my only true confidant."

"Thank you Sir. You don't know what an honor it is to have you say that. And you must know that my admiration and loyalty to you is truly genuine."

"I know that about you, Ollie . . . and the day may come when that loyalty will be severely tested."

Hill looked at Byrd quizzically, but didn't respond because the Admiral had just abruptly made a mid-course flight maneuver for which Hill wasn't prepared. Ollie grabbed his seat for stability and tried to get his bearings from the jolt of the sudden lurch of the airplane. A bright and blinding light covered the split windshield, Ollie was momentarily blinded and averted his eyes.

As Hill regained his regular vision, and the light settled off the plane's windshield, what he saw next was so incredible and unbelievable that he was speechless and almost panicky. His excited and broken words blurted out an octave higher than his normal voice.

"Admiral, what the hell was that?"

Byrd didn't immediately answer and appeared very calm. To the port side of the plane was a strange circular craft keeping pace with them, and in which was a man staring back at the two of them! Both occupants were able to see the distinct face of the craft's pilot, an obviously tall and blonde-haired humanoid, with strong Nordic features. The craft hovered next to them for a frozen instant with the alien pilot's smiling face very apparent and clear to both of them.

The Admiral, still calm but much more animated than usual, was grinning and, to the amazement of Hill, waved to the craft's pilot as the man waved back in greeting. The craft disappeared abruptly in what seemed to be a microsecond – even more quickly than it had appeared.

Hill was absolutely nonplussed and dumbfounded by what he just witnessed. Stammering, he exclaimed, "You KNEW that man, He waved to you!"

Admiral Byrd looked over to his young officer, smiled and quietly whispered in a low, calm, and very sincere voice, "Ollie, I wasn't planning on testing your trust so soon. It appears that you and I will need to have a serious talk."

Hill, still shaken from the experience, muttered his bewildered reply.

"Yes sir, that would be extremely appreciated, sir. Yes sir, it would. It surely would . . . be appreciated . . . sir" as he settled hard back into his seat speechless, his mind racing and clouded with disbelief.

Chapter Notes:

1. *Operation Highjump* was an American Naval operation in Antarctica. The mission consisted of three naval battle groups which departed Norfolk, VA, on December 2, 1946. It is also believed to have involved a British-Norwegian force as well as a Russian force. Australian and Canadian forces were also involved to some extent. It was initiated at a curious time, shortly after the conclusion of World War II when the country may have been at its peak military weakness as the armed forces were mustering out to go home. And, it was just a few months prior that the Roswell incident of a crashed saucer in 1947 had been reported and quickly hushed up.

   Officially, the instructions for the operation were issued by then Chief of Naval Operations, Chester W. Nimitz indicating that they were to: a) train personnel and test material in the frigid zones; b) consolidate and extend American sovereignty over the largest practical area of the Antarctic continent; c) determine the feasibility of establishing and maintaining bases in the Antarctic and to investigate possible base sites; d) develop techniques for establishing and maintaining air bases on the ice, (with particular attention to the later applicability of such techniques to Greenland) and; e) amplify existing knowledge of hydrographic, geological, meteorological and electromagnetic conditions in the area. Admiral Byrd's team of six R4-Ds (aka C-47's or DC-3's) were fitted with super-secret *Trimetricon spy cameras* and each plane was trailing a magnetometer. On the last of many "mapping flights" where all six planes went out, each on its own certain pre-ordained paths to film and measure with magnetometers, Admiral Byrd's plane was three hours late. The cause officially stated that he lost an engine. All data was discarded from the plane except the films themselves and the results of the magnetometer readings. Sorting through both the public and private accounts of what actually took place, this would be the time when Byrd allegedly met with representatives of the *Aryan extraterrestrials* and a contingent of German scientists working on the reverse engineering and construction of *flying discs*.

   The mission, expected to last for between six and eight months, came to an abrupt and early end and all units were hastily withdrawn from Antarctica by March, 1947, a mere eight weeks after arrival. The Chilean press reported that the mission had "run into trouble" and that there had been "many fatalities" (not what was reported by the U.S. Navy).

   From on board the ship Mt. Olympus, the newspaper "El Mercurio" of Santiago, Chile, quoted Byrd in a headline article during an interview with Lee van Atta: "Admiral Byrd declared today that it was imperative for the United

States to initiate immediate defense measures against hostile regions." He further stated that he didn't want to "frighten anyone unduly," but it was a "bitter reality that in case of a new war, the continental United States would be attacked by flying objects which could fly from pole to pole at incredible speeds." Not long after that statement, Byrd recommended defense bases at the North Pole. These were not isolated remarks as Byrd repeated each of these points of view, resulting from what he described as his "personal knowledge' gathered both at the North and South poles, at a news conference held for the International News Service.

Operation Highjump prompted questions of what the actual purpose of the mission was and why Byrd was "hospitalized" shortly thereafter and not allowed any more press conferences. Still, in March 1955, eight years later, under President Dwight D. Eisenhower, Byrd was placed in charge of *Operation Deepfreeze* which was part of the International Geophysical year 1957 – 1958 exploration of the Antarctic. He died shortly thereafter in 1957, some suggest not naturally.

2. The military equivalent of a civilian Douglas DC 3 or C47.

3. A blinding weather, atmosphere and surface condition that blends all distinguishing features as white.

Chapter 3

THE BRIEFING ROOM

Washington D.C.
March, 1947

*I*t was merely a month later that Lieutenant Oliver K. Hill arrived in Washington D.C. He had not seen or talked to the Admiral for the past couple of weeks as each was preparing for departure from the Antarctic base. The task of bringing men and material home was not a part of his duties and he was singled out to report directly to the Pentagon for his debriefing. Ollie played over and over in his mind the events of that fateful day with Admiral Byrd and the amazing and almost incomprehensible circular craft and humanoid being they encountered.

Of course, that was why he was called to appear at all. Radar from Little America, the home base of all American Antarctic activity, picked up the movements of the strange craft and had scrambled two fighter interceptors to confront the potential intruders. Finding nothing, they returned to base. Admiral Chester Nimitz, the head of all operations for Operation Highjump, subsequently ordered both Byrd and Hill to Washington for debriefing on the incident. One thing was for certain: Admiral Byrd had asked him to keep his confidence about that experience and Lieutenant Hill was not going to embarrass his superior with any outlandish tales about flying discs . . . or about strange beings piloting a strange craft. Byrd could count on his loyalty.

18

The Pentagon was a bustling hive of activity. The entire military complex has its leaders and support personnel housed in this huge five-sided building. Navy briefing rooms, even in the Pentagon, however, are strikingly stark. Hill sat in the entry office on the bottom floor where he was ordered to wait until he was called. The waiting room was devoid of any real décor with the exception of occasional navy combat craft photos on the walls and various credentials displayed by the ranking officers in charge. Of course, there was the mandatory photo of President Harry S. Truman hanging on the back wall.

There was a disinterested young ensign at the reception desk shuffling papers and answering the telephone when it rang. He occasionally would make a call, but seldom looked up to acknowledge the presence of Lieutenant Hill who was dressed in his officer navy dress whites. Hill mused that the young ensign's job was the epitome of boring military bureaucracy.

After a wait that seemed longer than it was, Hill noticed the turning of a doorknob and saw none other than Admiral Richard E. Byrd, corncob pipe dangling from his lips, exiting from the only adjoining room. He was accompanied by an unfamiliar and unusually tall man with striking Nordic physical characteristics, further distinguished by an unkempt beard and a prominent silver front tooth. The man regarded Hill with a knowing and unforced smile. The reception desk officer quickly snapped to attention as the Admiral and his companion entered the entry office area. Byrd closed the door gently behind them, smiled and walked over to Hill and put his hand on Hill's shoulder in an encouraging gesture. Byrd looked directly into Hill's eyes and winked.

"Your turn, Ollie," he said in a calming voice.

Hill, wondering what to say to his commander in this situation, uncomfortably responded with, "How did it go, Sir?"

Byrd politely ignored Ollie's question while he turned to his bearded companion.

"Let me introduce you to Sven Olafsson. He is a particular friend of mine. I wanted you two to meet. Sven might become handy for you to know one day."

Ollie shook Sven's hand, somewhat puzzled. He was nearly seven feet tall and towered over all around him. The man gazed deeply into Ollie's eyes without saying a word and simply nodded his head. Clearly this was a man of few words.

Byrd grasped Ollie's hand firmly, clasping his left hand over Hill's right hand in a double embrace. He again looked Hill directly in the eye and replied,

"Just tell'em what you saw," he whispered, "Within reason, of course."

Pausing momentarily and intently gazing into Ollie's eyes, Byrd encouraged the young lieutenant by saying, "Go on in, they're waiting for you."

Byrd watched Hill closely while Ollie glanced at the door leading into the briefing room. He looked back at the Admiral, nodded, and entered the adjoining room from where Byrd had just emerged. The Admiral and his Nordic companion quickly exited the building as soon as Hill entered the briefing room.

If Ollie thought that the entry area of the briefing room was stark, the adjoining room was completely devoid of any character whatsoever. The windowless room had no pictures or credits on the walls, no calendar, no signs of the room ever being designed to be comfortable or pleasant. The room, fairly small, yet well lit, seemed to Ollie to be a place more likely used for storage rather than for meetings. A medium-sized rectangular wooden table stood in the middle of the hardwood floor with a few straight-backed oak chairs randomly placed near the table. The only other semblance of human comfort was a large glass pitcher of drinking water, a half-empty coffee maker, three cups, and a few glasses.

There were three men in the room awaiting young officer Hill. They were impeccably dressed in form-fitting black silk suits, were clean shaven, with short cropped hair, accenting their well proportioned physical frames. Each wore a black felt fedora slightly tipped to one side suggesting some fashion consciousness. Hill was curious why none of them were in uniform, but dismissed that as a quirk to the Pentagon. Two of the men were standing at either side of the table while the third was sitting at the desk. Hill could not help but notice how straight and erect the two men were standing and how the one seated at the table also exhibited a noticeably erect sitting posture. All were wearing dark sunglasses that completely covered their eyes. This in itself was curious to Ollie as there was no sunlight coming into the windowless room and the overhead lights were not so bright as to be disturbing. Each of the men's movements was profoundly deliberate and without the normal easy flow of what one would expect from a normal person. The seated man gestured to Ollie to sit at the table in front of him. Ollie complied and took the seat with some obvious discomfort.

The man sitting at the table spoke first. The first few words out of his mouth sounded almost mechanical as he emanated a stark, staccato voice pattern of speech. His mannerism matched the ambience of the room.

"Welcome, Lieutenant Hill. Please sit down and make yourself comfortable. May I offer you a cup of coffee?"

"No sir, thank you."

"Perhaps some water then?"

The man in black poured a glass of water for Hill, not waiting to hear whether he wanted one or not. To be polite, Hill simply nodded his head in thanks.

The interrogator got right to the point with his questions. There were no other introductory pleasantries of any kind.

"As you are well aware, Admiral Byrd just gave us his report on what occurred on that flight last month that you and he shared over Antarctica. Would you please tell us what you saw?"

Hill was rapidly sizing up his interrogators. He was suspicious, but he had just talked with the Admiral a few moments before and figured that he was in proper company and would cooperate. He felt he wanted to be consistent with the report that Byrd gave, but was initially unsure of just how to proceed. He decided to respond with a military-style listing of facts without any embellishment. "Well," Hill began, "the Admiral and I were flying on a scheduled reconnaissance and survey mission on February 23rd at 0900 hours. We were on a southeasterly heading when the Admiral, who was piloting, banked the plane steeply to make a port turn. At approximately the same moment I was jostled in my seat and temporarily blinded by a bright light and, after a moment or two, I saw an unmarked aircraft fly very close to us and quickly disappear."

"Were you able to identify the craft?" the interrogator asked.

"No sir," Hill replied, "it happened so fast that, unprepared for the sudden maneuver, I was jolted by the steep turn and I only caught a glimpse of the aircraft. I could not identify the type of aircraft or whether it had any markings."

The MIB [1] paused, shuffled a few papers in front of him and asked,

"Had you ever seen an aircraft such as the one you glimpsed prior to that February day?"

"Well, as I told you sir, I didn't get a clear look at the aircraft. All I remember seeing was a glimpse and it was suddenly gone. I couldn't identify the craft."

One of the MIBs standing to the left of Hill walked over to where Hill was sitting and filled yet another glass of water from the water pitcher and placed it in front of Ollie. Hill thought the maneuver to be somewhat strange inasmuch as he already had a glass of water in his hand. The MIB quietly studied Hill and sat down beside him. He took off his sunglasses briefly to wipe them clean and deliberately looked directly at the startled young Lieutenant. His eyes were unlike any Hill had ever seen before. They were almost cat-like with wide, vertical pupils and a piercing blue hue, suggesting an inhuman quality. Hill was transfixed by the eyes yet tried to hide his shock and discomfort. The man put his dark glasses back on, smiled and in the same mechanical and staccato voice as his companion, addressed the young Lieutenant.

"Lieutenant Oliver Kendall Hill? Correct?"

"Yes sir."

We have been very interested in you since Admiral Byrd told us you were with him on that flight of February 23rd. The Admiral speaks very highly of you. He trusts you."

Hill began to feel a touch more comfortable with those words and replied, "I'm honored by him. I have nothing but respect and admiration for Admiral Byrd."

The MIB, still sitting in an overly erect posture, then spoke, peering directly into Lieutenant Hill's eyes.

"Then we know that you will honor his request to keep this conversation between us."

"Yes sir," Hill quickly responded.

". . . and you will not discuss this in any further detail with anyone else – not anyone. Do we understand one another?"

"Yes sir, the Admiral can depend on that!"

"Thank you, Lieutenant. That will be all. Thank you for your cooperation . . . and please give my regards to the Admiral . . . should you see or hear from him again."

Somewhat puzzled by the MIBs closing remark, Hill simply replies, "My pleasure, sir."

Hill stood up as he prepared to leave feeling somewhat ill at ease because he was torn whether he should salute or just leave. After all, these men were not in uniform. He decided to simply leave.

The sense of tension that he had been feeling immediately subsided as he closed the door of the small briefing room behind him. He donned his military cap and started to exit the front door when two uniformed naval officers entered.

The first officer paused upon entering, delaying Lieutenant Hill and said, "Excuse me, Lieutenant Hill? Were you about to leave?"

"Well, yes sir, I was."

"But you are here for the debriefing, are you not?"

"Yes," Hill replied, "But I thought you were through with me."

The first officer seemed puzzled by Hill's remark.

"Through? What do you mean through?"

A thoroughly confused Hill blurted out, "But what about those men I just talked to . . . in that room?"

"What are you talking about?" the somewhat surprised and slightly irritated officer asserted. The naval officer opened the door to the room in which Hill had just been interrogated by the three men in black. All three inspected the room.

"As you can see, Lieutenant, there is no one here . . . and there is no other exit."

Puzzled, the officer asked Hill, "Are you feeling O.K. Lieutenant?"

Hill struggled momentarily to regroup his thoughts, turning over in his mind what had just happened and his unintended blurting response.

He centered his thinking and replied to the two naval officers, "Yes, of course. I guess my mind is really fatigued at this time. I am very tired from our rapid return from the continent. Please accept my apologies."

Both officers regarded Hill with concern for a critical moment, but then seemed to accept his explanation.

"Of course, you must be exhausted," the officer retorted, his tone now much more conciliatory in nature. "We'll try and make this as brief and painless as possible. I'm sure you would like to get home to your family as soon as practical."

"Yes, I would sir, thank you."

****

Ollie Hill left the de-briefing room after reiterating to the naval officers essentially what he shared with the three men in black and re-entered the reception room. After carefully going over what he witnessed with the naval officers, taking care not to reveal too much detail, he took a deep breath and stepped outside. He pulled out his sunglasses to compensate for the bright glare off the cream-colored buildings surrounding him. Across the narrow plaza leading to the street he noticed a man a few feet away dressed in a black silk suit and cradling a large jet-black cat in his arms. The cat and Hill's eyes instantly met and Hill was momentarily transfixed by the similarity of the feline's eyes to the eyes of the man in black standing near him. The man released the cat and the animal quickly darted away with a screeching reprise. Hill watched the cat bound off while feeling overwhelmed with a strange and curious internal intensity. What in the world was happening today? The mysterious man in black, standing just a few feet from Hill, smiled sardonically at Hill, displaying his own, now familiar, catlike eyes as he meticulously put on his sunglasses.

Hill was mesmerized by this new strange moment. Another man in black? A comrade of the three inside? A coincidence?

"Hmm, not likely," he opined to himself.

His attention turned quickly to the cat now staring back at him from some distance away. Ollie took a deep breath, adjusted his sunglasses, cleaned them with his handkerchief and gazed up at the sky to ponder the moment. Abruptly, he turned around only to see that the man in black – and the black cat – had completely disappeared.

Chapter Notes:

1. MIB's are biologically engineered robots, emissaries from the inner earth of Asgarth. They are commissioned by the Arianni to gather and synthesize information. They wear the black suits, have vertical blue pupils, drive older black luxury cars and have precise accents and seem frightening, matter of fact, and vaguely non-human to the average person. They are known as the "silencers" and may perform magical demonstrations to entice humans not to talk about unusual sightings. They have no history of hurting anyone. They appear seemingly out of nowhere, control objects with their minds and seek to influence human minds. They most often appear in threes. They seem to know all about the people they visit and are commissioned to destroy evidence, if necessary. Even though they appear evil, MIBs may appear to be comical also. They are often ill at ease, ask strange questions and do not seem to reflect natural human traits or reactions.

Chapter 4

THE PROTEST

1968

Berkeley, California

The San Francisco Bay Area is truly a sight to behold on its often crystal clear days. The geography of the area is such that the large inland bay seems to accentuate the beauty of the surrounding land as it stretches north, south and inland to the fertile San Joaquin Valley. Beyond the valley lies the great Sierra Nevada range with its multiple rivers and streams that feed into the navigable Sacramento River which then empties into the bay. The Pacific Ocean provides the bulk of the Bay's water as the salt water intrusion is evident in the northern smaller inlets and bays as it meanders up the Sacramento River, each picturesque inlet gracing the region with a watery elegance. By 1968, the landscape of the area was covered on all sides of the bay with bridges, ferryboats, sailing craft, and cargo ships criss-crossing everywhere.

With the city of San Francisco occupying the prominent peninsula forming the bay's Western entrance, the East bay features the maritime and industrial cities of Richmond, Berkeley, and Oakland. The region enjoys a moderate climate that seldom reflects the extremes of the coastal weather one might find elsewhere. The weather is ideal for a populace that utilizes the bay and the surrounding area as a scenic playground and workplace.

The streets of Berkeley extending all around the University of California were pleasant and inviting and the local housing was plentiful and well designed for the comfort of its occupants. It was a family oriented city with an academic flair that catered to a wide and diverse population with its abundant recreational and occupational opportunities.

It was this peaceful and beautiful part of the country that Commander O.K. Hill called home.

In July of 1968, a U.S. Postal mail delivery truck rumbled down a typical urban Berkeley street as the driver searched for the delivery address. He was in the uniform of the U.S Postal Service, driving slowly, wearing dark sunglasses and searching for the location. He stopped in front of Commander Hill's home and got out of his truck with a small wrapped package in his arms, walking slowly and deliberately to the front door. The name on the mailbox near the front door identified the residence of *The Hill Family*. Hanging on the front door was a small MIA (Missing In Action) flag, its prominence signaling a family in potential mourning. The postman glanced at the flag, adjusted his glasses, and rang the doorbell.

From inside came an immediate vocal response to the doorbell's chime from a deep-throated and obviously agitated dog. The door opened slowly, but only part way, as Hill attempted to quiet and calm his rather large and imposing German shepherd.

"Sorry," Hill apologizes to the postman, "he always barks at uniforms. He thinks you're military."

The postman did not react at all but simply stared into the dog's eyes after removing his sunglasses. The shepherd immediately stopped his barking, lowered his ears, began to whine, and retreated quickly into the back room, obviously upset.

"Lieutenant Oliver Kendall Hill?" the postman asked, putting his glasses back on, "I have a special delivery for Lieutenant Oliver Kendall Hill."

"It's Commander Hill . . . Wow! He's never done that before," he said amazed by the antics of his usually unflappable shepherd.

The postman restated his delivery mission. "This package is for *Lieutenant* Oliver Kendall Hill."

"Yes, that's me. But it's Commander Hill now. I haven't been a lieutenant for 20 years."

Hill paused, still puzzled by his dog's reaction, "Do dogs always act that way around you?"

The postman regarded Hill carefully and paused in what became a truly awkward moment as if he didn't fully comprehend what Hill was asking. He quickly reprocessed his thoughts, reexamined Hill, and handed Hill a pen to sign for the delivery.

"Of course, you are, indeed, Commander Hill. Please sign here."

Hill took the pen and form presented to him, signed it somewhat clumsily and looked carefully at the postman with curious eyes. The postman stared intently at Hill through his dark glasses. Hill studied the mail carrier and visited a familiar, uneasy feeling. The postman handed him the small package and began to walk away. He then stopped, turned back towards Hill and took off his glasses.

"Have a good life, Commander Hill."

Hill held the package and looked up as the postman spoke, immediately struck by the blue tint of his eyes. He well recalled those eyes. He remembered the postman. He had not aged since twenty years ago in the Pentagon briefing room.

Standing alone on his front porch, Hill retreated indoors and slowly unwrapped the package. He had no idea what he would find, but he knew it would be significant. Thoughts and images of 1947 cascaded through his mind as he relived the moments of the flight with Admiral Byrd and the time he had spent at the Pentagon briefing. The package revealed a leather-bound medium sized notebook, a diary filled with scribbled handwriting and a small crystalline gem that was unfamiliar to Hill. Ollie Hill unfolded a carefully wrapped detailed map of the North Polar Region that revealed an air route to a potential entrance to the inner earth at the Northern polar cap. A small hand-written note tumbled from the pages as he quickly skimmed through the diary. The note was signed by Admiral Richard E. Byrd, whom Ollie knew had passed away in 1957, over ten years earlier.

The note read, *Here's the rest of the story, Ollie.*

Commander Hill immediately recognized the Admiral's unique hand. Ollie sat down in his favorite armchair, donned his reading glasses and examined the contents of the delivered package. Included was another short note detailing a flight plan to a polar hamlet known as Spitzbergen, situated off the Arctic coast of Norway. Byrd let Ollie know that Spitzbergen was the storage place where his Fokker was hangered under the watchful eye of Sven, the silver-toothed emissary of the Arianni, entrusted to maintain the plane for any emergency flight to the pole. Ollie recalled his somewhat inept meeting with Sven at his briefing those many years ago.

The crystalline stone was of a curious texture which Ollie had not seen before. He fondled it gently in complete bewilderment as to its significance or purpose. Here, in Ollie's hands, though, was Byrd's personal diary. In it Byrd revealed his astonishing experiences traveling into the center of the Earth through an opening in the North Pole territory, meeting representatives of a central civilization and being hosted by Thal, the commander of the unique flying disk.

"So that's how he knew the pilot of the craft!" Hill exclaimed to himself after carefully skimming through the Admiral's diary.

Hill gazed carefully at the stone which had the words *The Key* inscribed carefully on the base with no further information. Perplexed by the array of fascinating items, Ollie closed his eyes and pondered aloud, "Why was this sent to me? What am I supposed to do with all this?"

****

Commander Oliver K. Hill's home was a comfortable Craftsman designed bungalow, with a roof covered front porch and a multi-windowed front door leading directly into a small entry room with a living room situated just to the right of the entry. The living room featured a large three-paned picture window looking out on the quiet street lined with mature, white-trunked birch trees. In the living room stood a large river stone fireplace that was used often by the Hills during the chilly winters that visited the usually mild climate of California's Bay Area featuring several photographs of family members on the mantle. Most of the photos were relatively recent and featured the family of four in happy times. One could appreciate the closeness of the family simply by viewing the photos so prominently displayed. On the right of the substantial mantle was a glorious wedding picture of Ollie and Jackie, his wife of 23 years. There were also several photos of Hill in his military garb with both their sons, Jared and Garrett, posing in front of a small Cessna 150 civilian airplane, taken when both boys were finishing flying lessons. One large photo displayed on the mantle was that of Jared, the eldest son and a pilot in the U.S. Air Force, who was listed as missing since 1967 during the early military action in Viet Nam. The room was dotted with sports trophies earned by both boys, high school football pictures, and other family memorabilia.

Off to the left, on an obscure end table, was a singular photo of Garrett, the youngest son, clothed in the typical current rag-tag protest clothing symbolic of the times. His long brown hair was tied in a pony-tail with a small, but wild beard covering most of his jaw and cheeks, an ongoing concern of the elder, more conservative, Commander O.K. Hill.

Jackie Hill, the loving and caring mother of two sons and a strong supporter of whatever her husband or sons attempted, sat home alone in the mid-afternoon on another beautiful weekend morning in Berkeley. Ollie was across the Bay in San Francisco for the day and she was busy at the kitchen table writing letters to friends with whom she had corresponded for many years. She has grieved mightily at the disappearance of Jared over a year ago. It seemed impossible to come to grips with Jared being missing and presumed dead or captured. Writing letters was one of the ways that Jackie could express her feelings of loss. The sun was trickling through the kitchen window casting streaks of light throughout. The television was on in the background, within sight, but Jackie was not paying particular attention to it.

Her interest in writing, however, was suddenly distracted by the blaring sound of an all-too-familiar voice coming from the T.V. She could scarcely believe her eyes and ears. It was Garrett! He was shouting, almost incomprehensively, while being handcuffed and dragged away from the television cameras while an eager reporter kept a microphone near his mouth.

We will not be intimidated! We will not be ignored! We will never give up until this illegal and unjust war comes to an end!

Absolutely captured by the images and sound of her son's struggling and panicked voice, Jackie was astounded by the scene unfolding on the television screen. Garrett's shouting into the microphone was rapidly fading as the camera panned the hundreds of young protestors running, throwing objects and shouting from all directions.

Jackie screamed directly at the television with an impassioned and shaking voice.

"Garrett? Is that you Garrett? . . . What are you doing?"

Her son's TV voice gave way to police sirens and the scuffle of uniformed police officers moving rapidly into the scene with their billy clubs raised and swinging almost indiscriminately. She heard the sound of an electronic megaphone shout with authority.

> *This gathering has been declared an illegal assembly. You are all ordered to disperse immediately!*

On the screen a disheveled and struggling reporter described the scene to the viewing public. Tear gas canisters thrown by the police had begun to permeate the air causing a number of the protesters to move away from the scene, many holding cloths over their eyes in an attempt to evade the stinging effects of the gas. The TV reporter shouted into his microphone,

> *I'm standing here at the corner of Telegraph and Shattuck Avenue and I hope you can hear me. There are police in full riot gear with plastic face shields moving in a military V formation dispersing the crowd with their riot clubs. There are many injuries and bloodied young folks here as the bulk of the protesters are retreating and throwing rocks and other objects at the police. There is complete bedlam in the area as the police are landing some direct and severe blows to the students.*

Jackie watched in horror as she saw her son standing in front of the moving police line being clubbed as he dropped to the ground.

She screamed at the sight and in one motion frantically ran to her car. She speeded out of the driveway and onto the street frantically scanning the radio dial for news coverage. She found it. The radio announcer's voice broadcasted in mid-sentence loudly over the high volume of the car radio.

> *. . . trying to establish order. The police are now handcuffing some of the protesters and forcefully loading them into vans and driving them away . . . presumably off to jail. Ambulances are arriving at the scene and those who need assistance, according to the drivers, are being taken to local medical relief facilities. I have one young student protester who was at the scene. What did you see, Miss?*

The young protester, angry and flushed with tears sobbed out her story.

> *"They didn't have to hurt anyone. They kept swinging their clubs and really enjoyed it! Those pigs!"* she shouted, *"This is America. My God, so many are hurt badly."*

Jackie couldn't take anymore. She turned off the radio, crying hysterically.

"Garrett, what have you done? Where are you? Please be all right. Please God, let him be all right."

The repeated scenes of ambulances arriving at local hospitals monopolized the news. Garrett, one of the victims, was unloaded from one of the ambulance vehicles onto a hospital gurney, his head bandaged indicating a potentially severe injury from the blow of the police clubbing. He was gasping from the effects of the tear gas.

****

The emergency room had a special ward, with six to eight beds housing various wounded protesters as well as a couple of holdovers from a bar fight the night before. There was a quiet shuffling of concerned relatives attending to their young sons and daughters, each recovering from their various injuries. Jackie breathlessly entered the ward frantically searching for her own progeny. Her eyes were red and swollen revealing the emotions she had experienced watching her son's misadventures on television and driving frantically to the hospital. She quickly found Garrett lying on a bed near the back of the room looking weary, but conscious, displaying a weak smile for his obviously worried mother. A doctor attending to Garrett was about to wheel him out of the room "for some further tests."

The doctor calmly reassured Jackie that the tests would not take long and she should wait for him in the adjoining lobby. Jackie reached her hand out to touch Garrett and he managed a frail grin as he was taken from the ward.

Moving through the hospital corridors on the gurney, Garrett's thoughts were with his fellow protesters and his concern for them clouded his mind. The doctor wheeled him into a small, secluded room that did not seem like a room conducive to medical tests as it was small, dark, and had very little room for medical staff to maneuver. He glanced up at his doctor and was distracted by the dark glasses the doctor wore, which was strange – especially because the room itself had no lights. It was at that moment that he lost consciousness and was dazzled by incredibly bright lights that blinded his natural vision. The events suddenly collapsed into an all-too-real dream. The room somehow transformed into a cosmic elevator of sorts, one filled with colored lights and sounds that lifted Garrett into what seemed like another world. In an instant he felt himself standing in what appeared as a strange aircraft that defied his full comprehension. He was no longer on the hospital gurney, but was standing in front of a tall Nordic appearing man who was dressed in a form-fitting, whitish colored uniform constructed from material that was foreign to Garrett. The man, over six and one-half feet tall, was smiling at Garrett and immediately greeted him.

"Greetings, Mr. Garrett Oliver Hill. Welcome to the Asgarth Terrestrial Probe. My name is Thal, the master of this craft."

Garrett nodded his head in acknowledgement while asking himself what kind of dream he was having. He stood quietly, frozen in thought, frozen in speech. He could not seem to open his mouth to respond or ask where he was. He realized he had encountered a mystery he was absolutely unable to fathom.

Thal continued to speak, exhibiting a friendly, yet strong ethereal voice, accompanied by an assertive body language that enhanced his physical stature.

> *"I am an emissary from Asgarth, the Citadel near the inner Sun. I have brought you here to deliver a message from the central earth. You have been chosen to carry our message to the surface world and to act for us. You were chosen for many reasons as we have been watching you and your father for some time. It is you who must act in his place now.*
>
> *We have chosen to live apart from your world of turmoil and war. You are now threatening our own existence in the center world. Your peoples are learning the secrets of atomic energy and have shown their propensity to use it in a destructive manner. This cannot continue or we will have to interfere with your patterns of life and behavior. There is still time, but you must lead the way.*
>
> *You are a man of peace. But know that no man can have peace without knowing the grail . . . and one cannot win the grail,*

*but must be called by name to the grail . . . Garrett Hill, it is
from this place we call upon you. You must choose between good
and evil. You will be shown the vehicle of that power. I present
you with your key. Keep it with you at all times. Your father
can show you the way. Beware, many have fallen before you.
You will only vaguely remember this conversation, but it is fixed
in your subconscious for later retrieval. You are trusted to choose
to act for earth's salvation. You must always reject the path to
evil. You will have the choice. We can help you.*

*I have placed a small pebble in your pocket. You will find it useful
as a key at the appropriate time. Keep it near you at all times.*

Return back to your moment. We will meet again."

Jackie had become increasingly worried and impatient during
Garrett's absence from his room. She approached the nurse's station
to inquire as to when Garrett would be finished with his tests as she
had not had a chance to speak with him yet. The nurse checked the
records and stated that Garrett should still be in the ward as no patient
just admitted had been scheduled for any tests. The nurse accompanied
Jackie back to the ward to find Garrett in bed as if he had never left.
The nurse curtly informed Jackie that she must have misunderstood
as her initial records indicated that he had not been scheduled for
further tests and no doctor had as yet been assigned to him.

Although still slightly confused, Jackie was jolted back to reality
by the sight of her son in bed; his head still bandaged in the same
way he had been when he was taken from the ambulance. She quickly
dismissed her confusion blaming it on the anxiety caused by the
stressful situation. Garrett had fully regained consciousness and was
pleased to see his mother who held his hand, comforting him. Garrett was somewhat disoriented and had difficulty reconciling whether
his *abduction dream* was real or imagined. He absentmindedly put his

hand in his jeans pocket hanging alongside his bed and pulled out a small crystalline pebble. His awe would not let him connect his confused dream with the physical presence of the pebble.

The touch of Jackie's hand refocused his attention and he dismissed the ethereal experience as a heavy dream brought on by the traumatic circumstances of the past few hours. After a few quiet moments between them, Jackie gazed lovingly and sympathetically into her son's dark brown eyes.

"Are you feeling better, my dear Garrett?"

Garrett, finally emerging from his alleged dream state, replied softly, "I think so, Mom. I sure have a goose egg after getting conked on the head by one of the cops. Thanks for coming."

Jackie relaxed into her chair overlooking the end bed of the emergency ward where her son lay. She had calmed down somewhat from the frantic ordeal and was relieved that Garrett seemed O.K and not seriously injured as she had feared. After a few moments, she quietly pleaded,

"Garrett, is it worth it?"

Garrett sat up a bit in his bed, felt the top of his head and grimaced. His eyes wandered a bit before he finally spoke. He knew he had to be gentle, yet he knew his mother could understand his motivations.

"Mom," he said lovingly, "You know it is. I know you believe in what we are doing . . . even though Dad thinks I'm some kind of traitor."

"Garrett, he doesn't think that! He just doesn't understand why it is so important to you. You know how much he loves you."

"Sure Mom," Garrett answered sarcastically. "That's why he always supports me in whatever I do. Yeah, he loves me all right . . . he just wishes I was Jared."

Jackie glared at Garrett and admonished him, saying, "That's not fair . . . and you *know* that's not true."

Garrett paused a moment, considered again what he said, softened his words and quietly replied, "I know. I guess you're right. I just wish he would understand that what I do is the most important thing I can do . . . saving my friends from dying . . . for no valid reason. I'm also doing this for Jared. I loved him too, you know."

Jackie managed a slight smile. She, of course, missed Jared incredibly, but didn't want to risk losing yet another son, her beloved youngest. Jackie lovingly squeezed Garrett's hand and sat looking at him for a long moment and finally reached into her purse. She produced a couple of letters addressed to Garrett.

"Your letter from Sweden came today. It looks as if you may have gotten the response you wanted."

Garrett excitedly snatched the letter from his mother's outstretched hand, quickly scanned it and broke out in a wide grin.

"This is it, Mom! Now we've got a place to go. . . Looks like they can provide shelter, food . . . political asylum, and look at this! They will help anyone get a job. You see, this is hope for hundreds, maybe thousands."

He paused, and looked at his mother with grateful eyes.

"Thanks, Mom. I couldn't have done this without your help . . . does Dad know about this?"

Jackie paused again, thoughtfully, "Well, I don't think so . . . but, you know, he saw the letter addressed to you and handed it to me without comment. He looked me right in the eye and said . . . I think this belongs to you and Garrett."

"And he didn't say anything else?"

"No . . . he didn't."

For a moment, Jackie and Garrett looked at one another quizzically. Both wondered silently what Commander Oliver K. Hill, loving husband and devoted father was, indeed, thinking.

****

It was the next morning. Ollie Hill emerged from the bathroom into the kitchen and poured himself a cup of hot coffee and strolled over to the kitchen counter, gently kissing his wife softly just behind her left ear. Jackie smiled at her adoring husband while putting the finishing touches on a tray of food to bring to her son, Garrett. He had come home late last evening after his dad got him released from the hospital. His injuries turned out to be relatively minor, just a goose egg on his head and a pounding headache. The doctor advised a few days rest while the symptoms diminished. Ollie was the first to speak.

"How is he this morning? He was really a sight last night when we brought him home."

"Well, he seems fine . . . but I'm going to baby him for a day or two just to be sure."

"Well," Ollie said playfully, "that's a good mom for you! I could do with a bit of that babying treatment on occasion too."

"I always baby you," Jackie lovingly protested.

Jackie put down the tray and glided over to give Ollie a big hug. She looked at him with her darting brown eyes and said, "Thanks for last night."

"Thanks for what?" Ollie quietly responded, knowing just what his wife was thinking.

"Thanks for being you. You didn't judge him last night."

Ollie pondered her words for a moment, sipping another swig of the hot coffee, but didn't immediately respond.

"It appears I didn't have to. His arraignment is next Tuesday."

"How do you think it will go?" Jackie worriedly responded.

Hill paused once again before answering. He stared at the newspaper's morning headlines chronicling the mêlée that occurred the day before.

"Well, it *is* his third arrest. Remember what the judge said last time? This could be serious."

Anxiety swept over Jackie and she addressed her husband before she considered what she was asking.

"Oh, Ollie, What can we do? I couldn't stand the thought of Garrett going to jail. Is there something you can do? You are so well respected, maybe . . . "

Her voice trailed off before she finished her sentence. She knew that it wasn't fair of her to ask her husband to use his influence to intervene. Ollie was much too principled to "pull rank," even for his son.

"I'm sorry, Ollie. I know you can't do that. I shouldn't have said that." .

Ollie took his wife in his arms and spoke lovingly into her ear.

"You're his mother, Jack. I would expect you to do all you are capable of doing. He's my son too. I can only do what I'm capable of doing . . . you know that."

They embraced one another tenderly. Jackie kissed Ollie gently on the cheek whispering, "I love you," as she carried the breakfast tray off to their son's bedroom.

Chapter 5

ICELANDIC ADVENTURE

San Francisco to Iceland
1968 - 1969

*T*he arraignment and subsequent legal proceedings of the protesters were eventually dismissed, including those of Garrett. His
public attorney was able to convince the local district attorney to drop
all charges under the premise that there was not enough evidence to
convict him or single out his direct responsibility for the violence. The
attorney pleaded that it was a peaceful assembly and the students had
a right to protest. Although the local police disputed the decision, the
matter was formally dropped.

The protest movement, however, was now in full swing across
the nation. University and college students were engaging in almost
daily demonstrations that garnered much attention from the press as
well as distain by various levels of government. Young Garrett still
felt the sting of the government's role of trampling on what he and
others felt was their right to protest an unjust war. Many of the young
male protesters were displaying their displeasure with the Viet Nam
War by burning their draft cards in public gatherings. Garrett was
no exception. In fact he became an advocate of boycotting the draft
and leaving the country if one was drafted – rather than supporting an unpopular war effort. His vocal leadership in the movement
brought him much publicity, mostly negative, from the local and

national press, and overwhelmingly praise from his university peers. He took it upon himself to contact countries such as Canada and Sweden seeking to find refuge for young men wishing to protest and escape the war and the draft. With the tacit support of his sympathetic mother, he wrote several letters to various anti-war groups in Europe seeking their assistance. He appeared regularly on local and national television proclaiming his impassioned message. He soon became very prominent and recognizable in the anti-war movement and was tagged as a government *person of interest* in view of his very public persona.

As was happening with many of his fellow students and young men of his age, the day of reckoning came via the postal service. He received his draft notice from the Selective Service Board and was ordered to report to his local Board in two weeks. Garrett was faced with the decision he knew he would one day have to make. It was not a decision where Garrett felt he had any real options to ponder. He had engaged in several intense and uncomfortable conversations with his parents, each of them giving him their thoughts and opinions of what he should do. Commander Hill suggested that he consider becoming a medic to avoid combat and to keep his principles intact, yet not be subjected to prison for refusing to serve. Jackie, however, was torn. She knew the military traditions of their respective families and saw how Garrett's decision could tear apart the very fabric of her family. She had lost one son to war and didn't want in any way to risk her youngest son falling to the same fate.

Jacqueline Pendergast Hill, an attractive, university educated, and poised woman in her forties, had been raised in a strict military family herself and understood the expectations that were tradition-ally required in a military marriage. Her father, himself a retired naval lieutenant commander, had been deployed in several foreign outposts during the World War as an attaché to the Department of War. The youngest of three daughters who had each married military husbands, Jackie saw the flaws in the military way, but tolerated the vicissitudes of navy life because she did not want to upset or alienate the other members of her family. She certainly wanted Ollie to succeed in his chosen career and would do whatever it took to make her husband happy, including playing the dutiful military wife. As a young girl, she was always irreverent towards the military pomp and circumstance, but went along with what she considered silliness because she continually refused to be the cause of any family turmoil. Her father, Commander Joseph P. Pendergast, a decorated war hero, insisted on a relatively strict adherence to military custom, even at home. Dinner, for instance, always included a military salutation along with the family prayer. Jackie found it tolerable to accept the practices because of the love and deep respect she had for her father. There was no doubt in her mind that her father loved her, as he often showed subtle hints of admiration and enjoyment of her somewhat rebellious side. She was her dad's favorite daughter, and she knew it. The disappearance of Jared in Viet Nam and the possible defection of Garrett, however, put her in a position of scrambling her emotional priorities and perceived duties to follow her heart and choose being a mother first.

Ollie understood his wife's reticence to send Garrett off to a war that even he had growing misgivings about. He knew that Jackie was helping Garrett find a political refuge for his friends, so he chose to not be insistent on Garrett following his direction. Lately Ollie was having concerns about the direction the Southeast Asian war was taking and found it difficult to challenge both Garrett and his

wife on the principles they were defending. His own military training, which presupposed absolute loyalty to the government he took
an oath to defend, had become a gut-wrenching clash of long-held
values, tumbling towards a path where he would be forced to choose
between his sworn oath and his son.

Garrett, as one might expect, knew precisely what he would do in
the likely event he were to be drafted into military service. He now
had contacts in Sweden where he set about making arrangements to
go there and assist others to join him. It was a given rather than a
decision as far as he was concerned; yet his impetuous youthful enthusiasm didn't fully prepare him with what it would mean to leave his
home and family . . . or his country.

Jackie assisted Garrett in making the travel plans. She realized
that there was no persuading her son to consider any alternative.
Her emotions were peaked at the thought of sending Garrett to an
unknown country without the guidance she wanted him to have.
She relented only because she saw no alternative, yet committed
herself wholeheartedly in support of her young son. It was through
her tenacity that Garrett was able to book a flight out of San Francisco to New York and connect with Icelandic Airlines for the final
leg of his trip to Sweden. There would be an overnight stopover in
Reykjavik, Iceland as service directly to Stockholm was not always
available. Jackie wanted to pack suitcases full of clothes for any and
all occasions, but Garrett would have none of that. He insisted on
taking only what he could carry in his backpack to accommodate his
perceived need for flexibility. Garrett had already converted some
U.S dollars to Swedish Krona for his immediate needs in Sweden.
His mom offered more, but he felt that leaving was his decision and
he wanted to be responsible for himself.

Ollie and Jackie bade good-by to their son at the airport and, for the first time, it struck Garrett that he was actually leaving the comforts of his home and family. His resolve only weakened for an instant.

****

The trip to New York was relatively uneventful and Garrett arrived with a new confidence in himself. He was wearing his missing brother's air force flight jacket which Jared gifted him after he earned his wings. Sewn on the lapel and sleeves were various anti-war slogans along with several political buttons displaying his disgust for the war. His backpack was equally covered with patches and university logos. As he deplaned at LaGuardia Airport, he once again was confronted by reporters who insisted on him giving a statement. He was an unusual sight at the airport with his anti-war slogans pasted all over his possessions and his scraggly beard and long hair accentuating his youthful face. Surprised by the unexpected attention, Garrett gave what now was a well rehearsed diatribe on the evils of the Viet Nam war. Local television in New York pounced on the story and it became a first-page lead in the morning news, a fitting damning tribute, Garrett thought.

The headline read:

Student Protester Leaves Country to Evade Draft

Garrett rushed to his connecting flight and settled quickly in a window seat near the rear of the Boeing 707, the pride of the Icelandic air fleet. He was anxious and relieved that he was finally on his way. Garrett paid little attention to the other passengers but gave fleeting notice to the quirky, darkly dressed man in the seat just across the aisle, still wearing his sunglasses. He was sitting very erect in his seat and thumbing through a magazine – scanning it upside down. He was eating what appeared to be a cracker of some kind and was holding it with both hands chewing on it as a rabbit would chew a carrot. Garrett, somewhat amused by the man's idiosyncrasies, chuckled to himself. And people thought he was strange with his beard, long hair and backpack, he thought to himself.

His eyes, however, were primarily focused on the attractive airline stewardess greeting those boarding – a gorgeous Icelandic blonde beauty with an engaging smile and soothing voice giving emergency instructions to the passengers as they taxied down the runway. As the plane reached the end of the runway, the stewardess finished her required talk and sat down on the aisle seat next to Garrett, strapped on her seatbelt, looked at Garrett, smiled and whispered, "Here we go!"

The large lumbering jet plane gathered speed over the runway as it prepared for takeoff. Suddenly, the bumpy runway vibration gave way to the rumble of the landing gear retracting into the belly of the plane. The grinding sound of the mechanical gears briefly overrode the competing sounds of the whining engines. The plane was in the air.

As the 707 leveled off, Garrett stared out the paneled window on the starboard side of the plane, the wing partially obscuring a panoramic view of the New York environs. He was well aware of the beautiful stewardess sitting beside him. The stewardess stole an occasional interested glance at the young American. She ventured a question to Garrett.

"Will you be staying in Iceland long?"

Garrett turned his attention to his attractive seat mate. He was struck by her radiant face, deep blue eyes and flawless skin.

"I'm on my way to Sweden . . . a one way journey. What's your name?"

"Guthbjörg Gudmunsdottir . . . You may call me Gugga."

"Hi Gugga, I'm Garrett," he replied with a wide grin, "That's a very interesting name. Does it have any special meaning?"

Gugga giggled slightly and looked at him with amusement.

"Yes, it means the right hand of God."

"Well, it looks as if God did himself proud." Gugga is once again amused by his retort and chuckles.

"Most Icelanders are named after the Nordic Gods of Asgarth."

"Asgarth, what's that?" The puzzled Garrett quizzically responded.

Gugga smiled at Garrett, "Ah, one of Iceland's many mysteries. You have an overnight stopover in Reykjavik before your flight to Stockholm; perhaps you will take a tour of our beautiful city."

"Yeah, why not, I certainly don't have a tour agenda."

Gugga smiled sincerely at an admiring Garrett. "I must attend to the other passengers," she informed Garrett.

As she rose from her seat, she squeezed Garrett's hand and said in Icelandic,

"Perhaps God will guide your tour."

Garrett watched her glide away to her duties and slowly closed his eyes in an attempt to sleep.

His attention, though, was diverted more than occasionally to the strange passenger in black sitting directly across the aisle from him. The clumsy actions of the man continued to amuse and befuddle him. Garrett continually closed his eyelids only to be disturbed by the antics of the weird character across from him. The man had finished his meal, but was seemingly uncomfortable sitting in the somewhat cramped airline seat and constantly readjusted himself in uncoordinated motions. He refused any accommodation from the flight attendants and constantly stared out of the narrow window next to his seat.

When he took off his sunglasses, ostensibly to clean them, Garrett almost freaked out. A bright blue essence shined prominently from his now exposed eyes and revealed cat-like vertical pupils that shocked the young traveler. Realizing that Garrett was looking at him, the stranger managed a contorted smile and quickly replaced his glasses over his eyes and resumed his constant gaze out the window. "What a weirdo," thought Garrett as he slowly drifted into an uneasy slumber.

****

A few hours later, the Icelandic Airways plane touched down outside the picturesque city of Reykjavik. Garrett quickly grabbed his backpack, put on his colorful flight jacket and slowly walked off the plane. The temperature was markedly cooler than New York and the snow on the distant mountains covered the peaks. The mountains reminded him of the Eastern Sierra Nevada range that he visited so often while living in California. The western parts of the Sierra offered a variety of ski opportunities where his family often would travel for family vacations. He wondered whimsically to himself if the mountains in Iceland offered that kind of opportunity.

City of Reykjavik

Traveling lightly, he didn't have the burden of waiting for any baggage to be retrieved and he proceeded directly to the streets outside the terminal. The air was chilled, but not unbearable and Garrett took the opportunity to take in the view. The mountains were beautiful and imposing with jagged peaks interlaced with snow and ice. Apparently it never got consistently hot enough on this intriguing island to completely melt the white coverings. The streets were not the bustling activity that one would find in a large American city. In actuality there were but a few autos on the main street outside the terminal. As Garrett contemplated boarding a local tour bus to kill some time before he found a place to sleep for the night, he felt somewhat disoriented. He was anxious to get to Sweden and wished he had been able to get a direct flight. His attention was quickly interrupted by the sound of a car horn as a small sedan pulled along next to the curb with the driver waving to him. It was Gugga. She leaned out from the car window, and with her wide smile, caught Garrett's eye.

"Come," she yelled over the competing traffic noise, "I can give you a personal tour if you like."

Garrett suddenly abandoned his ambivalence seeing Gugga beckoning to him. Delighted at the prospect of spending time with her, he quickly put his backpack in the back seat of her car and settled into the front next to her.

As they drove into the central part of Reykjavik, Garrett suddenly felt extremely fortunate to be sharing some personal time seeing the city with Gugga.

"Thanks, this is so great! I thought about how boring a tour bus could be and I almost decided not to see anything and just find a place to sleep until tomorrow's flight."

"You're welcome. I am so happy that I saw you standing on the curb. Welcome to Reykjavik."

After a few self-conscious moments of silence, Gugga started the conversation as a tour guide.

"Democracy. Did you know that Iceland is one of the oldest democracies in the world?"

Garrett shook his head, still a bit bewildered at his situation, but delighted to be with her.

"It's over a thousand years old and has the oldest parliament, the *Althing*. Did you know that our president is a woman?"

"Is she blonde and beautiful too?" Garrett answered re-adjusting his sitting position to look more directly at his delightful companion.

Gugga laughed easily and accepted the indirect compliment from her handsome passenger. They continued a drive around the city with Gugga pointing out various points of interest and making general comments about Iceland. She was proud of her country and continued her description of the physical beauty and lifestyle of her people.

"Iceland has a 100% literacy rate, the lowest death rate in the world as well as the highest birth rate in all of Europe. Forty per cent of our births are, as you Americans say, illegitimate. It will be dark for about six months during the winter months . . . and we have virtually no crime."

"Hmm, I didn't realize that Iceland was considered part of Europe . . . and dark for six months? What do you people do in the dark for six months?"

Gugga contemplated his question for a moment and almost impishly she replied,

"We read a lot."

Garrett realized the double meaning of her answer and blushed slightly. Gugga watched him and laughed while he exhibited a sheepish grin. Garrett's attention was temporarily diverted as he noticed steam rising from what appeared to be a long covered culvert pipe stretching for miles along the side of the highway leading to Reykjavik.

"What's that?"

Gugga nonchalantly smiled again and commented, "Oh, that's hot water from the volcano. Iceland has over 200 active volcanoes. All of Reykjavik's water is heated by volcanoes. There are hot springs all over the country. We swim in warm water all year round. You could take an all-night shower in volcano-heated water if you wish."

Garrett jokingly lifted his arm and pretended to smell his armpit.

"Well, it seems I could use an all night shower."

They both laughed and glanced back and forth at one another aware of their obvious chemistry. Gugga stopped near a volcanic beach as Garrett's attention became fixed on a large distant mountain, an ice-capped glacier that stood prominently on the near horizon. It was further enhanced by the darkening sky as Iceland was moving into the fall/winter season. He was transfixed by the sight of this mountain image and fell silent as Gugga explained.

"Remember Jules Verne's book, *A Journey to the Center of the Earth*? Verne described a party of explorers who entered a volcanic shaft, and, after traveling for some time, arrived at the center of the earth."

"Yeah, I remember that book . . . saw the movie too! I guess I was about ten years old. They found a whole civilization there."

"Yes, and Verne believed that prior to the destruction of the ancient civilization of Atlantis in the Atlantic Ocean, some of the Atlanteans escaped and established subterranean cities in the interior of the earth. His party entered a volcanic mountain shaft on that mountain you see. It's called *Snaefellsjokull*."

"Schniefiel . . .what?" an amused Garrett retorted.

"Snaefellsjokull." Gugga repeated.

"Gesundheit!" Garrett mischievously countered.

Gugga snickered at Garrett's weak attempt at humor. The subject was, to her, a serious and historical matter although she realized that most visitors to Iceland would scoff at the Icelandic legends. Gugga went on in an attempt to clarify the meanings and the legends.

"It is an ancient belief among Icelanders that the mountain is a gateway to another world, much like Jules Verne's fictional book and movie. "You probably have not heard of Halldor Laxness?"[1]

Garrett shook his head indicating complete ignorance of such a man.

"He is Iceland's Nobel Prize-winning author. In his book, he describes the spiritual life of a community beneath the glacier. He sometimes ridicules modern Icelandic religious beliefs and he also refers to the mystical powers which long have been attributed to the glacier. He says that beneath the glacier, people are different."

"You don't believe all that . . . do you?"

Gugga simply flashes a winning smile and continued.

"The Icelandic legends also tell of Odin, the Sky God and Allfather. He was known by his blue cloak, grey garments, one eye, and long, white beard. He lived in Asgarth, Citadel of the Gods in the center of the earth, and rode the clouds on an eight-legged horse. It is said that from his seat, he could see the entirety of the whole world."

"Odin sounds a bit like the God I was raised on . . . you know, the long, white beard and all."

Smiling even wider, Gugga continued.

"Yes, and he had two ravens known as Thought and Memory. They flew over the world every morning and returned to whisper to Odin of what they had seen. The Valkyries, his warrior maidens, rode the air over battlefields and brought the souls of dying warriors to Valhalla, his hall."

"So Gugga is the daughter of Odin . . . Does she have any brothers or sisters?" Garrett queried.

"No, I'm an only child. My mother disappeared in Germany during World War II. My father, I have no idea what happened to him. Apparently he was a German officer . . . but Odin had a son," she continued. "His name is Thor. He is identified by his red beard, blue eyes and he carries a huge hammer. Thunder is made from the rumbling of his goat-drawn chariot."

Garrett continued his probing questions, increasingly aware that he was dealing with a philosophy and history he had not encountered before. He was becoming more and more curious about this strange land, and especially about his new companion.

"These legends," Garrett pondered, "Do most of the Icelanders believe in them?"

Gugga looked at Garrett more deeply, sensing that he was genuinely interested in what she was saying. There was no question that she was attracted to him, but to find him actually interested and curious about the ancient legends of her people was extremely enticing. She wondered how much more she could peak his new-found curiosity.

"Well, our history tells us that King Olaf of Norway, around the year 1000, forced the Icelanders to become Christian. Norway was the only country that Iceland could trade with and with the violent threats from the King, they eventually complied. Most of the inhabitants of that time originally came from Norway. Because of Olaf, most Icelanders are Christian."

Garrett was highly focused on Gugga's stories.

"If you had more time, you might want to speak with Sveinbjorn Beinteinsson.[2] He is the official spokesman for the *Asatru*, the religion of pre-Christian Iceland. He is properly called the High Priest or Prophet-King."

Garrett was more than intrigued. He had studied philosophy while a student at Berkeley and glossed over Nordic legends to which he was exposed, but never truly developed an intellectual or spiritual interest in what he perceived to be fantasies. His mind was attempting to bring forth whatever he could remember. He recalled that he had often wished he could actually talk to people who propagated such interesting or outlandish stories. And now, he was being offered a chance to do that.

"You mean I could actually talk to him, in person?

"Of course," Gugga replied "He is available to anyone. If you were here longer, I would be able to arrange an audience with him. You would find him extremely fascinating."

"Let's stop up the road at Thor's Café and have a cup of hot chocolate. Actually, it's only a short walk from there to where I live."

"Thor also has a café?" Garrett grinned, "He must be a latent capitalist!"

Garrett and Gugga stopped at the small café, Garrett was intrigued by his companion in ways he could not explain. They sat serenely, staring at the mountains in the background gently sipping on a large, dark, steaming chocolate drink. Each of them exchanged glances with one another enjoying their new-found relationship, feasting on the sights and sounds of the magnificent surrounding landscape. Garrett almost forgot that he was on his way to Sweden, captured by the unexpected moments and the very interesting young woman sitting across from him. He was so taken by the conversations they shared, the story of the mountain, the interior of the world, the mystical beauty of Gugga that it felt as if his interior world was changing to adapt to the new surroundings. After a seemingly short stop that was actually over an hour in duration, Garrett decided he wanted to learn more about his very interesting tutor. As they left the café,

Garrett slid his hand into Gugga's and posed a question to Gugga, not knowing how she would respond.

"You said you lived near here. Is that correct?"

"Not far, actually only a short walk from here."

Garrett fidgeted for a moment before asking her. "You know, I really am enjoying being with you, having this wonderful personal tour and listening to your beautiful stories about Iceland. I would like to spend a little more time with you, walk along this enchanting path and perhaps I could walk you home."

Gugga broke out laughing, her eyes lighting up in delight as she grabbed Garrett's arm playfully.

"Why are you laughing?" Garrett exclaimed, not detecting any humor in his remarks.

"Because you want to walk me home," Gugga responded, trying to control her giggling.

A puzzled Garrett could not figure out what was so funny. "What's so hilarious about walking you home?" Gugga hesitated for a moment and revealed to him the irony of his request.

"Because, it is a custom in Iceland that when a man asks a woman to walk her home, and she says yes, it means they will sleep together that night."

Garrett backed away from Gugga slightly, feeling terribly embarrassed for his cultural ignorance.

"I'm so sorry, I didn't mean . . ."

"Don't be sorry. I'm flattered, even if you don't know our customs."

Garrett mused about the situation he had stumbled into and contemplated his next move. He truly wanted to get to know this new lady better and knew he could always catch another plane to Stockholm. He wasn't on a strict schedule.

He turned to Gugga and said, "Gugga, may I walk you home, no matter how I interpret your customs – and no expectations?"

Gugga now regarded Garrett with a new perspective. She didn't have a current beau and was very attracted to her new acquaintance. She, too, wanted to get to know this handsome American boy and quickly decided that spending time with him could be a wonderful interlude.

"Well, my next flight is a few days from now. I can get you on the plane of your choosing. I would love to have you walk me home."

****

Gugga's home was a small upstairs flat above a theater where short play performances were held on holidays and special occasions. As they climbed upstairs to her dwelling, Gugga was carrying her flight bag as Garrett was hauling his back pack up the winding stairway. She unlocked the door with a small key, looked back at Garrett and entered. Gugga immediately set down her personal belongings, walked over to a floor lamp to light the small room and, if as one motion, turned up the heat.

"Welcome to my home," said Gugga. She planted a quick kiss on Garrett's cheek and directed him to place his back pack on a small table. As he did so he rummaged through his jean's pocket and found a crystalline stone. He was perplexed as to how it got there as his memory of the visit to Thal's craft had faded over the months. But, he had a deep sense that he should keep it with him.

"Make yourself comfortable while I fix us something to eat. You must be very hungry, are you not?"

"I am. Thanks."

He watched her move about the flat with grace and charm and

marveled at how beautiful she was. He had never met a woman like her in his life.

He walked around the room studying the décor, pictures of local scenery, photographs of her and various friends or relatives. One photo was that of a young Nordic featured man, probably in his twenties. Garrett looked at it with interest.

"Boyfriend?" he said aloud so Gugga who was in the kitchen could hear.

Gugga stepped from the kitchen area to see to whom he was referring.

"No, he is a childhood friend. His name is Magnus Magnusson. We still write occasionally and send photos to one another. I believe he now lives in Munich and attends the University there. I haven't seen him in years."

Garrett continued browsing around and came to a photograph of a young German Naval Officer in a Kreigsmarine uniform, vintage World War II.

"Who's this?"

Gugga came all the way in from the kitchen area carrying a couple of plates of food. She set them down on a square table set against a window with an open view of the city and a small lake to the left and invited Garrett to sit with her as she acknowledged the photo.

"My mother gave me that photo when I was a young girl . . . before she disappeared. She said it was my father. I don't know. I have never seen him or heard from him. I've assumed he was killed in the war."

"Do you know what happened to your mother?"

"You ask a lot of questions, don't you?"

"I'm sorry," Garrett responded, "I'm just curious."

Gugga was intrigued by his inquisitiveness and set the plates down. She glided over and caressed Garrett's face between her hands and kissed him gently on the lips. He welcomed the soft kiss and put his arm around her waist, pulling her closer as they embraced each other. After a moment, Gugga gently pulled away, placing two fingers on Garrett's lips as she slowly retreated from their embrace.

"You need to eat before it gets too cold." Gugga suggested quietly.

They settled into their meal and slowly began to munch on the delicacies that Gugga had prepared. During the meal both of them continued exchanging glances and smiles, thinking to themselves how wonderful it was to be together. Gugga was the first to speak.

"My mother went to Germany. I think to look for my father. I was just a very little girl. She never returned and I never heard from her again. I lived with my grandmother for many years until she passed away nearly a year ago. I've lived in this flat ever since."

"And you never heard anymore about your mother . . . or your father?"

"No, except . . . ," her voice pausing thoughtfully.

"Except what?"

"Well, it's strange. When my grandmother died, I started getting checks sent to me from an unknown benefactor . . . postmarked from America. When I went through my grandmother's things, I found records showing that these checks had been coming since I was a small child. Someone has been supporting me for all these years and I have no idea who. Sometimes I fantasize that they are from my mother who somehow can't get back to me, and sometimes I think that they may come from my father's estate. But in truth, I really don't know . . . what about you?"

"Me, what about me?"

"Why are you going to Sweden?"

Garrett regarded her closely and thought about what he should tell her.

"Oh, what the hell. I got my draft notice and rather than go into the military and fight in Viet Nam, I decided to go to Sweden."

Garrett looked directly into Gugga's eyes to detect an adverse reaction to what he just revealed. He got none.

"Apparently," he continued, "I became well-known for my anti-war activities in Berkeley and the government thinks I'm dangerous to the country . . . do you think I'm dangerous?"

Gugga blurted out emotionally, "For not wanting to kill or be killed in an unjust war? No, I don't think you're dangerous. I think you are very brave . . . and your family, how do they feel about you leaving?"

Garrett began to open up, feeling her trust through her empathetic reaction.

"My mom helped me with my protest activities . . . at least as much as she could. She cried when I left, but she knew it was my decision. The thing I remember most was her saying to my dad as they were seeing me off in San Francisco, *Now I've lost both my sons.* My older brother, Jared, was, or is, I don't know which, a pilot in the U.S. Air Force and was shot down somewhere near Hanoi. He is listed as M.I.A. Mom's words keep echoing in my ears. It's hard to ignore. Of course I can't help but wonder if I made the right decision."

"And your father?"

"You mean COMMANDER O.K Hill, U.S. Navy?" Garrett emphasized, pausing thoughtfully. "My father knew I was leaving. He didn't approve. It was his idea that I should become a medic or something so I wouldn't have to kill anyone. I told him that it was still wrong for me to fix others up from their wounds just so they could go out and kill someone. It's the same thing as far as I am concerned."

"But didn't he try to stop you?

"No, he didn't. My dad is hard to figure out. There are times when I think deep down he might actually agree with me, and other times when he acts like the military man he is. When I left, he didn't say anything to stop me. He just looked at me with a longing gaze, hugged me and stepped back so I could give another hug to my mom."

"What did you want him to do?" Gugga asked inquisitively.

Pausing, Garrett stammered, "Hell, I don't know. All I know is that I had to leave . . . Say, what is this I'm eating?"

Gugga looked down at the meal she served Garrett, pointing to the bowl. "This is Plokkfiskur, a fish soup with potatoes, white sauce and a couple of strips of Hardfiskur from the Sea Wolf for dipping. Also a slice of rye bread with a generous topping of Svith . . . made from boiled sheep heads and a dab of Skyr . . . what you call yogurt, on the side."

She paused and looked for a reaction from Garrett.

"Well, you have a meal *almost* fit for a Viking," she announced. Garrett quizzically looked up at her and said, "Almost?"

"Yes," she replied, "You can become an honorary Viking if you can eat this and a small piece of Hakarl."

"Do I dare ask what Hakarl is?" as Garrett reacted almost apathetically to the strange concoctions already before him.

Gugga continued her narrative vaguely challenging him with suggestive voice tones to adjust to the new tastes presented to him.

"But, of course, you will need a few swallows of Brennivin, also known as *Black Death*, to eat the raw, rotten, Greenland Shark soaked in urine for several months."

Garrett looked up at her animated face, absolutely traumatized by her chilling description of Icelandic traditional food habits, and uttered, uncomfortably, "Uhh, No thanks, I think I'll pass on the urine Viking thing."

Not wanting to hear any more about unappetizing Icelandic food traditions and wanting to change the subject, he seemingly out of the blue, blurted out, "By the way, did you notice that weird guy dressed in black who sat across the aisle from me? He distracted me for the entire flight – his crazy blue eyes and gawky movements. Who was he?"

"Just another passenger," replied Gugga who was much too focused on assuring Garrett's comfort to give any thought to strange passengers, a phenomena that occurs frequently in her duties as a flight attendant.

Gugga laughed, once again amused by Garrett's frequent questions and quaint responses. Garrett found Gugga absolutely irresistible, moved towards her and kissed her slowly with deep feeling. She willingly responded. After a moment or two, she pulled away gently, looked deeply into his eyes and began to unbutton his shirt. His eyes closed as he enjoyed the moment. Gugga slipped off his shirt and whispered quietly into his ear.

"First, let me draw you a bath and bathe you. You must be exhausted from your travels."

Garrett slowly opened his eyes as Gugga turned and moved towards the bathroom. He soon heard the bathwater running and waited with a heightened sense of anticipation. Gugga returned from the bathroom wearing a short robe highlighting her long, slim legs and well proportioned body. She gently took his hand to take him in to the bath.

She sampled the temperature of the bathwater and invited him to slip in. He took off his remaining clothes and slid into the water while Gugga tenderly began to wash him with a soft sponge. Garrett quickly fell into a majestic state of ecstasy, as the sulphur-scented steam from the hot bathwater obscured his eyes. His mind was soothed and he relished the quiet as he luxuriated in what seemed to be a spot in paradise. Gugga dropped her robe and joined him in the oversized tub.

****

Garrett toweled himself off next to Gugga's soft bed which was tastefully adorned with feminine doilies and silk pillows. There was a heavy home-made woolen quilt for warmth even as the little flat was now heated to a comfortable and pleasant temperature. Gugga was toweling her hair dry, looking sheepishly at Garrett as if about to tell him something.

"I saw you on television," she confessed.

Garrett stopped his drying, and exclaimed, "What are you talking about?"

Gugga explained,

"I recognized you when you got on the plane in New York. Not too many people wear the clothes you wear and look like you and burn their draft cards on national television. On our many layovers in the U.S., television is often our only entertainment."

Garrett was shocked. He pondered her words for a moment, and broke out in a wide grin.

"You knew all the time, I can't believe it."

He was genuinely surprised at what she related, but felt delighted that she had taken notice of him and quietly pursued him without his realizing it. He playfully grabbed her in mock anger as they both laughed and fell playfully together on the bed.

****

It was early the next morning when Garrett shifted his body and stretched to begin waking up. He reached over to find Gugga, but she was gone. He stumbled out of bed, went to the kitchen area and poured himself some hot tea that Gugga had prepared. Going to the main window overlooking the street from the flat, he stared at the new morning, unsure of what time it was. He laughed to himself thinking that it really wasn't important what time it was as he no longer needed to be aware of it. While dressing in his familiar clothes, he contemplated where he was and how he got there. He wandered over to Gugga's bookshelf and pulled a book that had a cover featuring a drawing of a hollow earth. A photo of the globe with openings at each pole fell out and onto the floor. The book recalled his earlier conversation with Gugga when she hinted at Icelandic legends and a hollowed earth. He was intrigued and began to read aloud passages from the book.

He heard the turn of the door lock as Gugga had entered with some groceries. She immediately put down the groceries and embraced Garrett with a tender hug. She noticed that Garrett was examining the book.

"So you found my mysterious book," she said, slipping her arm around his waist. "Do you find it interesting?"

"I've never even heard of the earth being hollow. It's just an Icelandic legend, right?"

Gugga began to put away the few items of food she brought home. She nonchalantly answered his question. "Perhaps," she offered, "Perhaps it is more than legend."

"Well that would be a historical coup," he exclaimed. "It would turn mankind on its ear. Fascinating! What if it were true?"

Gugga simply smiled as Garrett contemplated what he just said and he fell into deep thought studying the extraordinary pictures in the book. He ambled across the room to the window and lifted his eyes towards the receding Northern Lights with a new and intriguing interest that he had not contemplated just twenty-four hours ago. He didn't yet realize that it was his destiny to stay with Gugga in Iceland, creating an entirely new purpose in his young life.

Chapter Notes:

1. **Halldor Laxness:** Born 4/23/1902 died 2/8/1998. Icelandic novelist who was awarded the Nobel Prize for Literature in 1955. He was considered the most creative Icelandic writer of the 20th century. He published a series of articles with topics drawn from the social life of Iceland. His modernistic style marked the beginning of his disassociation from Christianity.

2. **Sveinbjorn Beinteinsson:** 7/4/1924 died 12/23/1993. A native of Iceland, also known as The Prophet or the King of Iceland. He was instrumental in gaining recognition by the Icelandic government of the pre-Christian Norse religion. He acted as *godi* (priest), of an organization that was officially recognized as a religious body in 1973.

Chapter 6

ICELANDIC MYSTERIES

1968 -1980

*L*iving in Iceland was not in Garrett's plans when he left the United States in protest of the war in Viet Nam. Iceland, however, offered Garrett the opportunity to restart his life and still operate a small enterprise to assist fellow defectors. His Swedish contacts were more than happy to work with Garrett and he reveled in the unexpected serendipity wherein he and Gugga became live-in partners. Her schedule with the airlines and his volunteer work with potential defectors gave them both ample time to be alone and together. Garrett was also able to secure a part-time teaching job at one of the local secondary schools, who were delighted to have a competent native-speaking American teacher to help their students learn English. English was a required course in Iceland and most Icelanders spoke it relatively fluently. Garrett's knowledge of American customs and social culture gave him a unique status among his fellow instructors and delighted the students. Gugga and Garrett were both supremely happy and Garrett was quickly accepted as the mate of Gugga's by her friends and colleagues. Their new life was a magnificent dream come true.

A pleasant surprise for both Gugga and Garrett was to discover that she was pregnant. Garrett became the attentive father-to-be while Gugga's beauty grew even more pronounced as the pregnancy developed. Finally, just nine months from when Garrett arrived, the baby was born. The happy couple doted on their new healthy young daughter. In keeping with Iceland's tradition, the blonde-haired blue-eyed child was named Thora, after the ancient God, Thor.

Settling down in Reykjavik, Garrett spent many of his leisure hours studying Norse legends, especially those that related to a hollow earth. He read as much as he was able to find and then sought out Icelandic folks who still adhered to the ancient customs and beliefs. His curiosity became a new obsession. His teaching job was a joy to him as he loved working with young and eager students. His volunteer work was satisfying, even if not directly in Sweden. He was able to keep in touch with the world news, particularly the progress of the war in Southeast Asia. His mother would regularly send him the newspaper from San Francisco to keep him up on current events. The *San Francisco Chronicle* seemed to express a bias towards ending the war as the growing protests ramped up the pressure on the political system.

Gugga and Garrett initiated and maintained a close relationship with his parents, often talking on the phone for lengthy periods of time. Garrett enjoyed it when his mom and Gugga talked with one another on the phone. They found much common ground in their conversations despite the differences in cultures. Garrett would regularly converse with his father, mostly about flying and various sports in which both had maintained an interest. Garrett was able to persuade an acquaintance, a fellow airplane enthusiast named Bjorn Ericksson, to let him fly with him over the Icelandic glaciers in his small plane. Garrett assured his father that he would not neglect his flying skills; there were endless wonders to explore in Iceland. Ollie would inquire as to how Garrett was getting along and exhibited a forgiving and loving interest in the welfare of his son. There seemed to be a mutual acceptance of one another's personal choices, and an easy rapport between the two was soon reestablished. There was still no word or confirmation, however, regarding Jared's status or fate. That subject remained a dark sadness to all of them.

****

Garrett's interest and experience in flying led him to visit the Reykjavik airport where he looked forward to being near small planes and nourish his visceral thrill of flying. On several occasions he took his young toddler, Thora, with him. It was Garrett's hope and dream that he could instill his love of flying in his inquisitive young daughter and this was a perfect opportunity to spend precious time with her. She enjoyed watching the various aircraft taking off and landing, giggling and pointing to each aircraft as it came and went, as they sat on a wooden bench near the small craft hangers.

It was on a Tuesday afternoon when Garrett and Thora were delighting in the airport activity when Garrett noticed a young man near his age working on a private aircraft's engine. Garrett observed him intently while Thora, elated in her laughter, reacted as the man dropped one of his wrenches and yelled an obscenity. Suddenly embarrassed, the young man nervously glanced over at Garrett and awkwardly offered a muted short distance apology. Garrett simply laughed and nodded back to him and waved his acceptance.

The man descended his ladder propped up near the engine, picked up his wrench and walked over to Garrett and Thora.

"I'm terribly sorry for that," he exclaimed. "I realize that you have a young child with you. I'm very embarrassed inasmuch as I have a young daughter myself."

"Not a problem," responded Garrett, "She's heard my indiscretions before. I have my moments also."

"My name is Bjorn. I live here in Reykjavik, born here actually. I can tell by your accent that you are not an Icelander."

"No, I am an American, been here for about two years, living with an Icelander. My daughter's name is Thora."

Bjorn tenderly greeted Thora with an affectionate acknowledgement.

"Do you get a chance to fly often?" asked Garrett.

"Oh yes, I have a contract to deliver mail and supplies to some of the towns on the north side of the Island. So I fly a few times a week. Been doing this for a few years now . . . took over my father's routes after he died."

Bjorn and Garrett spontaneously engaged in a spirited conversation each revealing to one another their interest in planes and flying and comfortably discussing their personal lives. Their easy manner with one another was genuine and personal. Both were about the same age and seemed to have much in common. Bjorn revealed that he and his girlfriend were not married but they had lived together for several years and had a young daughter by the name of Meda, now about four years of age. His live-in girlfriend, Marit, was a research assistant in heat induction and worked on various geo-thermal heating systems and projects throughout Iceland.

"I occasionally take Marit with me on my flights north, just for company. I've even taken my daughter up a few times for short runs. Do you have a plane?"

"No, not here. I learned to fly in California. My father is a pilot and made sure my brother and I both learned when we were young. My brother is missing in Vietnam, presumed dead. It was his inspiration and the absurdity of the war that brought me to Iceland. I do miss the feeling and thrill of flight and the majesty of being free in the heavens above."

"Well, said Bjorn, "Perhaps you might want to join me on one of my flights. I could sure use the company and, if you can fly this thing, you can assist me. What do you think?"

"I'd be delighted and thrilled . . . and I can help you with the maintenance and repair of the aircraft. I'm quite a good mechanic."

"We'll do it then," an excited Bjorn responded.

"Perhaps we can meet first together with our families. We don't get to visit much with folks. I will check with Marit and we can have you and . . . your lady's name?"

"Gugga," answered Garrett.

"Wonderful! Garrett, Gugga and Thora. My family will be so delighted."

To the surprise of both Gugga and Marit, each recognized one another through social activities within the city. Bjorn and Marit proved to be a wonderful match with Garrett and Gugga. Thora was delighted by the antics of her slightly older friend, Meda, who in turn, entertained Thora with her dolls and rock collection. Marit and Gugga found much in common and each was fascinated by the other's profession.

Bjorn was a tall wiry blonde-haired Icelander, definitely of Nordic extraction as his countenance echoed classical Scandinavian features. He was soft spoken, well mannered and seemed especially devoted to his ladyfriend and daughter. He spoke Icelandic, Norwegian, English and German, as was the norm in most of Iceland. He had inherited the mail and supply contract through his father's business after his death. He did so mostly to honor his father, but soon found it as addictive a profession as his father had. While the job did not make them rich, it provided adequately for his family, especially coupled with Marit's additional income. He was a happy man and delighted to have a new friend that shared his passion for flying.

A week after the two families met for dinner at Bjorn and Marit's small bungalow, Bjorn invited Garrett to accompany him on one of his sojourns on the North Island. They would make stops at the West Coast town of Blonduos and fly further North to Saudarkrokur, a city of about 2,000 people, to deliver medical supplies as well as a week's mail and other products and materials that were difficult to get in the small northern settlements. Garrett immediately accepted and met Bjorn early the following morning. The weather was clear, with some clouds forming in the North which promised a chance of rain, ice, or snow. Bjorn was well aware of the conditions but felt that it was still good weather to fly. He had flown in much more inclement weather then was forecast for this trip. Garrett also examined Bjorn's flight plan and certainly trusted Bjorn's assessment of the weather condition.

He bid Gugga and Thora adieu in the early morning hours and arrived at the scene to observe Bjorn warming up the Cessna 180 and doing a last minute air worthiness check. Garrett already knew that Bjorn was meticulous regarding his aircraft, and stood admiring Bjorn's attention to the minutest details in preparing for the flight, much like Garrett's father who had drilled him on the protocols and the steps in departure. Bjorn had shared with Garrett that he bought the Cessna because it was his father's delivery route that the government bestowed on him after his father crashed and was lost on his way to Saudadarkrokur some years ago. Bjorn flew commercial routes three to four times a week. He was grateful that he had a job that not only honored his father, but allowed him to fly regularly and be paid enough that he still had time to enjoy his other hobbies and duties. Bjorn was a history buff and spent much of his non-working time studying Norse history. He was often sought after to share his historical insights with local school children. This was intriguing to Garrett – yet another commonality that they shared. Garrett's own curiosity about Icelandic history had become a deep and abiding interest – especially after his early introduction from Gugga's own knowledge and practices.

Almost immediately after the flight plan briefing, the two boarded the plane and taxied to the runway awaiting permission to take off. The lack of air traffic at that time of day allowed a prompt take-off and the Cessna 180 roared to life, gathered speed along the runway, and lifted gently into the morning sky. As the craft leveled off they began their Northern flight to the west coastal town of Blonduos. It was a trip of about two-hours, mostly uneventful – save a slight edginess regarding the weather – a constant challenge when flying the unpredictable skies of Northern Iceland.

Blonduos was a small hamlet with a population of five-hundred or so. They landed on a small and somewhat rough airstrip and immediately taxied to the terminal – a set of steel huts that were surely remnants from World War II, now more than a generation ago. Bjorn quickly began the unloading process as a truck pulled alongside his plane to take the deliveries and load up outgoing mail and material to go on to Saudarkrokur or back to Reykjavik. Meanwhile, a refueling truck pulled up and began servicing the Cessna. Quite an efficient operation, thought Garrett, especially for a small outpost in an isolated spot in Iceland. The fuel truck driver brought some hot coffee to the flyers as, apparently, was the routine for Bjorn's frequent visits. All knew that the plane needed to get on its way relatively quickly in order to meet the time schedules specified by the flight plan.

Garrett felt exhilarated to be in the air with Bjorn. Although it was a bit difficult to hold a deep conversation due to the continual roar of the engine, both young men thoroughly enjoyed their time together.

The flight from Blonduos to Saudarkrokur was a bit bumpier as the weather was changing in anticipation of a potential storm. As they approached Saudarkrokur, the wind was blowing quite intensely and ice began forming on the wings. Both men recognized that they needed to land as quickly as possible. As they were approaching the airstrip in a mild descent, the airport warned of crosswinds and a potential icy runway. The visibility was rapidly getting worse and Bjorn expertly touched down smoothly. The craft made a violent shift as they touched down and both men were suddenly thrown against the cabin doors as the plane spun slightly into a skid onto the icy runway. Bjorn deftly brought the Cessna to a stop just outside the terminal and looked over at Garrett with a sigh of relief.

"Well, that was fun," Bjorn said with an impish smile. "We must choose not to do that again sometime," he joked. "I think, though, I may have injured my left shoulder," he groaned.

Garrett quickly unbuckled his seatbelts and assisted Bjorn in doing the same. "I think you better have this looked at," Garrett suggests, "It might be broken."

"Well, I hope not," Bjorn retorted, "You would have to fly us back."

The terminal crew immediately sent out a medical truck and personnel to assist with any issues or problems that the boys had.

"I think we need a doctor," Garrett shouted out to the airport personnel. With that, the airport driver quickly loaded Bjorn and Garrett into the truck to take them to the medical facility – with Bjorn stoically enduring whatever pain he felt.

"I'll see to your plane," one of the men yelled through the now substantial snowfall. "It doesn't seem to have incurred any damage."

"By the way, we don't have a doctor on duty tonight. You will have to see a medical assistant," said the truck driver.

Within minutes they arrived at the medical facility. Garrett carefully helped Bjorn out of the truck and they made their way inside.

The "facility" was the epitome of stark. There were no decorations, signs, or art to identify its purpose, with only a few medical brochures on the waiting room counter to even give hints as to its purpose. Nonetheless, Garrett guided Bjorn into the building and rang a small bell on the counter.

A moment later, much to the surprise of Garrett, a man dressed in a black suit wearing dark glasses and a hastily donned white smock appeared from a back room. Garrett was speechless. No, it was not the same man Garrett had seen on the plane, but certainly his odd character bore a startling resemblance to that strange individual, the memory of whom was immediately revived. Re-gathering his wits, Garrett explained to the man that his friend was hurt and had injured his arm or shoulder in the landing a few minutes prior. The medical man said nothing, but gestured to both of them to come behind the counter into a small examining room. He assisted with the removal of Bjorn's jacket and shirt and carefully probed the areas of concern.

After a moment or two of touch and manipulation, he turned to Bjorn and said, "It is not broken and the bone is merely bruised. The pain will subside with time."

Garrett listened closely and could not help noticing the man's staccato and halting voice patterns. His mind jumped back and forth from the present encounter to the strange memories that jumped into his mind of that weird character he observed on his flight to Iceland.

The strange man gave Bjorn a small bottle of white pills and directed him to take two at a time when experiencing severe pain. He put an ointment on the bruise and sent them on their way.

They were scheduled to stay that night in a small hotel near the airport. They checked in for the evening, settling into their room as each recounted their impressions of the experiences of the day.

Garrett couldn't wait to get Bjorn's opinion on the strange medical examiner.

"Did you get a good look at him, hear his speech patterns?" Garrett exclaimed. "I've seen a man like him before . . . really weird, all dressed in black wearing dark glasses at times when glasses are not needed. The man I saw before had blue eyes that were shaped like vertical slits – quite strange. I didn't get to see this guy's eyes, but there was definitely a blue tinge emanating from them through the glasses. Who – or maybe what should be the question – do you think he is?"

Bjorn touched Garrett on the shoulder, pondering how to answer his new friend's legitimate queries in a way he could logically accept.

After a moment of contemplation, Bjorn quietly and gently suggested to Garrett, "I think you need to sit down and listen carefully to me. I am going to share with you something that may cause you to think that I've taken leave of my common sense."

Bjorn took a deep breath and slowly offered the following to Garrett.

"Those types of men are not uncommon in the Northern part of Iceland. We acknowledge them for what they are. They are not from Iceland, they are not Norse. And . . . Bjorn paused for a moment before asserting, "They are not truly human.

"They have been with us for many, many years. We have come to accept them for what they are. They are harmless creatures – strange, but harmless. As our ancestors got used to them, we have also accepted them as part of our Northern society."

"Bjorn, you are blowing my mind. This is too weird. Who are they? What are they? Where are they from?"

"I know you may think I'm crazy, Garrett, but these men are part of the Nordic mysteries. They are real, but they are not human.

As you know, I am also an historian. I've researched many Nordic legends, myths, and religions. I can tell you, at the risk of you never trusting my word to you again, that they are said to be biologically engineered robots that are sent here from Asgarth, the civilization in the center of the earth. We believe they are here to watch over the human population, to keep tabs on what we are doing. Apparently, they are fearful of what the human population is doing, especially now with the advent of nuclear energy and mankind's seeming willingness to use it for destructive purposes. From what I have learned over the years, they are watchful because whatever occurs on the surface that disrupts the outer earth has a direct effect upon the peaceful population within."

"Wow," Garrett exclaimed, "I knew Iceland's secrets were profound, but having these weird episodes happening to me just scrambles my brain. It's really weird that I can accept what you are telling me while still disbelieving my acceptance. It's a strange psychological space to be caught in. It's difficult to accept my own rationality."

"A significant number of people know what just what you are experiencing as they have gone through the same transformation of thought. After acceptance, one simply knows there is more to our existence than we are commonly taught to believe. We deal with that knowledge while still going through our somewhat normal lives. It's like having a subconscious link to yet another dimension where a new aspect of our existence is revealed. I'm not fearful of these phenomena, but, I know that one day the truth of all this will be revealed to the outside world, and anticipating that revelation and its effects is somewhat daunting. The existence of an inner earth population has become, as you say, an open secret – one that we seldom share. I only tell you this because you are my friend; you have questioned me and I feel that you will respect the integrity of my explanation. You now join a very select group of people who are aware of Asgarth – aware of an inner earth."

The flight back to Reykjavik was smooth and comfortable. Their flight from Saudarkrokur to Blonduos was mostly silent as both Bjorn and Garrett reflected quietly on the events and conversation they shared. The final leg back to Reykjavik found Garrett probing for a bit more information from Bjorn, now convinced that he had been blessed with a true friend, one who not only shared the thrills of flying, but also who shared his intimate thoughts freely and generously.

Garrett could hardly wait to tell Gugga about this new information, thinking how amazed she would be about all the revelations regarding the mysterious men in black. Garrett bubbled inside just anticipating her reaction.

Arriving back to his home, Garrett greeted his companion with enthusiasm and excitement. He spoke of the journey he and Bjorn had just finished, detailing almost every moment of their time together. After his enthusiastic recount of the trip, Garrett finally got around to telling her the truly exciting news he learned.

"Gugga," Garrett began, "do you remember that weird guy that sat across the aisle from me when we first met? When I mentioned him to you before, you passed him off as just another strange passenger. Well, I now learned from Bjorn that he wasn't just weird, but was a real visitor from Asgarth, from the center of the earth. I couldn't wait to tell you that I met another one with Bjorn and he, somewhat reluctantly, told me an incredible story about a number of these weird guys who are here to keep an eye on our human events. I was blown away!"

Gugga listened intently to Garrett's animated story as she helped Thora take a bath. She didn't appear as excited as Garrett had anticipated and he was a bit puzzled by her lack of enthusiasm.

She finished assisting Thora, went into the kitchen area and poured a cup of coffee for both herself and Garrett. She fidgeted around with some meaningless chores and finally sat down with Garrett.

As she sipped from her cup, she looked quietly over at Garrett and softly said, "What you say does not surprise me. I've known about them for some time now. When you brought it up before, I purposely ignored it and changed the subject. I knew you weren't ready as yet. They are, indeed, part of the mysteries and lore that I mentioned to you when you first arrived. I am surprised and delighted that Bjorn is one of those who know, inasmuch as only a select few have that knowledge and insight. I am delighted that you are now aware. I have been reluctant to share that with you because there is so much that I have shared that I sometimes think I am overwhelming you with mystical information about our culture and you may think that I am losing touch with so-called reality. I know you are interested in this lore and I look forward to embarking with you on a provoking quest. You truly have a love for Nordic legends and history. We'll study it hand in hand, together. I do so love you!"

Garrett relaxed in solitude after hearing Gugga bearing her soul to him. He understood her early reluctance to share all her mystical feelings with him, but he began to look at his beautiful consort with new and appreciative eyes. He realized that he had a lot more to learn. And now he had both Gugga and Bjorn to help guide him.

Chapter 7

THE SPIRIT OF ICELAND

1968 - 1979

*O*ver their early months and years together, Gugga had introduced Garrett to many of the prominent research and spiritual leaders in Iceland. He had the good fortune to meet such world-wide luminaries as Halldor Laxness, the Nobel Prize winning author of the book, *Beneath the Glacier,* as well as Svienbjorn Beinteinsson, the high priest and prophet that Gugga had mentioned on Garrett's first day in Iceland. He was amazed at how easily the leaders of the country, political, spiritual, and social, would manage to find time to talk personally to him and Gugga. But, he reasoned, the whole of Iceland had a population of less than 300,000 people, substantially less than the San Francisco Bay area with which he was familiar. There were definitely advantages living in a small country. Garrett soaked up the experiences with great enthusiasm and quizzical interest.

His experience with Svienbjorn Beinteinsson was perhaps the most enthralling of the meetings he had so far. As he and Gugga entered the ornate home of *The Prophet-King,* he was struck by the host's clothing. Beinteinsson wore a traditional red and black velvet-lined cloak, clearly of some ancient origin, while sporting leather sandals over heavy stockings wrapped with fraying twine – just as described in Nordic legends. Garrett judged him to be in his mid forties or early fifties, a graying beard that tended towards the wild side.

Beinteinsson smiled genially and grasped both their hands as he led them into his museum-like home. Old spiritual relics and symbols of unknown origin dotted the furniture and a multitude of photographs and ancient paintings hung in the hallway and adjacent rooms. The house was heated by two iron radiators that emitted steam from their mechanical innards.

Garrett was fascinated beyond belief. Gugga drank in the impressive array of artifacts and wondrous paintings. On the back wall was a curious framed sketch of three Runic[1] symbols arranged in a triangle with a gemstone placed at the center. Garrett peered at the drawing and stared at it with an intense interest. He was fascinated by the alphabetic symbols of the Runes as they seemed very different from anything he had encountered in the past. Gugga was so captivated by the drawing that she took out a small pad and pencil and sketched it in her notebook, carefully noting the markings on the runes. Her thought was to artistically reproduce this work of art to compliment her collection of artifacts of Nordic legends.

"What does this drawing represent and what are those interesting markings on each of those three stones?" Garrett asked respectfully.

The Prophet paused and put his hand on Garrett's shoulder. He studied him for a moment as if to determine Garrett's readiness to receive the mystery contained in the drawing. This particular piece was something only a few would pause to examine, and even fewer would be drawn to enquire as to its meaning. The Prophet instantly knew that Garrett was one of the few. Gugga was clearly touched by it as well.

"That, my son," the Prophet extolled with solemnity, "is the key – the key that unlocks the many mysteries of the universe. It is called the *Runic Triangle*. It is said to have the power to open locked tombs, bypass blocked entrances, unveil the secrets of the inner earth, and reveal the power of the pyramids. Each runic symbol – there are twenty-four total – can contribute to the power of the triangle and activates the key. The three depicted in the drawing are the primary gateways to the power of the triangle. Once mastered, one who understands runic power and has the knowledge and ability to energize the triangle, has the magic of the key at his disposal. Nothing physical or mental or spiritual can be blocked or locked from him or her."

Svienbjorn Bienteinsson
The Prophet King

"Wow!" Garrett exclaimed, "How would one access the means to energize it? Is it something that is learned or is it a gift that is given only to those who have been initiated in some way?"

"The power to energize the triangle is bestowed by the gods when the right to receive it has been earned. He who earns it may not know he has the power until he attempts to use it. How and why the gift is given remains part of the mystery, part of the Universal conscience. To activate the power, one would need to arrange the three runes in a precise ordered triangle and then place the energizer piece in the direct center of the triangle. The power of the mind, a gift from the universal consciousness, commands the action desired and the barriers disappear."

"But what is the energizer? How does one find the energizer?" Garrett probed further.

The Prophet turned Garrett towards him and solemnly stated, "He will know."

Finding the Prophet's explanation both highly interesting and deeply mysterious, Garrett conjured up myriad scenarios in his overly active mind before being distracted by yet another painting in the Prophet's large rooms.

Gugga and Garrett stopped in front of a large, almost life-sized oil painting that depicted Jesus the Christ nailed to the cross. Surprised that the Prophet would keep a Christian oriented piece in the most prominent spot in the largest room, both were taken by the majesty of the scene.

The Prophet stepped forward in front of the painting and remarked to the curious pair, "The soldier with the spear who stands before the cross was a Roman Centurian who had loyally and bravely served his country for many years. He was a distinguished veteran officer of the Roman Legions. His name was Gaius Cassius."

The two visitors listened intently as the Prophet detailed the scene revealed by the painting. As Beinteinsson quietly spoke, the two listeners unwittingly let go of their logical minds and lost themselves in the narrator's tantalizing and ethereal voice as if they were witnessing the incredible event themselves in person.

"The spear which he holds in his hand had a special quality. It never rusted and was always sharp. All who tested the Lance considered it to be almost magical, the finest weapon in the Roman army.

The Prophet pointed directly at the spear and continued,

"The spear was presented to Gaius Cassius' grandfather by none other than Julius Caesar as a special reward for meritorious service during the conquest of Gaul. It had been carried by his father in the service of Germanicus Caesar and in turn handed down to Gaius Cassius. He was nearing the end of his long and distinguished career as a professional soldier of the Roman Empire, with his health failing and his eyesight growing dim. In order to complete his final year or two of service, he was assigned to a non-combative duty in the political observation corps in Jerusalem. As a ranking centurion and political observer under the command of Pro-Consul Protectorate, Governor Pontius Pilate, he was free to come and go as he pleased in the province of Palestine."

"Why does Gaius Cassius hold such a place of importance in history?" Gugga asked.

"It's a bit of a complicated story," the Prophet retorted as he continued, "Gaius Cassius' attention, while he traversed the area in his role as observer, was attracted to a small slender man with light, flowing hair and pale, compelling blue eyes who called himself Yeshua, or Jesus of Nazareth. This man was invariably followed by a growing group of disciples and large crowds gathered wherever he appeared. His reputation as a teacher, or Rabbi, spread throughout the land. Some claimed that he was the reincarnation of John the Baptist, while others maintained he was a king who sought to overthrow the power of Rome.

Gaius Cassius began to follow this man's movements and observe him from afar. He noted the words the Rabbi spoke were those of peace, yet his message was troubling and difficult to interpret. Gaius Cassius stood on a low hill and watched as the disciples seemingly manifested enough food for a multitude from two small baskets of bread and fish, and he heard Jesus say:

> *Blessed are the merciful: for they shall obtain mercy; Ye have heard that it hath been said, an eye for an eye, and a tooth for*

a tooth; but I say unto you, whosoever shall strike thee on thy right cheek, turn to him the other also.

"To a soldier of Rome, and indeed for many of the followers of Jesus," the Prophet continued, "these words were incomprehensible. He spoke words of peace and yet it seemed he was threatening to destroy the temple."

The prophet paused a few moments, searching the eyes of his new pupils to assess their comprehension of his story. He was satisfied that Garrett and Gugga were receiving his impromptu lecture with marked attention.

"During the weeks that followed, the centurion watched as Jesus healed the sick, cured the crippled and the blind, cast out demons and even raised the dead. He also listened to the words of Jesus as he related to his disciples,

I am the way and the light, and No man cometh to the Father save by me.

Gaius Cassius began to believe that this man was either a god or a prophet . . . or a gifted charlatan.

And then one day, finally," the Prophet said, raising his hands for emphasis, "He approached Jesus and asked him to heal his favorite servant who was old and ill. When he arrived home that evening, to his surprise the servant was well! At that moment, the centurion knew that he had spoken with the son of God."

During a casual pause from the Prophet, Garrett couldn't resist asking a question. "What happened to Gaius Cassius after the healing of his servant?"

The Prophet-King leaned on a chair in front of the painting, and stared at the painting as if he were seeing it for the first time. Despite his having shared this story dozens of times with inquiring individuals and friends, he himself occasionally could not resist succumbing to the majesty of the story.

"Gaius Cassius was deeply moved when this man Jesus was brought before Pontius Pilate to be judged. As he had anticipated, the Governor found no fault and washed his hands of guilt when shockingly the crowd chose to free the criminal Barabbas and to condemn Jesus . . . . Then followed the crushing assignment which he always loathed. He, Gaius Cassius, was to command the crucifixion squad. Good soldier that he was, if it must be done, he dedicated himself to doing it well. He watched as they stripped Jesus and two others and nailed each to a cross. There he watched Jesus die. But, it was clear the other two were not yet dead. The temple guards were ordered to break the legs of the two that still lived so that they might be taken down before the Sabbath, as was the custom of the time. But as they came to Jesus, Gaius Cassius, with the spear in hand, stepped forward and pierced Jesus' side to show that he was already dead and his legs need not be broken.

"As an act of mercy, he thrust the keen point of his spear into the right side of Jesus. His mark was true to the Roman skill of piercing the chest between the 4th and 5th rib to prove that a wounded enemy in battle was truly dead. It was known that blood did not flow from the body after death . . . but forthwith out came blood and water from the lifeless body of Jesus. Thus the miracle of blood flow after death occurred and the lance which had brought it forth became a Holy Lance . . . and in that moment two other miracles occurred: Gaius Cassius's sight was restored and the tip of the indestructible lance suddenly cracked and fell away signifying that it was never again to be used as a weapon or draw blood for any reason.

Gaius Cassius embraced Christianity at that moment and, as the foremost witness to the shedding of the Holy Blood, he became highly revered by his new brethren. He was referred to thereafter as Longinus (The Spearman) and his Lance became known as the *Spear of Longinus* or *the Spear of Destiny.*" [2]

The Prophet, his disarming lecture complete, led both of his guests into the sitting room where he invited them to contemplate what he had just shared with them. Garrett, overcome with curiosity, tentatively asked the Prophet what he considered to be an obvious question. "What does this all mean? What happened to the Spear?"

"A proper question," replied the Prophet to his inquisitive young student.

"I will attempt to explain. It was this account of the story that birthed the legend of the Lance. That is, that he who holds the Holy Lance in his hands controls the destiny of all mankind . . . but only if he understands the power of the spear and acknowledges the miracles from which its vitality flows, including the miracle of resurrection."

"Hear this prophesy!" the Prophet bellowed in a God-like voice,

"Whosoever possesses this Holy Lance and understands the powers it serves, holds in his hand the destiny of the world for good or evil. And if thereafter the sword and Lance come into evil use, to him who holds them will they turn to his fall and death."

It was at this point that the young couple gathered themselves together and prepared to take their leave. They grasped the hands of the Prophet, their eyes tearing up with emotion, as they bid their sincere good-byes and quietly left the home of the Prophet-King.

Gugga took Garrett's arm as they walked to their car. "We'll come back another time and he'll tell us the legends of the hollow earth."

****

The years slowly passed and Thora was growing up to be a virtual physical replica of her mother. She possessed the same gentle personality one would expect of a thoughtful and intelligent young girl, while loving and admiring her father in a way that allowed her to deeply consider everything he was learning himself. On many occasions, Thora and Garrett became intensely engaged in reading together, each delighting one another with their interpretations and imaginations spurred by the many Icelandic legends and spiritual teachings they were exploring. Garrett would often look at Thora and remark to Gugga how much she seemed to know and how much she was like Gugga. Garrett was intrigued by the intuitive side of both females in his life and giggled in delight at both Thora's and Gugga's insights and understandings that often seemed to be much deeper than his own.

More than occasionally, his thoughts would trail back to a dream that seemed to have taken place while he was in the hospital. He still couldn't determine if it was a dream . . . it was so real. The remembrance swept over him like a flashback more often than he would have wished. At times he would wake up from a deep sleep in a cold sweat that jolted him awake, the residue of the dream permeating his suddenly conscious thoughts. Who was Thal? What was it he meant? Where did he come from? Was someone really watching him? Was the stone he still kept in his pocket the one that Thal actually had given him? There must be a logical explanation for that little pebble . . . and what was this premonition regarding good and evil between which Thal indicated he would one day have to choose? Garrett became obsessed with figuring what was happening in his mind. He had related to Gugga the substance of his dream and how confused he was by it. She always had calming words for him, probing him with questions relating to what he thought the dream meant to him. Gugga had heard stories since childhood of flying saucers coming from the center of the earth, and while she didn't bother to embrace or dismiss them, she encouraged Garrett to always keep his mind open to the possibility. The stone could be symbolic of something important. Garrett's generally non-intuitive, logical, sequential mind, however, could not reconcile it as easily as his partner. His mind continued with its inner turmoil until some other distraction relieved him.

****

It was 1980. Garrett and Gugga had been together for over ten years. Thora was now almost eleven years of age and maturing rapidly, not only in her striking physical characteristics, but intuitively and spiritually as well. She was different from many of the other young girls her age and had always professed to Garrett and Gugga that she had a unique destiny. Both parents would often exchange bewildered looks and had no trouble realizing that Thora was indeed special.

The war in Viet Nam was essentially over. The United States gradually withdrew its troops as the war lost its initial acceptance. Later that year, Jackie called Garrett to inform him that President Jimmy Carter had granted amnesty to all war protesters and that he could, at last, come home. Garrett was pleased at the political turn of events, but he had grown so accustomed to life in Iceland that going back home seemed like a distant fantasy. He always assumed that he would want to go home sometime, but now? He had a new life, and going home to him meant being with Gugga and Thora. He realized, however, that neither of his parents had ever met Gugga or their granddaughter, even though they spoke by telephone to one another regularly. Of course, Garrett and Gugga were not officially married and the subject had never come up at any time between them. Garrett, however, after talking with his parents and hearing their desire to have a real relationship with Thora, began to give thought to a wedding.

When he brought the subject up with Gugga, she was taken off guard. Marriage had never occurred to her, nor was it an issue, but the thought of an official union with Garrett became increasingly pleasing to her. After some deep thought and consideration as to the wisdom of such a union, they both happily agreed that it would be a wonderful celebration and acknowledgement of their life together.

That night they called Jackie and Ollie to tell them the news. Garrett touched his mother's heart when he told them they wanted to get married in Iceland and travel to Berkeley for their honeymoon. Jackie cried with delight and Ollie enthusiastically shared their collective joy. Garrett pleaded with them to come to Reyjkavik and be the guests of honor at the wedding. Ollie and Jackie quickly agreed to the arrangement and made plans to travel as soon as Ollie could get away from his military duties. He had accumulated a substantial amount of leave time and predicted he could make it happen. Garrett and Gugga, of course, had not as yet set a date for this momentous occasion, but they did so immediately now that they knew both parents could attend.

It had been many long years since Jackie had seen her son, and many years of not seeing and holding her granddaughter. It was a dream come true for Jackie and her heart palpitated at the very thought of it becoming a reality.

Garrett, his heart now bursting with joy at the idea of marrying his true love and the happy anticipation of reuniting with his parents, made as his first priority the finding of an engagement ring in keeping with the customs of his native land. Gugga bubbled with delight when she thought of the upcoming marriage and journey. She felt honored and privileged to be given a ring in commemoration of such a momentous occasion. Thora, who had consistently lobbied to visit her American grandparents, became so excited about the wedding that she thought she should have a ring also. After all, she reasoned, she should be an official part of the wedding. Garrett lovingly assured her that she would have a ring too. After all, he concluded, all three of them were joining together in a family partnership.

Gugga happily began making the plans for the wedding and was thrilled with the anticipation of meeting Garrett's parents. Her unexpressed regret, however, was that neither of her parents or her beloved grandmother would be there to witness this milestone in her life.

"We must have the wedding on a Friday," Gugga cooed. "It's a tradition from Iceland's ancient pagan times to wed on a Friday in honor of Frigga, Goddess of Marriage, who considered the day sacred. Ancient Icelandic wedding celebrations can last nearly a week and include a special Icelandic drink called Mead, a smooth ale brewed with honey. It has been considered the Icelandic wedding drink since the early Viking days. At one time it was a legal requirement for newlyweds to drink the honey ale in the weeks after their marriage; in fact, that was the origin of the term *honeymoon*."

"A Friday it will be!" exclaimed Garrett, bubbling over with joyful anticipation. "And we will drink until we can no longer stand."

Years ago it was customary to give the whole of the bride's family a *morning gift*, usually a gift of appreciation in honor of giving their daughter away in marriage. However, due to the anomaly that Gugga's parents were no longer thought to be alive, she would accept and honor the ring from Garrett in place of the tradition. Following modern Icelandic tradition, Gugga would also present a gift to Garrett. In this instance, she would choose to give him a ring, honoring customs from both cultures. Garrett was delighted with the arrangements as well as with Gugga's wish to follow as many traditions of his adopted homeland as possible.

The stage was set. They would be married in a month and travel to America to celebrate the event. The joy that permeated their hearts, from California to the mid-Atlantic, was palpable.

Chapter Notes:

1. *Runes* were an alphabetic system that predated Latin and were inscribed on stone or wood. The lines were drawn only vertically or at an angle because horizontal lines cut into substances could crack wooden or rock scriptures. The earliest 24 runes dated from 150 AD and were known as the Elder Futhark. There are two additional rune groups called the Anglo-Saxon Futhork (400 – 1100 AD) and the Younger Futhark (800 – 1100 AD). The earliest runic inscriptions remain a linguistic mystery. Because of this mystery, early runes were used not as a simple writing system, but rather as magical signs to be used for charms, divination or as an oracle. *Rune* means secret or something hidden, the knowledge of which was esoteric or restricted to an elite. Modern (1980) times include a blank rune, but it is not considered useful except to replace a lost rune in a set.

   The Runic Triangle does not appear in any historical folklore. However, the signs arranged as a triangle, opens locked doors, tombs, caves and caverns if energized with an appropriate energy force. For example, in the story, the pebble acts as the energizer and pulsates and gifts the bearer with the power to enter closed spaces with one's mind.

   The first rune, placed at the top of the triangle is known as ANSUZ, which means to be ready for unexpected changes and to practice one's sensibilities. The second rune is placed at the bottom left of the triangle form and is known as PERTH, meaning mysterious powers are taking place and it is a time for reflection. The final rune, completing the triangle, is known as INGUS and is placed opposite the ANZUS. The meaning of INGUS pertains to breaking up old relationships and making ready for a new start. It could be dangerous. The image of the Runic Triangle appears on the cover of this book.

2. The Spear of Destiny, The Spear of Longinus or The Holy Lance. An image of the spear is featured on the book cover.

Chapter 8

THE RETURN OF THE LANCE

Germany to Antarctica

1974 – 1979

*T*he voyage of the U-530 in 1945 had officially ensconced the Antarctic cave-vault into Nazi Germany's lore. Preservation of the most meaningful relics and artifacts of the Third Reich were assured by sending them to the South Pole hideaway which was a high security storage area serving the collapsing Reich. It was reasoned, however, that these items could be collected again if the necessary conditions changed with time and circumstance. There were other U-boats which made the trek transporting escaping Nazi personnel who would be disembarked on the beaches of Argentina before the boats were either surrendered or scuttled.

It was shortly after the departure of the U-530 that yet another U-Boat, the U-977, captained by Heinz Shaeffer and directed by Colonel Maximilian Hartmann, left for Antarctica on May 1st, 1945, tracing the U-530's sojourn and carrying additional artifacts and personnel to Antarctica.

****

A mysterious contact between a member of the U-530 and Rudolf Hess in 1957 led to top secret information being smuggled out of Spandau Prison from Hess. A key to a storage box in a Swiss bank containing information provided by Hess produced a triad of secret letters. The envelopes were brought to and opened by Hartmann. One of the envelopes contained instructions directing Colonel Hartmann to reorganize and regroup the order of the *Knights of the Holy Lance.*

"I must bring together again the Knights that were informally disbanded some years ago and recommit them to meet again," Hartmann muttered to himself, fully understanding the new and historic mission that needed to be undertaken. A coded message in one of the letters from Karl Haushofer, with an addendum by a trusted associate, Karl Müeller, gave the exact location of the meeting.

Hartmann's efforts required him to discreetly contact key members of the dormant *Holy Order of Teutonic Knights*, who were spread throughout Europe. The quest required him to personally travel to each Ritter's (knights) home residence to advise and recruit each to join his mission to travel once again to Antarctica to recover the Holy Lance. He had been waiting for this moment for nearly 30 years, as he was one of the original nine leaders of the 1945 adventure to transport the Lance and other Third Reich artifacts to the sequestered cave in the Muhlig-Hofmann Mountains of Antarctica.

In 1974, Maximilian Hartmann called the first meeting of the thirteen Knights of the Holy Lance in Munich. They met to reaffirm their dedication to the cause of world peace with the companion herculean task of recovering the Holy Lance from its sequestered cave in Antarctica bringing it back to Germany. In order to carry out this quest, a secret expedition was formed consisting of four men who were chosen to be the leaders of the group.[1] Each of these men were hand-chosen as men of integrity, great moral strength and character, who were linked together by their war time bonds of the past. They were considered the cream of the Holy Ritters. The mission would represent the completion of the German operation of *Valkure Zwei*, (named originally by Adolf Hitler as *Valkure Eins*) which was initiated so long ago after the first ventures into the Mulhig-Hofmann cave.

On May 19, 1979, Colonel Hartmann and the expedition leaders boarded a Lufthansa flight from Munich bound for Sao Paulo, Brazil. This would be first leg of the journey.

Traveling in business suits and carrying briefcases, the three Knights were careful not to don any kind of attire that would give rise to even the slightest suspicion regarding their historic mission. After spending an overnight in Sao Paulo, they boarded a small twin-engine plane that took them to the settlement of Bahi Thetus, on the very tip of South America, Tierra del Fuego. From here, Expedition Hartmann would be launched.

The lumbering twin engine McKinnon flying boat, the *Aerius*, flew southward with the first destination to be a half-way point over the Weddell Sea. Here they rendezvoused with a small diesel pow-ered trawler, the *Fortuna*, which acted as a refueling station along the way before a second rendezvous with a 70-foot fishing trawler, the *Annelise*, especially modified so that her afterdeck contained a platform on which rested the *Taifun*, a helicopter. The crew stayed aboard the *Annelise* until they arrived at the coordinates where they could board the helicopter and fly to their ultimate destination.

Everything went according to plan. They reached the valley where the landing would take place. The landing itself was unremarkable except for some heavy cross-winds that buffeted the craft. Once on the ground, the crew began quickly preparing for the trek across the frozen ice and tethered the copter into the ice with mooring pins. Hartmann directed the crew to put on their respective backpacks and other gear to begin their trek to the cave.

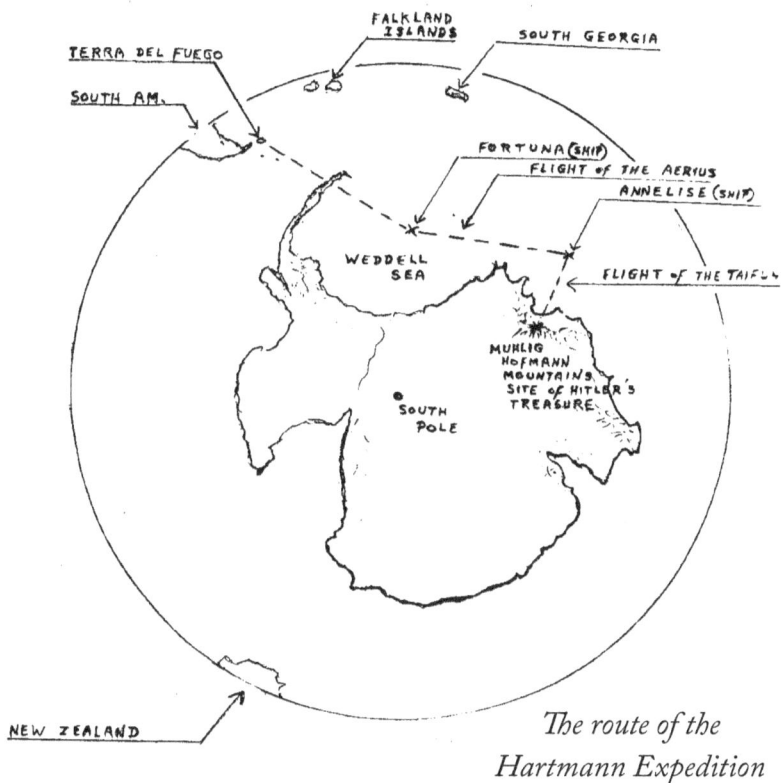

FALKLAND
ISLANDS

SOUTH GEORGIA

TERRA DEL FUEGO

SOUTH AM.

FORTUNA (SHIP)
FLIGHT of THE AERIUS
ANNELISE (SHIP)

WEDDELL
SEA

FLIGHT of THE TAIFUL

MUHLIG
HOFMANN
MOUNTAINS,
SITE of HITLER'S
TREASURE

SOUTH
POLE

NEW ZEALAND

The route of the
Hartmann Expedition

Following the map provided to the expedition from the bank box, the crew reached the coordinates within the hour. Working in groups of two, each man started digging. They managed to break down through the ice nearly a meter and drove four special thermal tubes loaded with explosives around the area. As planned, they took cover a few dozen meters away and activated the caps. The explosions from the tubes sent ice and snow debris upward, leaving a large hole in the designated area.

As the men waited for the air to clear, they cautiously turned their hand torches towards the hole.

"Success!" Colonel Hartmann exclaimed enthusiastically, as the outline of an iron doorway appeared at the bottom of the hole. Klauss proceeded to pour a special thermal liquid around the edges and they waited another ten minutes or so before he nodded to Hartmann, alerting the group to start prying with crowbars. After an exhausting effort, punctuated by the Antarctic cold, the crew finally heard a screeching sound of movement. The door slowly opened.

Quickly, they moved the iron door back and peered in with electric torches. Hartmann was the first to enter, followed by Klauss and Lothar. Heinz remained outside as pre-planned in case of any mishap. The cave extended for approximately 10 meters and at the end was a large cavernous area. It seemed tepid to the group as they searched the cavern with their lights. They moved into the cavern about 300 meters and arrived at a smaller cavern which circled to the right and ended in a room approximately 80 meters in width and 10 meters in height.

At the entrance to the small cavern that housed the brass boxes was an obelisk, about a meter in height, marking the spot. On it was an inscription which read:

> There are truly more things in Heaven and "in" earth that man
> has dreamt.
> (Beyond this point is AGHARTA Haushofer, 1943.) [2]

Their lights immediately fell upon the treasure that consisted of eight medium-sized bronze chests. Hartmann surmised that the four of them could not carry all of the chests and he made the decision to identify the most important and carry them to the helicopter. He also reasoned that the copter would not be able to carry the additional weight of all eight boxes, even if they jettisoned all their other equipment. The group selected four boxes and carried them out single file to the awaiting helicopter.

Shortly before they were ready to leave, the chest containing the Holy Lance was opened. Each watched with profound fascination as Klauss knocked the bronze pin from the clasp. Inside the chest was a faded leather case along with a variety of other items. It was there, The Holy Lance! The spear that pierced the side of Jesus Christ! It was noted by Lothar that this memorable day was July 30th, 1979.

Hartmann held the Holy Lance aloft in his hand and, without thinking; the words simply flowed from his mouth,

"The Holy Lance points ever towards our beloved homeland."

Amid the elated cheers from his companions, the Lance was replaced in its container and the last box was loaded aboard the *Taifun*. The expedition returned by the same route by which it had arrived. The boxes were sent to Germany where they were secretly sequestered at Wewelsburg Castle in Westphalia, West Germany.

Lothar and Heinz returned directly to Germany via Sao Paulo. Klauss and Hartmann continued their journey to the United States via New Orleans where they chartered a plane and flew to a small town in the State of Missouri. It was here where they met an old friend and colleague from the U-530.[3] Because of this friend's extraordinary help in planning the expedition and his familiarity and participation with the placement of six of the eight bronze boxes in the cave, the colleague was presented with some meaningful gifts. The gifts included a log of the Hartmann expedition. The thrilled and grateful friend was allowed to hold the Holy Lance in his hands as a tribute. Several days later, the Holy Lance was once again in Germany. *Valkure Zwei* was completed.

Chapter Notes:

1. Dr.Lothar Manfried Zweick – navigator and pilot, Helmut Unger, Klauss Ortner, Heinz Loser.

2. Sign in Antarctic cave, left by Karl Haushofer in an earlier trip to the cave/vault.

3. Purported to be Wilhelm Barnhart.

Chapter 9

Trust and Friendship

Germany and Iceland
Spring, 1980

*T*he University of Munich, referred to often as LMU (Ludwig Maximilian University) founded in 1472 and named after Duke Ludwig IX of Bavaria. It is one of the most prestigious universities in Germany, producing thirty-six Nobel Laureates and a host of noted scholars throughout its existence. Such luminaries as Werner Heisenberg in Physics, ex-Chancellor of Germany Konrad Adenauer, and Sociologist Max Weber all were products of the University.

The goal of a European education and matriculation at LMU was paramount to a young Magnus Magnusson who, in spite of his simple roots forged in culturally isolated Iceland, had dreamed of attending and contributing to the intellectual and world-wide society of mainland Europe. Magnus' attraction to LMU was his interest in Political Sociology fashioned from his admiration of Konrad Adenhauer and the exciting growth occurring in Southern Germany after World War II. Germany was rapidly asserting its economic power and structure and the thrill of national restructuring was incredibly enticing to a young and impressionable student of international politics.

The Great Hall (Grosse Aula) was one of the most attractive buildings on the vast campus that somehow survived the war. Outside the Hall students would gather at mealtimes and mix and study with each other while drinking in the immense majesty of the surroundings.

Magnus was generally a loner, one who liked the ambience of intellectual pursuits and enjoyed engaging with others in discussions of political events. On this day, however, he was deep in the study of one of Sir Muhammad Iqbal's poems. Iqbal, a graduate of LMU, was known as the *Poet of the East* and *The Thinker of Pakistan.*

While reading and sipping one of Bavaria's famous dark beers, Magnus was gently interrupted by an older, bearded man, who sat down across from him at the table. Magnus glanced at the slim, industrious looking man and nodded a welcome to him as he was sitting. The man immediately rose to his feet and extended his hand in salutation to young Magnus, introducing himself.

"Hello, permit me to introduce myself."

He spoke English fluently with a notable clipped German accent.

"My name is Otto Wermoutt, Captain Otto Wermoutt, formerly of the *Reichsmarine,* at your service."

"Hello, pleased to make your acquaintance Captain. My name is Magnus, Magnus Magnussen," mirroring his new companion's introduction. "Please feel free to join me."

"Thank you," the Captain replied. "I know you are a student here at the University. What is it you are studying?"

Magnus contemplated his new acquaintance for a moment before answering.

"Yes, I'm a student. I've been here for three years now, hoping to graduate in the future with a degree in Political Sociology. I'm originally from Reykjavik, Iceland. I was born and raised there."

The Captain paused for only a moment before fixing his piercing gaze directly into Magnus' eyes as he said, "Yes, I am aware of that. You are the reason I am here. I have been looking for you because I would like to offer you an intriguing service opportunity that only you can perform."

Magnus shifted his full attention from his book to stare quizzically at the man across from him, attempting to ascertain whether or not he was being preyed upon by some brazen solicitor.

"Excuse me," Magnus declared a bit abruptly, "How could you possibly know who I am or where I'm from?"

"I know this is a surprise to you and I apologize if my directness startles you. But I am on an important and time sensitive mission. We have been able to research your life in Reykjavik and have determined you to be the proper individual to assist us. We wish to offer you a lucrative and limited contract."

"Look, I don't know who you are or where you come from, but I'm probably not who you are looking for. I don't have any special knowledge or abilities that would lead to seek out and contact me like this. I lead a simple life as a student and my focus is my education."

"Please let me explain," the Captain continued. "You have a special quality that I am sure can be of great service to us. It will simply require that you return to Reykjavik for a short period of time, perhaps two or three weeks, and report back to me your observations. You would be paid very, very well – enough to finish your education and launch yourself into whatever career you choose."

The Captain then reached into his jacket lapel and produced an envelope stuffed with high denomination German currencies. He handed it to Magnus and stated,

"The job is very simple and will cause you no personal risk. When you return with your final briefing, another payment will be made to you of equal amount. Are you interested?"

Magnus was shocked and suspicious but nonetheless intrigued by what his companion was proposing, along with the impressive amount of currency he had produced.

"What is it you want me to do and whom do you represent?" he queried solemnly while staring at the contents of the envelope with disbelieving eyes.

"I wish to keep my associates confidential at this time, the Captain began. You grew up in Reykjavik and were a close friend and schoolmate of a Fraulein Guthbjörg Gudmunsdottir or Gugga Gudmunsdottir, were you not?"

"Yes," he answered haltingly, "Gugga and I were friends for years until I left to come to the University," replied Magnus, amazed that this stranger would know anything about him or Gugga. "We have been in occasional correspondence over the years. What does she have to do with this?"

"She is now living with a young American in whom we have a great interest. We are considering him for a momentous position and need to know more about him without his knowledge. You will not be expected to meet with him, in fact we discourage any personal contact with him whatsoever, but only to re-connect with Gugga and solicit some information about him and report back. We will be asking you to keep your presence in Iceland a quiet secret. You will be instructed to not reveal your presence to anyone except Gugga. When you have the information we require, you will return to your studies. This is a convenient time for you because the University, as you are well aware, is beginning an academic break for nearly a month. I assure you that neither you or Gugga, nor her boyfriend, will be placed in any physical danger. And, as you can see, you will be handsomely compensated. You have but two days to make up your mind. I have already booked you for a round-trip flight to Reykjavik. I will give you the ticket, the currency and written instructions when you agree. Do you require anything else?"

Magnus' heart was pounding. Was this for real? Was this actually happening? His first instinct was to dismiss this persuasive stranger as a crank, but after listening to him, seeing the money, the tickets and written instructions, he realized that he needed to revisit his initial impressions.

"No, I think you've made yourself quite clear. When do you need an answer?"

"I will return to this table tomorrow. If you are here at the same time as now, I will know you have accepted the terms and I will deliver the envelope to you with everything you will need. The instructions will tell you how we will communicate after you return to Reykjavik."

****

The flight to Reykjavik passed quickly as Magnus recalled and relived his times in Iceland, musing over the many interactions he and Gugga had over the years. They were good friends growing up. Magnus was always attracted to her but never acted upon his attraction because of his plan to leave Iceland and study at the University of Munich. They had corresponded on a few occasions since he moved to Munich, and they had exchanged photographs with one another, always vowing to stay in touch.

He found it difficult to fathom his sudden good fortune that essentially paid for the rest of his education and promised much more. It seemed so serendipitous, but here he was, returning to Reykjavik, with a new opportunity completely unanticipated – all because of his familiar association with Gugga. He vowed he would take full advantage of his new bounty and use it to enhance his ultimate dream of working in a social-political institution, making use of his diplomatic and social skills.

The written instructions were precise, leaving little doubt as to their meaning and desired results. The document directed him to make contact with Gugga at the airport, feigning a chance meeting by accidentally bumping into her as she exited her flight from New York. He would then elicit information from her gradually about Garrett while leading her to believe he was on a top-secret mission and that no one should know, especially Garrett. He would have to concoct a reasonable story to gain her confidentiality and trust. This is why the Captain approached him. Magnus was, indeed, uniquely qualified to carry out this mission. He would do it, he decided, with finesse.

****

Flights between New York and Reykjavik were relatively common and one could easily arrange passage at least three times a week. Icelandic flights were efficient and the airline prided itself in its positive history. One could count on their arrival being on time if there were no extenuating circumstances and Magnus would use this Nordic efficiency to his advantage. Gugga was still actively working for the airline and usually worked two or three flights a week. She loved her job and the opportunity to meet new people and brag about her homeland. She was a proud emissary of her tiny nation.

Gugga and Garrett had settled nicely into their relationship, giving respect and love to one another while together raising their deeply spiritual daughter. They had developed a trust that made them inseparable and focused on the agreeable life they had created. Neither would ever think to hurt the other with angry words or gestures. Their love transcended daily practical problems and formed the stout foundation of their solid relationship.

Magnus found and rented a small innocuous flat just outside of the Reykjavik Airport and settled in for what he anticipated to be a lonely but relatively short duration. He was instructed by the Captain to not venture casually out in public and chance running into someone he may have known. He was to focus entirely on his specific task of finding and attracting Gugga into his confidence.

After meticulously checking the arrival schedules from New York, Magnus began setting up his *chance* meeting with Gugga. While he was not sure if she would be on every flight on the schedule, he randomly chose the next day after his arrival to appear at the airport and, hopefully, find Gugga. He was sure he would recognize her as her image was clear in his mind.

The Icelandic Boeing 707 aircraft glided slowly to the terminal and Magnus watched the passengers disembark, each apparently looking for someone who was to greet them. He knew the crew would exit the plane soon after the passengers went to claim their baggage. Magnus would wait around for the crew and appear to surprise Gugga. He had guessed right. There she appeared, pretty as ever, dragging her uniform case with her as she headed for the crew's lounge. He stood directly in her path, glancing away, until she herself looked up to avoid running into him. Her recognition of Magnus came quickly and she stopped in her tracks and emotionally screeched, "Magnus, Magnus, Is that you?"

"Yes, yes it is!" he countered, feigning his surprise.

"What are you doing here – have you come back to stay?"

They immediately embraced one another, Gugga truly surprised and delighted by this seemingly accidental meeting with her old school chum and friend. Her excitement in seeing him was palpable and her mind quickly reminisced through the many adventures and meetings of their childhood relationship.

As the brief reunion became more noticeable in the public surroundings, with Gugga exclaiming breathlessly thoughts and exclamations of past events, Magnus quickly embraced her tightly and whispered into her ear.

"Let's please hold our emotions here in this public place. I am here on a government mission and I am supposed to be incognito."

Gugga immediately calmed down. She wanted to respect his needs and gestured for them to leave the airport before anyone would notice.

They briskly left the airport as Magnus bade them to find a quiet place where they could talk freely. Gugga immediately invited him to come and stay with her and Garrett. Her enthusiastic greeting gave him the opportunity to quickly explain to her that his mission had to remain secret, his presence unknown, as he was here to carry out a mission that he could not discuss with her.

Gugga could not imagine why such secrecy would be needed but, out of her trust and respect for Magnus, agreed to his needs for his stealth behavior and her cooperation. Magnus quickly laid out the ground rules letting her know that she could not even tell her mate. Gugga balked initially at that suggestion, but soon, after the pleading urging of a now somber Magnus, agreed she would go along with his suggestion.

This kind of clandestine arrangement was very foreign to Gugga as she and Garrett always shared everything with one another. She was reluctant to keep a secret from Garrett, but rationalized that she knew she would eventually tell him the whole story . . . no matter what Magnus may ask.

The small café just outside the airport was an ideal meeting place as it offered a secluded booth that was out of the public eye.

They spent over an hour joyfully reminiscing special memories of their common upbringing and remembering fondly some of the activities and people that dotted their relationship through the years. Magnus enjoyed the time with Gugga more than he anticipated and would occasionally imagine that he might want to renew and enhance an old relationship. Gugga felt as a child again, remembering the innumerable instances that the two cavorted together in their pasts. Often, throughout the conversation, Magnus would inquire about Garrett, asking what appeared to be innocuous questions of natural curiosity, but in truth were probes as to the character and practices of her husband as directed by his agreement. Gugga answered him graciously and enthusiastically, mainly because she was so proud of Garrett and wanted Magnus to know what a wonderful man Garrett was.

Gugga suddenly glanced at her watch and realized that it was getting late, as Garrett and Thora would have expected her home some time ago. She quickly let Magnus know of her tardiness and got up to leave.

Magnus, delighted that his plans were working so smoothly and that he had apparently rekindled Gugga's trust, stood up to give her a hug before she left and said, "This was so much fun. There is so much more to talk about. How about we meet again, perhaps next week when you return from New York? I could fix you a snack at my flat which is not far from here. It would be so wonderful to reconnect."

Gugga paused for a moment to contemplate his invitation. Yes, she did enjoy his company again and would indeed look forward to more conversation. He was the kind of friend who knew so much about her that it was interesting to hear his perspective on the myriad of things they held in common. She did not perceive any harm in meeting him again and agreed to do as he suggested. They bid good-bye and Magnus embraced her in yet another hug, this time one that lingered a bit longer than usual. Gugga felt no alarm from the extended hug. After all Magnus was an old, old, friend.

She went back to the airport, changed out of her uniform, and drove home with somewhat mixed emotions. She was excited about seeing Magnus again but disappointed that she could not share the news and excitement with Garrett.

"Just for a short time," Gugga thought, "and I can share my excitement about seeing Magnus. I can wait."

From her flights to and from New York, Gugga always relished her homecoming knowing that Garrett and Thora were waiting. This time, however, she was a couple hours later that her normal arrival time home and she found herself making a pretext for her late arrival. Garrett, however, was simply happy to have her home again.

It was a week later on a Tuesday when Magnus again met Gugga and, as promised, had prepared a snack so they could comfortably relax at his flat. He felt that in a calm, non-stressful atmosphere, with the initial excitement of their meeting behind them, he could probe more deeply into the actions and personality of her husband in a more intimate setting.

With Gugga settling in comfortably on his couch, Magnus placed himself next to her, ostensibly to share some photos that he thought she might take pleasure in. He found that he enjoyed being physically close to Gugga and, with their close proximity, he would occasionally touch her in conversation. Gugga began to notice his more familiar demeanor but passed it off as brotherly affection.

At this juncture Magnus began a deeper probe regarding Garrett. He asked questions that belied his casual interest, but explored into personality traits that her husband had – such questions pertaining as to how he treated her, how he treated his daughter, what hobbies he pursued, how often he taught at the local schools, and what subjects he taught – all suddenly seeming to be the focus of their conversation.

At first Gugga was pleased to share her personal life and her relationship with Garrett. As the questioning continued, she began to wonder why the sudden intimate and probing interest in Garrett. Her internal red flags began to emerge. She became a bit disconcerted when it came time to leave and Magnus embraced her with a full-body hug. This time his embrace was more physically felt prompting Gugga to scrutinize what was apparently changing in this supposed happy reunion of old friends.

She returned home that night carrying an uncomfortable feeling about her visit with Magnus and wanting to share it with Garrett, but decided it wasn't quite the time. She had agreed to meet Magnus one more time and felt she would be able to decipher what his intentions were by that time.

Garrett, meanwhile, was becoming curious as why Gugga had come home twice so much later than had been her routine. He decided that she must be working too hard and thought he would surprise her at the airport the following week and take her to share a nice dinner at one of their favorite restaurants. He would get a baby-sitter for Thora and make a special evening out of it.

He somehow missed her as she disembarked from the plane, but lingered in a small waiting area nearby. The crew lounge was adjacent to the public restroom and Garrett began to rise from his booth as he saw Gugga emerge. He started to walk towards her when a man he did not recognize approached her at the door of the lounge, kissed her on the cheek, and led her away outside the airport. Garrett stepped back with a mild shock of disbelief. He secretly followed them out of the terminal as they walked and entered a nearby flat together.

Confused as to the meaning of what he observed, he drove home alone and waited. Gugga returned a bit later and acted normal as if nothing was wrong. Garrett pondered what to say – how to say what he needed to know.

He finally blurted out, "Who was that man you were with at the airport and accompanied to that flat? I came to surprise you to take you to dinner and I saw you together!"

Gugga was caught off guard. She stammered and broke into tears, knowing that Garrett must think the worst. "I knew this would happen. I told him tonight that I couldn't keep his secret any longer."

"What secret, what are you talking about? Is this man a lover of yours?"

"No, no, no, not at all. That's him," she said, pointing to the photo on the shelf. "That's Magnus Magnussen. He is a childhood friend. I've mentioned him before to you. He is definitely not a lover of mine. He surprised me one day at the airport and confided to me that he was here on a secret government mission and I could not mention to anyone that he was here. He was especially concerned that you not know. I invited him to stay with us, which he refused. I trusted him. He is an old and dear friend. I am so very sorry I did not tell you. He told me that his life would be in danger if anyone in Reykjavik knew he was here. I believed him. He even said he was somewhat sorry that I had recognized him and hurried me out of the airport. He invited me to his flat where we could talk without danger. I was so excited to see him again that I didn't think clearly. You must believe me, I love only you!"

Garrett leaned back in his chair, pondering the story his trusted lady had just blurted out. Gugga had never shown any propensity to lie . . . to anyone. His inner concern slowly melted away as he listened to her impassioned story, his uninvited jealousy quickly subsiding. Of course he believed her and his trust for her quickly returned.

"What does he want, why is he here?" Garrett softly posed as a question supporting Gugga.

"I truly don't know. But he has been getting much more familiar each time we met. I only met him on three occasions, including this afternoon, and it was always on Thursdays that he appeared. I was becoming very uncomfortable with him with his seeming insatiable need for intimate details of our life. I had told him that I couldn't see him anymore under these circumstances and that I had to let you know. At that point he became somewhat agitated, so I left. I don't know that I will see him again.

That was the last time Gugga heard from Magnus. As time passed, both Gugga and Garrett passed the interlude off as an interesting but unimportant interval in their otherwise happy lives.

Meanwhile, Magnus realized he had gotten as much information as was possible regarding Garrett and returned to Munich without risking any graceless good-byes. As promised, he met the Captain once again for a final debriefing. The Captain was generally pleased with Magnus' report, thanked him for his diligent work, and delivered another envelope with cash in an amount matching his original payment. Magnus had provided the Captain with confirmation of Garrett's trustworthy character and habits. Magnus never saw or heard from the Captain again.

Magnus often reflected on his adventure at the behest of the Captain. It left him with a mixed set of feelings and emotions. He was thankful for the financial windfall, giving him a chance to build his importance and resume, yet acknowledging an inner feeling of guilt for his covert role culminating in a now damaged or severed relationship with Gugga.

Chapter 10

THE WEDDING

Reykjavik, Iceland

1980

*T*he wedding in Reykjavik was planned to reflect the traditions in Iceland as closely as possible with additional cultural heritage traditions from America. Garrett and Gugga had been planning the occasion for weeks with Thora assertively interjecting her thoughts on the proceedings. Gugga knew the church she would pick. Following Nordic traditions, Gugga chose the oldest church in Iceland for the events picturesquely settled in the shadow of the mystery mountain of the ancients, *Snaefellsjokull.* The wedding was to take place beneath the magical canopy of the early season appearance of the Northern Lights under the array of dancing atmospheric waves of mixed hues of green, blue, and red scintillating lights against the cool crisp sky. This is the fantasy wherein the prominent Icelandic poet, Einar Benediksson in 1897 recites,

> *Does the son of the dust know anything more beautiful than the palace of the gods in electrical flames?*

Gugga and Garrett invited many friends to attend. The guest list was large, as Gugga and Garrett had often involved themselves with friends and local officials in a number of community activities, private dinners, and general recreation. And, of course, Thora had her own circle of friends through school. Reykjavik was a relatively small community and common citizens mingled freely with social and government officials. Garrett, due to his area research, teaching, and considerable social talents, had met and befriended many of them.

The most honored guests, of course, would be Garrett's parents, Ollie and Jackie Hill. After a dozen year hiatus from his family, Garrett was thrilled at the thought of presenting Gugga and Thora to them. All three would go to the airport to greet his parents. Gugga, with her airport social and employment connections, arranged a special welcoming party and greeting for them as they got off the plane.

Ollie and Jackie were equally excited. Jackie pondered over and over what clothes and items to pack. Garrett had suggested that she dress for chilling weather, so Jackie fretted over not having the proper clothing as well as what dress she would wear for the wedding. This was a moment that she had dreamed of since both boys were born. She was aware that attending Garrett's wedding would help salve the inner wound she carried knowing she was unlikely ever to see Jared again, let alone attend his wedding. And to hug and caress a grandchild – the sweet young Thora – was a fantasy of which she had only dared to dream. Jackie was beside herself in anticipation as her mind raced over and over about what she needed to do to prepare. Ollie did his best to calm her down on several occasions when the excitement was almost more than she could bear.

Ollie was inordinately excited himself, but his military demeanor would not allow his emotions to explode into outbreaks that could disrupt his logical and practical thought processes. His training had prepared him well in emotional situations in order to keep his wits about him. Flying to Iceland for a social gathering, however, was a new adventure for him. He had traveled to many countries and regions of the world in his naval career, but never to Iceland. Jackie's concerns regarding the temperature or conditions did not faze him. After all, he spent several months in Antarctica and survived and flourished in that harsh environment. What could be more difficult than that?

Ollie's heart swelled with delight when he imagined seeing his son again, even though Garrett had left under circumstances of which he didn't completely approve, Ollie had put those concerns far behind him. He missed his son very much and tenderly looked forward to connecting with Gugga and Thora. This would be a momentous journey to reunite his family and to reconnect with his son. Indeed, he was excited.

****

"What Icelandic customs shall we include in our wedding?" Garrett curiously asked his newly betrothed partner. Relaxing at the kitchen table and scribbling thoughts into her ever present notebook, Gugga had been thinking the whole ceremony through and was anticipating keeping as close to traditions as possible. She thoughtfully included the inherent customs of America out of honor and respect for her new in-laws, as well as for Garrett. She anticipated a mixture of old Nordic customs coupled with modern practices that favored both Icelandic and American conventions.

"Well, my love," Gugga replied, "Today Icelanders have adopted many American and European customs and wedding traditions. Traditional Icelandic weddings were much more elaborate. Icelanders, even today, take marriage as a very serious proposition. Long engagements are expected, sometimes for many years as young couples are urged to not rush into matrimony."

"It seems that we've followed that tradition very well," Garrett chuckled. "What's it been, twelve years now since we moved in together? I'd say we can score one point for Icelandic tradition."

With both of them staring at one another realizing the solemnity and humor of their situation, they held one another closely in a loving embrace each in affectionate anticipation.

Gugga had moved closer to Garrett from her place at the table of their small bungalow that they now occupied since Thora was a toddler. Thora was visiting for an overnight with Meda, her new friend and daughter of Bjorn and Marit. With an appealing smile Gugga suddenly turned and disappeared into their bedroom. After a lingering moment she reappeared wearing a short sheer nightgown, similar to the one she wore on her first encounter with Garrett. She moved towards him gracefully and suggestively sat on his lap snuggling up to Garrett with a enticing smile and mouthing a gentle kiss at the base of his neck while playfully reaching under his shirt to sample his warm skin.

"I think we should score, as you Americans tend to say, some more points right now," Gugga giggled.

Garrett reached around Gugga's inviting waist and pulled her close to him as she gingerly pressed her genial body against his bare chest. Garrett, having no mind to resist, instantly embraced her and slowly removed her nightgown top to reveal her ample charms. They gazed deeply into one another's eyes tasting the physical connections they had come to relish together. Gugga's alluring smile, soft kisses, and velvet skin excited Garrett again as they fell together on the couch with Gugga caressing Garrett fully with her half-naked body. Garrett paused for just a moment and whispered in her ear, "I love these Icelandic traditions." They both giggled happily and immersed themselves in their lovemaking.

****

Gugga's flat had become too small to comfortably accommodate a young child. After a year or so of making due with limited space, they searched and found a larger five-room secluded home not far out of the city. The home was relatively simple by Western standards, cozy, yet yielding a larger sense of space because of the impressive expanse of the Ocean waters and glacial mountains as an outside backdrop. Thora had her own room and relished her sense of independence. She had begun her own collection of stones and gems, just like Meda, and proudly displayed them in prominent spaces near her bed.

Their unfenced yard consisted of some hearty plants that barely survived each cold winter, but provided Thora room for outside exercise and play. Having the privacy of another bedroom, Garrett and Gugga often used it as a retreat from family togetherness, each occasionally utilizing it as a necessity for time alone. With ample windows on all sides, the home was always bathed in natural light, especially in the winter months as the moon reflected its image off the glacial ice-covered mountains. This was home, a place to live and raise a family. Garrett and Gugga felt that they had reached a point in their lives where harmony, presence, and love prevailed.

Gugga arose from the couch, straightened her hair and put on her bathrobe. She was relaxed and drifted closely behind Garrett and teased him by continuing to explore plans for the wedding as if nothing had just transpired between them. Garrett, vaguely able to pay attention, tried somewhat to listen attentively to her. However, due to his relaxed state, he was not especially successful. Gugga, acknowledging his condition with a slight giggle, continued with her thoughts.

"Sometimes the tradition required they hire toastmasters to keep the toasts going on and on for days. That might be one Icelandic tradition we could temper a bit."

"I don't know, that could be a great deal of fun," Garrett answered, slowly retrieving his senses. "But I agree with you, it also would be a bit tedious and become too exhausting for everyone, especially my parents."

"Who will you choose for your best man," Gugga probed gently.

"Oops," Garrett exclaimed, "I've never thought of a best man. I had somehow always assumed it would have been Jared, but . . . " his voice trailed off in silence to his early childhood memories of Jared. He paused for a lingering moment and then blurted out, "I'll ask Bjorn Ericsson. He and I are good friends since we have done so much flying together, and I think he would be happy to stand up for me. I'm sure he will do it."

Garrett's remembered how Bjorn had become one of the first townspeople he had befriended. He marveled at Bjorn's haunting historical interests and general enthusiasm for life on many occasions while flying together exploring the hinterlands of Iceland. Garrett considered Bjorn his best friend.

"My parents will be arriving at the airport two days before the wedding. That would make it on Wednesday, August 16th. We'll all plan to greet them as they arrive. I want them to feel completely honored and welcome."

Gugga could feel the excitement in Garrett's voice. She had already planned to make some special arrangements at the airport for Ollie and Jackie's arrival. Her close connections with the airline allowed her some special leeway in her planning. She also wanted to do something special for them when they arrived in Iceland for the first time. After all, she was welcoming her new and only family.

Garrett, Gugga, and Thora gathered at the arrival gate that Wednesday afternoon. They searched the airport approach lanes for the first glimpse of the arriving plane.

The massive 747 suddenly appeared in the cloudy sky much like a graceful swan would in its approach to landing before setting down upon a peaceful pond. It seemed as if it took forever for the landed plane to approach the disembarking gate assigned to the flight from New York. Garrett, Gugga and Thora were so excited that their collective hearts were beating seemingly out of control in anticipation.

Ollie and Jackie were having a similar reaction to landing. Even though they were weary from the long trip from California, the expectation of seeing their son after so long a time was palpitating. And to meet Garrett's lady and their eleven year old daughter, their granddaughter, became the highlight of their lives. Yes, they had talked to all three of the young family by telephone on many occasions, but now it was almost surreal.

"I think I'm going to throw up," Jackie whispered loudly to Ollie. "I'm so nervous." Ollie gripped her arm tightly as the plane came to a stop. They began their exit from the craft and slowly made their way to the gate.

"You'll be fine," Ollie reassured her as they stepped out of the plane.

The air was crisp but the temperature was mild in Reykjavik on that afternoon. It was a summer day and Iceland had come alive after a typically long winter and a breathtaking spring. As soon as they stepped from the plane they immediately could hear a small band playing a welcoming tune that sounded much like *America the Beautiful*, but with a definite Nordic resonance. Gugga, Garrett, and Thora, were standing with the band waving enthusiastically. Gugga had arranged for the band to help celebrate their arrival.

Jackie screamed and waved with delight as the couple quickly waded their way through the crowd as the family embraced one another tearfully and enthusiastically. No introductions were necessary, no stiff formalities, just pure love. The reunion was as natural as one could imagine.

As Ollie and Garrett embraced, the respect and love for one another quickly erased any misconceptions or concerns of the past. They were together again and that was all that mattered. Jackie couldn't take her eyes or her hands off Thora, holding her tightly and marveling at her attentive young granddaughter. Thora was immediately drawn to Jackie's embrace and felt such pride and happiness that she now had grandparents she could love and cherish.

And Gugga, her bright smiling face beaming with happiness, hugged Ollie and Jackie and said softly, "I'm so happy to have a mother and father again."

Jackie, already in tears, looked into Gugga's eyes and whispered, "Thank you for taking care of my son. I so love you. I have always prayed for a daughter and now my prayers have been answered."

After such an emotional day, it was difficult for all of them to retire for the evening. Garrett drove them to the hotel where they would stay while fielding non-stop questions soaring in all directions during the ride. Tomorrow, they would all meet for breakfast at Ollie and Jackie's hotel to share more questions and stories. After breakfast Garrett and Gugga would bring Ollie and Jackie to their bungalow home to relax and share memories and plans in anticipation of the wedding. And, if time permitted, they would take their new guests on a tour of the beautiful city of Reykjavik.

Ollie and Jackie were rapidly attempting to adjust to the culture in Iceland. They were impressed with the life that Garrett and Gugga had carved out for themselves. Getting to know Gugga and Thora proved to be the great delight they dreamed of as they continually showed the new in-laws their appreciation and love in a multitude of ways. Ollie and Jackie were welcomed as if they were royalty . . . and they felt as royalty within the new extended family.

****

The magical day, Friday, July 18th 1980, Garrett awoke from a sleepless night to begin the second and last day of the festivities. Gugga had spent the night with Marit and three other women friends as they dressed and bathed her in scented oils in preparation for the wedding and for her stroll down the street amongst the townspeople on her way to the church. The day before, as tradition offered, a multitude of friends had gathered at the reception site and toasted the couple with many speeches followed by several drinks of mead and a host of congratulatory comments. It seemed every person in the room needed to say something, and as the toasts got longer, the more mead was consumed. Garrett toasted along with the rest and his enthusiastic consumption of more than his share of mead left him with a lingering headache as he faced the next day.

He arrived at the church first to the sound of the ringing bells celebrating his arrival. Accompanied by Bjorn and his father as well as some local officials, Garrett entered the church to wait for the arrival of Gugga along with her handmaidens who were accompanying her. One of the local officials guided the bridegroom to a bench near the altar where he would await Gugga's entrance.

Garrett remarked to his father and Bjorn, "Hmm, I like the idea of being greeted by ringing church bells. It sounds so special, so honoring. I can hardly believe that this is happening."

Meanwhile, Gugga was happily dancing through her walk to the church accompanied by her four handmaidens, each complimenting Gugga's white wedding dress and adorned with summer flowers. As she ambled down the middle of the street to the church, local residents joined the procession by throwing flowers and ribbons and voicing greetings and salutations towards the bride to be.

"I feel like a princess," Gugga gleefully exclaimed. "What a thrilling time this is. I'm so happy."

The small procession moved slowly towards the church, gathering more onlookers as they lithely walked until they arrived at the entrance of the church. On the front steps of the church, The Prophet-King, Svienbjorn Beinteinsson, who was conducting the ceremony, took Gugga's arm and ritually escorted her into the church and seated her next to Garrett on the ceremonial bridal bench.

The inclusion of the Prophet in the wedding proved to be a singular coup for the couple as both Gugga and Garrett almost simultaneously wondered if they could be married by this mystic priest who gave them much encouragement and historical insight when inviting them to his museum-home. His acceptance and elegant presence in his traditional Asatru robes gave the aura of ancient Icelandic spiritualism to the wedding procedures.

Garrett marveled at how beautiful Gugga appeared and how gracefully she sat down beside him – her eyes locked with Garrett's. Ollie, Jackie and Bjorn looked at one another exchanging approving wide grins. Thora sat aside the happy couple and the three of them joined hands as the priest began the ceremonial rites.

The ceremony was very simple in keeping with the desires of both Gugga and Garrett. Garrett, at the prompting of the priest, produced two rings, the first he placed on Gugga's left ring finger and the second ring he put on the anxious hand of an adoring Thora to commemorate the official status of a complete family.

They exited the church, the church bells ringing triumphantly and were greeted once again by a throng of awaiting townspeople who were singing a traditional Icelandic song in honor of the newly married couple.

The process reflected a bit more Icelandic tradition after they arrived at the reception.

"I hope to have the reception at the old Hofdi House"[1] Gugga had remarked earlier. She had chosen this traditional building as it was a place where many wedding receptions have been held. They, with Thora alongside, were seated at a high table overlooking the guests, with the Prophet-Priest, Ollie and Jackie, Bjorn, and just a couple of selected toastmasters.

Gugga whispered into Garrett's ear, "My father and mother would have been sitting there also, but I am so honored to accept your parents as my own. They are simply wonderful!"

The dozens of guests were seated at tables that branched out from the high table. On an adjoining table was a simple, yet colorful, smorgasbord of breads and cakes. The guests were enjoying themselves immensely while Garrett and Gugga danced and partook of all the adulation they could. The family joined into the dances, even as some Icelandic traditional dances were not within Ollie or Jackie's expertise.

Suddenly, after a couple of hours of loud merriment, the four handmaidens, led by Bjorn's partner, Marit, snatched Gugga and whisked her away from the guests, explaining to Garrett that they were going upstairs to their honeymoon suite to prepare his new wife for the wedding night. Garrett, somewhat confused, reluctantly agreed to release her and puzzled as to when he could join her.

"We will let you know, Garrett, just stay here and enjoy the celebration," laughed Marit. "Here is where Icelandic custom becomes very intriguing, interesting – and exciting!"

Icelandic sunset in July was near midnight – and even then wasn't completely dark outside because of the occurrence of the summer months in the Northern Latitudes. Their suite, however, was darkened with heavy curtains which made the room so dim that one had to fumble his or her way around.

In was near midnight when Marit re-appeared and motioned for Garrett to follow her. They made their way up the winding stairs, meeting the three other handmaidens coming down, all with giggling grins on their faces. Bjorn, knowing what was happening, gave Garrett his only piece of advice. "You will enter a dark room and you will find Gugga waiting for you in the dim light. Just follow your instincts."

With that sage advice, Bjorn patted Garrett gently on the shoulder as Garrett trailed Marit up the stairs.

Garrett and Gugga have lived together for over 11 years, yet his anticipation of being with Gugga as his wife was overwhelmingly compelling for him. He opened the door to the suite and closed it quickly behind him. He stood there for a moment as his eyes became accustomed to the dimly lit room.

Then he saw her outline against the shadowy window. She was standing there, completely nude wearing only her bridal headdress. She extended her arms towards him as he slowly moved to embrace her. Bjorn was right. His instincts took over as he bathed in her scents so expertly applied by the handmaidens. As he touched her awaiting body, he couldn't help thinking, "God, I love Icelandic traditions."

Chapter Notes:

1. A historic building facing the sea in Reykjavik. It became famous in 1986 when Russian First Secretary Mikhail Gorbachev and American President Ronald Reagan met for a formal peace conference which, essentially, ended the cold war.

Chapter 11

DESTINY REVEALED

Reykjavik, Iceland

*I*t was a week after the wedding. The frenzy of the festivities had waned somewhat, although some of their Icelandic friends continued partying as was the Icelandic tradition. Garrett and Ollie were strolling together along a quiet street in Reykjavik, reminiscing earlier times and catching up with current events and family news. Garrett was proud to have his dad with him at a time of great fortune and happiness for all of them. He was no longer a child or adolescent in the eyes of his father, but rather a companion who, surprisingly, shared many mutual values. Getting to know his dad as an adult gave a different and comfortable perspective to Garrett. Their musings together found that they paralleled many opinions and values, often to the amazement of the other. Garrett was pleasantly surprised by his dad's commitment to world peace and they found much common ground in such diverse areas as politics, social mores, and attitudes. In Garrett's eyes, his father no longer represented the archaic vision that he held of him for so long. Dad had changed. Or had he? Maybe his dad had been that way all along and Garrett, in his stubborn youth, had refused to understand his father's position and background.

Ollie, in turn, was delighted at the intelligence and aptitude of his son and marveled at his openness toward him, a condition that was rarely evident in his son's younger years. He could feel the new connection with Garrett and realized that his son was no longer a child, but a young man to be admired. Ollie felt a new pride in his youngest son.

It was in the family plans to stay a week or so in Iceland to enjoy a perspective of the lives of the newly married couple. They would then travel as a group to Berkeley where Garrett and Gugga would be introduced to San Francisco Bay Area society. Thora was as excited as she could be anticipating traveling at long last to America. It had been her dream since she first heard the stories from Garrett while growing up.

As their walk allowed them to aimlessly wander around town, they both realized that they were getting hungry and stopped to contemplate a place to stop and eat. As they bantered a bit about food, a sleek, black, limousine pulled up alongside the curb. A tall, rather thin man with a carefully cropped white beard, dressed immaculately in a cut of clothes that indicated that he was a maritime officer, stepped out of the limo. His measured gait reflected that of an aristocrat. His wide welcoming grin and extended hand suggested that they would know him.

"Good Afternoon, my friends. My name is Captain Otto Wermoutt, formerly of the Kreigsmarine, and currently a resident of the United States," he said in English with a clip Germanic accent.

Ollie and Garrett glanced quizzically at one another, neither of them recognizing him nor understanding why he would specifically stop and address them on a street in the middle of Reykjavik.

"Good afternoon," Ollie replied, extending his hand, yet still perplexed at the suddenness of this man's appearance. "Is there something we can do for you?"

"I have some very intriguing news for both of you," Wermoutt suggested. "You will find it very interesting and it could contribute to your understanding of the workings of your friend and confidant, Admiral Richard E. Byrd."

"Excuse me," Ollie replied, "Why do you think I have any interest in Admiral Byrd?"

Wermhoutt looked directly into Ollie's eyes, smiled and glanced at Garrett. "I also have some very interesting news for you about your new wife's family. Won't you join me for a bite to eat? I know a cozy little biergarten down the street that serves authentic bratwurst and pomme frites. Of course, the beer is also good."

Without waiting for an affirmative answer, Wermoutt opened the back door of the limo and invited them in. "Please, join me. It will only be for a short time and I promise you will not be disappointed."

Both Ollie and Garrett were skeptical, but very much intrigued. What was it that this aristocratic, Germanic stranger knew about Admiral Byrd? Garrett looked at his dad with curious eyes, wondering just what this man knew about Gugga. After a bit of hesitation, Garrett gestured towards the limo. "Why not?" Garrett posed to his dad, "This could be interesting and it sure solves the problem of a place to have lunch."

Ollie nodded in the affirmative and both got into the stranger's limousine.

"A beautiful day, don't you agree, especially for Iceland?"

"Yes, a beautiful day," Commander Hill responded, "Who did you say you are again?"

"Wermhoutt, Captain Otto Wermoutt," he responded, pleasantly repeating his name, but offering no more, obviously not willing to talk until they reached the biergarten.

True to his word, Wermoutt stopped at a small Nordic/German delicatessen only a block away. No conversation took place in the limo. They entered and sat at a table in the rear that was somewhat secluded. Both Garrett and Ollie noticed with interest that the driver was dressed in a black suit, wore sunglasses and said nothing. They each remembered their earlier convergences with a man in black and each, without the other's knowledge, had their memories jolted by their earlier meetings with this strange man.

"First I want to congratulate you," Wermoutt began by addressing Garrett, "For your wedding. I want to let you know that I was there and witnessed the whole ceremony."

"I don't remember seeing you," Garrett responded. "Why were you there?"

"I'll get to that in a moment," the Captain said as their lunch arrived, served by a young man who proudly presented the plates to each customer. He then poured each man a generous stein of pale ale and quietly retreated to the serving counter.

Assured of their privacy, Wermhoutt addressed both men in a hushed and secretive voice.

"Commander and Mr. Hill," he began, "We knew you were coming soon after the wedding plans were made. I arranged to come here and meet with you at the earliest convenience. Naturally, I didn't want to interrupt the wedding festivities, but waited until I could speak to you alone, privately."

"We?" probed Garrett curiously.

"Yes, we will talk about that a bit later, if you don't mind."

Wermoutt turned and looked directly at Garrett. "You, Mr. Hill, we have been observing for many years."

Garrett sat back in his chair, stunned by what he just heard from this complete stranger.

"Watching? . . . Me? . . . Who is watching me? For God's sake, why me?" Garrett stammered.

The Captain spoke directly to Garrett with a soft, reassuring voice, "Don't be alarmed. Those that have been watching mean you no harm . . . they simply have tested you to make sure you can be trusted."

Garrett was nonplussed and intrigued. "Trusted? Trusted for what?"

The Captain ignored Garrett's surprise and turned his attention to Commander Hill.

"We weren't sure of you until after you saw Thal in the *flugelrad* and then we knew you could keep it in confidence . . . and, of course, you have done that."

Commander Hill was startled upon hearing this complete stranger, a German, and someone who could not possibly have known or been privy to this information, reveal this deep long kept secret. He felt an anxious vulnerability to his long held personal scrutiny and now his secret was subject to not only to the knowledge of his son, but to a total stranger as well. He noticed much the same anxiety rising up in him as when he was debriefed at the Pentagon so many years ago. This time, however, it was not a man in black, but a seemingly retired German Naval officer. He decided to maintain his facade of military reserve and professional nondisclosure for now – until he could understand the situation more completely.

"*Flugelrad*? What in earth are you talking about?"

"*Flugelrads*, flying saucers, as your country prefers to call them. February, 1947, an American C-47 flying near Little America piloted by your famous Admiral Byrd. You were his co-pilot."

Commander Hill was stunned as Wermoutt continued with his improbable tale. "It is interesting, Commander Hill, that you posed the term, *What in Earth?* If you remember, you looked directly into the eyes of the pilot of the craft. He caught more than a glimpse of you. You may soon see how prophetic your words will prove to be."

Garrett shifted uncomfortably in his chair and stared at his father, as seemingly hundreds of questions bounced around in his mind.

"Dad, is that true, did you encounter a UFO during Operation Highjump with Admiral Byrd?"

Ollie Hill, transfixed by the words from Wermoutt, leaned forward in his chair, almost knocking his stein of beer into his lap.

"How could you know . . ." his voice quickly trailed off as he caught himself and stopped to consider his words.

Garrett looked at his dad with a new set of eyes. Seeing him in another new light, he realized that there was more to this meeting than he could have imagined, and more to his father than he had ever considered. He continued to stare in amazement at his father, drinking in all the dynamics of this incredible conversation, and the insightful presence of their mysterious new acquaintance. Ollie, in a moment of resignation, looked and nodded towards his son, glanced at Wermoutt, sat back in his chair, relaxed his body and softened his speech.

"Yes, Garrett, it's true. I saw a flugelrad, to which our friend is referring."

A prolonged moment of silence gripped both father and son as they tried to reconcile to themselves what had just transpired. The tenor of conversation from that point on became more intimate and tensions began to temper themselves in the new common atmosphere.

"Garrett, may I call you Garrett?" The Captain spoke, easing his formality.

"I must tell you a story, a seemingly fantastic story . . . one that may so impact your life that you may never turn back. I shall begin with you. First, let me tell you that Gugga is my daughter."

Garrett's jaw dropped. He could not believe what he heard. Here is a man who just appeared from off the street and was claiming to be Gugga's father! His mind raced through his memory as he recalled the photo Gugga showed him of her alleged father in her flat the day they met. He conceded to himself that there could be a resemblance, but how could he be sure?

"I have not been part of her life because of my, shall we say, journey? I have watched her grow and mature without her knowledge. It is I who has assured that her financial well-being was provided. She does not know this. She does not know me. It is I, not incidentally, who has quietly led you and Gugga to the understanding of 'Nordic Legends.'"

Garrett interrupted, startled, "Then . . . What . . . you are claiming to be my *father-in-law!*"

"Well, yes, technically. Gugga's mother and I met briefly when I was in Iceland. We had a few intimate encounters and I went back to Germany. She, apparently, came looking for me to let me know she had our child. But we never connected and I never saw her again. The headquarters of the Kreigsmarine in Germany later informed me of her attempt to find me and to let me know that I had a daughter. I, of course, through my contacts found out about Gugga and wanted to care for her in the best way I could, but my mission would not allow me to raise her. I decided to send money to her Grandmother anonymously."

Wermoutt looked at Garrett with searching eyes, attempting to garner whether the young man could digest this new and life-changing information all at once. He decided that Garrett was a mature young man and could assimilate his story without major emotional upheaval.

"That is also why I have been watching you over the past several years. I know your background, your history and the story of your family, including the loss of your brother during the early days of the

Viet Nam war, a truly unfortunate incident. And, of course, you, Commander Hill, we have known about you since Operation Highjump and your flight with Admiral Byrd over Antarctica."

"Who the devil is the *we* you keep referring to, and what do you know about me?" Hill demanded.

Garrett fidgeted nervously, his voice almost paralyzed, causing him to stammer. He was still very startled. "You are Gugga's father?" he repeated with questioned awe.

Wermoutt smiled, slightly nodded his head to the stunned young man, and went on. "Let me begin," he paused, "from the very beginning." The Captain relaxed in his chair preparing to tell them his story. He looked around the café to ensure their absolute privacy and prepared to reveal to his reluctant students the information that would prove to be incredibly startling to them and change their lives forever.

"In the closing days of the war, I was assigned a final mission aboard U-Boat 530. We were to transport six brass boxes to Germany's secret base in Antarctica. One of the most treasured and valuable artifacts in history, the Holy Lance, or *Heilige Lance*, as we say in Germany, was taken there for safekeeping. Rudolf Hess and Karl Haushofer were aware of the mission at that juncture. Hess, of course, is still in Spandau Prison in Berlin. They were both the architects of our base in Antarctica and both aware of the Holy Lance and the power it bestowed. That knowledge, incidentally, is why Hess is still being held in complete solitary confinement without any visitors, not even his family. He knows too much and the victorious allies do not want any of this information to be leaked to the rest of the world.

We were accompanied by some very high-ranking Nazi leaders who, after the delivery to Antarctica, left the U-530 and disappeared into Argentina, with the help and cooperation of the friendly Argentine President, Juan Peron, and his wife, the popular Evita. The Lance remained in Antarctica until 1978 when a select group of *Ritters*, of the Knights of the Holy Lance, [1] traveled to Antarctica and retrieved it. This was successfully accomplished and the Lance is now in the permanent hands of the Ritters.

"Who are the Ritters and where is the Lance now," asked Ollie.

"I cannot reveal the exact location of the Lance to you at this time, but I can tell you that it is in Germany under strict guard and encased in an impenetrable fortress. As far as the Ritters, they are all members of a select group of men throughout the world who are aware of the power of the Holy Lance and have vowed to use it to bring and maintain peace in this world. If it fell into the wrong hands, as it has throughout history, more wars and possible total disaster and possibly even planetary annihilation could occur. The Arianni, the inhabitants of the inner world, have entrusted us to find the proper individual who can hold the Lance and in doing so bring peace to the world. Since the explosion of the first atomic bomb, the Arianni have recognized that their civilization is threatened by the misuse of atomic technology. They have intervened before and would intervene again if nuclear weapons were to permeate the world and become a threat to their own existence. That is our mission – to assure that peace becomes the world's unified purpose, rather than conflict and war."

"So, what is it you want from us?" Garrett wondered. "We are not Ritters nor are we affiliated with your Knights. Perhaps you have made a mistake in approaching us."

"No, there is no mistake. We have been in contact with Thal, the emissary of the Arianni, for some time, and we have agreed with him, after many consultations, that you are the *chosen one*. Thal and the Arianni know that you, Garrett, are a dedicated man of peace and are the one to be given the mantle and power of the Lance to guide the world. You will be initiated into the Teutonic Knights as a

Ritter. We, as your companions and comrades, will assist and follow your leadership as soon as you are confirmed by both the Knights and the Arianni. There is truly no other alternative at this time. We must act now to preserve humankind and avoid any dire actions by the Arianni that would impact up the surface world. The Arianni are dedicated to peace. They want to be left alone, but would be willing to share their magnificent institutions and technology if humankind can embrace harmony as a way of being. We can achieve peace. They are willing to assist us by granting the power of the Holy Lance to be vested in Garrett. Do you see what a magnificent opportunity we and the Arianni are presenting you? It is unprecedented."

"Am I to presume then, that you are also a Ritter?" Garrett opined.

"Yes, of course, I am your emissary from the Order of Teutonic Knights that has been entrusted to bring you back to our castle and begin the process of initiation for you."

Garrett's head was spinning. What kind of fantasy was this? This man, whose story, while fantastical, was compelling in a strange way especially after realizing that his strange dream now appears not to be a fantasy, but a phenomenal reality. He knew he would soon share his "dream" memory with his father. He reasoned that his dad would be fairly receptive now that he had revealed his own well-kept secret regarding seeing Thal in Antarctica, the same humanoid Garrett recollected meeting in his dream state.

****

The story spun by Captain Otto Wermoutt proved to be both fascinating and curious to Ollie and Garrett. Each of them realized that this was no tall tale from a crackpot, but a communication of significant proportions, one that portended enormous consequences for the world and for one another.

Ollie was the first to speak as questions were popping into his head like popcorn on a skillet.

"But what of the *flugelrads*, what does this story have to do with them? Were they German secret weapons? What happened to them?"

"No, they were not craft from Germany, although Germany was working on secret propulsion systems that could mimic the performance of the *flugelrad*. They are from *Asgarth*."

"Asgarth," Garrett pondered aloud, captivated by the moment, "Of course. Now I remember. In the Prophet's home when Gugga and I were enthralled by Nordic and Icelandic legends, the Arianni were said to come from Asgarth, the center of the Earth."

Garrett realized what he had blurted out and instantly remembered the many conversations with the Prophet and what he had taught them about the "inner kingdom."

"The *flugelrads* came from the center of the earth!" he exclaimed.

The Commander leaned back in his chair as competing ideas of reality danced through his head. All his military and historical logic had been defied; all his military training in observation and reality had been challenged by this bizarre and seemingly unbelievable story. Every logical bone in his body wanted to resist this fairy tale, yet . . . he had seen the *flugelrad* and had heard the story from Admiral Byrd. He had read it in Byrd's secret diary that Ollie pledged never to reveal.

"Yes, from the center of the earth," Wermoutt confirmed.

"Well," Ollie countered, "it is a fantastic story. How do we know that it isn't just that – a fantastic story?"

Wermoutt sat back in his chair, reached into his jacket pocket and produced a small crystalline gem and handed it to Ollie. The Commander picked it up and fingered it carefully, remembering a similar stone that was in the package that he had received years ago from Admiral Byrd. Garrett, his heart beating rapidly, recognized the amazing similarity to the stone he received in his *dream*. A gift from this man named Thal, the pilot of the craft wherein he was transported during his so called dream.

"My God," Garrett thought, struggling not to reveal his amazement. "I was transported to a space ship and given a stone just like this one. I was indeed abducted! Oh my God, It was real!"

"A curious little pebble, is it not? The Captain suggested.

"Yes, indeed, a curious little pebble. Where did you get it?"

"From Thal." The Captain replied.

"Thal?

"Yes, the figure you saw out the window of your plane with Admiral Byrd that incredible morning in 1947."

"The humanoid figure I saw in the spacecraft?"

"Yes, and he also observed you and has detailed images of you preserved from that day as a dossier of your life, before and since your encounter with him. That day initiated our interest in you. They have had an interest in you ever since."

"Why me?"

"They were looking for someone who could be taught and bring the fruits of the inner world to the surface world. You were a candidate, a confidant of Admiral Byrd."

The Captain turned to Garrett and spoke directly to him. "Frankly, it is you who is under consideration now."

Garrett squirmed uneasily in his chair, stunned, excited, frightened, and swirling with mixed emotions at the shocking words, trying to assimilate the implausible story in his mind. This was the most fantastic, wild proposition anyone could have come up with. The mantle of peace, forged by the Holy Lance, was being presented to him, Garrett Oliver Hill. Could it possibly be true? Had the legendary King Arthur of Camelot been granted the same phenomenal opportunity? Was the Holy Lance – the Spear of Destiny – Garrett Hill's magical sword?

Chapter notes:

1. Order of the Teutonic Knights: Leopold of Austria, the last of the Roman Emperors, quarreled with the powerful King Richard of England and decided the Lance should be hidden in some secret place. A group of Christian Crusaders formed a clandestine organization known as the *Knights of the Teutonic Order* and Leopold placed the Lance in their custody. More information regarding the history of the Order can be found in Appendix I and in the preface.

Chapter 12

INTO THE ABYSS

Reykjavik, Iceland

*L*eaving the biergarten, Garrett and Ollie respectfully declined Wermoutt's offer to drive them to their destination. Both had much to talk about and they relished the time they would have spent walking together back to Ollie's hotel where Garrett had left his car. Needless to say, neither of them could have fathomed the entire scene that unfolded just a few hours previous. But here they were, reeling from a situation that could only occur in make-believe. Yet, both realized that this fairy tale had enough substance to tilt their thoughts in directions that they could never have predicted.

"Dad, I have something to tell you," Garrett said hesitantly, "I visited Thal too!"

"You what?" Ollie replied incredulously.

"It was when I was in the hospital in Berkeley. Remember? I was in a protest and was clubbed by the local police breaking up the gathering. I remember Mom coming over while I was in the hospital ward with several other people and I was taken out of the room for tests. Thinking back, I don't believe that the man who wheeled me out of the room was a doctor at all. He was wearing dark glasses and a dark suit under his smock. I thought it was unusual, but I didn't give it much thought because of the circumstances. He wheeled me into a little room and that's when I had what I thought was a fantastic dream. I was suddenly in some sort of craft facing a tall humanoid with Nordic features and he was telling me that I had a destiny and *they* were there to help me. He, and I think he identified himself as Thal, said I was going to be faced with a choice between good and evil and he also mentioned the Spear of Destiny, the same Holy Lance that the Captain was talking about. And I remember him giving me a stone much like the one the captain presented to us today. I still have it! I tell you Dad, something strange is burgeoning and I'm both scared and excited."

"Well son," Ollie admitted, "I have to say that this has all the trappings of some hysterical dream. I can really empathize with what you are going through. I am wrestling with the same dilemmas, trying to separate truth from fabrication. I received a package from Admiral Byrd many years ago containing maps, a diary and yes, a small similar stone. I've been puzzled for years about the meaning and purpose of me receiving it. It appears that those memories are beginning to assert themselves. These men-in-black keep reappearing at odd moments as if they were sent to do someone's or something's bidding."

"Yeah dad, you're right on," mused Garrett. "I also saw one of those guys on the plane to Iceland but didn't put two and two together . . . until now."

"And then, of course, the Captain, he's the icing on the cake," added Ollie. "It's also significant that both of us have either seen or met the same Nordic humanoid, Thal, under very weird circumstances."

"What are we going to tell Mom and Gugga? Gugga might freak out when she realizes that her father attended the wedding and that we just had a long, bizarre conversation with him."

"I think we have to tell them everything," Ollie proposed. "They need to understand the whole story of what we experienced, both with

Thal and with Captain Wermoutt. We can't keep this from them. They might initially think we are crazy or launching an elaborate joke, but I know they will eventually understand. It will be an incredible awakening for us all as we piece our way through this."

****

Dinner that night proved to be an evening of extremes. It was not easy to chronicle what had happened earlier that day, let alone convince their wives that their crazy story was not an elaborate hoax. Both women repeatedly exchanged wondering glances, not sure what to think about their husbands' stories, or whether more unbelievably, they were playing a silly joke, or perhaps suffering from delusions from the beer they drank that afternoon.

Jackie was the first to comment.

"I know one thing. Neither one of you would pull a cruel or hurtful prank on us. You would never dream of telling Gugga that you had seen and talked with her father. You just would not and could not do that. There is no way I could not believe that what you have shared is true. You are much too honorable. Ollie, we've been together for many years; you have never lied to me. I believe you."

Gugga was stunned, perhaps more to hear that her father was alive than being concerned about the other aspects of the tale. She could fathom the flying saucer sighting and could intellectually accept the legend of the Holy Lance. However, that part of the story was secondary in her mind as she jostled her thoughts with visions that her father was not only alive, but here in Reyjkavik. That was the most unbelievable element that Gugga tried to reconcile in her thoughts after hearing the shocking words from Ollie and Garrett. She had not even begun to consider the implications of Garrett being the designated recipient of the Holy Lance.

"Gugga, do you want to meet your father?" Garrett gently proposed. "I know that this is a huge shock for you, even if it somehow turns out to be a hoax. It surely will take you some time to sort it out in your mind. However, I believe you will know when you meet him and if it feels right, you can then determine any next steps. He has consented to meet you if you would allow it."

"I've always assumed he was dead," Gugga thoughtfully reflected, slowly recovering from her initial shock.

"I never heard from him. I only had an old photo that you saw in my flat. What a revelation it would be if, indeed, it is him! I frequently fantasized that it was my father who was sending me money after Grandmother passed away. I should at least meet him and thank him for that."

Gugga smiled at Garrett and pointedly brushed back her long blonde hair as she pondered seeing her father. She grasped Garrett by the hand and assertively said to him, "Yes, I will see him. But I want to see him alone, without any distractions. I know you can understand that. Can you arrange to have him come to the dining room of your parents' hotel? I'm not as yet comfortable for him to come to our home."

"Of course," Garrett willingly agreed. "I'll make the arrangements for tomorrow morning. He can meet you for tea in the dining area. I'll call him this evening. I have his room number at the hotel where he's staying."

Both Jackie and Ollie were heartened and encouraged by the easy, loving, conversation between their son and his wife. They marveled at how sensitive Garrett was and how sweetly Gugga's request was delivered. It was so gratifying to see such a amiable demonstration of their mutual commitment and love. Ollie and Jackie secretly squeezed one another's hand under the table in quiet mutual admiration for their newly married children, while lovingly reaffirming their own commitment of over thirty years.

****

The hotel was elaborately decorated with both modern art pieces and ancient Viking paintings and murals on the walls. The lighting was pleasantly dim and reflected the glamour and majesty of the room. Efficient young waitresses and waiters roamed about with ample smiles while they went about their duties. It was quiet, without many morning distractions or interrupting sounds that challenged the ambience of the setting. The hotel would be a fitting place for Gugga and her alleged father to meet for the first time.

Gugga was nervous. She could feel her heart beating more rapidly than normal and attempted to calm herself by taking several deep breaths. She entered the dining room, glanced over to a far wall and gazed for the first time at the man who claimed to be her father. He was taller than she had imagined, although his formal dress and elegant manner were consistent with her image of him. He rose from his chair when he saw her, bowed slightly and extended his hand in greeting.

"So we meet at last," he said. "You are as delightful as I had imagined. Won't you please sit down and enjoy a cup of tea with me?"

Gugga accepted his hand which was strong and comforting. She immediately relaxed, smiled and sat across from this elegant man. He appeared to be in his late fifties or early sixties, very handsome and poised.

"Thank you," she politely murmured in a barely audible voice. "This is a highly interesting turn in my life. I am delighted to finally meet you."

Captain Wermoutt formally acknowledged her statement by nodding his head affirmatively as he sat down. He carefully poured them each a cup of tea from the carafe brewing on the table. He invited her to join him in a toast and they both raised their cups and took a sip of the teeming beverage.

"I know you have many questions, my dear Guthbjörg, and I will try to answer them to the best of my ability. Perhaps your first question might well be, 'What am I doing here, and why now, after all these years?"

"That would be a good start," Gugga replied, still unsure of where the conversation would lead.

"As I told Garrett and your father-in-law, I am here on a mission, a journey perhaps it may be termed, to escort Garrett with me to Germany to participate in an initiation ritual that will enable him to fulfill his dream of world peace. I was at your wedding and watched your every movement. It was a marked surprise to me that the fates brought you and Garrett together. I have learned, however, not to question such spiritual directives. When I arrived in Reykjavik, I realized that my past had caught up with me and I would meet you for the first time."

"Was it you that sent the monthly stipends to my Grandmother to care for me?"

"Yes," the Captain admitted, "I did so when I learned that your mother came looking for me in Germany. I must confess to you that she and I had a few liaisons during the small number of weeks or so we spent together. I was young and never truly got to know her well. I also never met your Grandmother although I tracked her down through my sources after I could not find your mother and learned that she had taken you in as a child. I knew that the path my life journey was taking me would not allow me to be more active in your life. So I did what I thought at the time was the best thing for both of us – as well as for your grandmother. I'd been living in Missouri, in the United States and made arrangements with a local bank to see that you received regular monthly checks to assure your survival and education."

"I appreciate that," Gugga quietly responded. "But what happened to my mother? Surely you know more than what you just told me."

"No, I really don't. The Reich's Ministry only gave me basic information telling me that they were not in the business of searching for unwed mothers. They said they had given me all the information they had and there was no other. It was my own curiosity and concern that led me to look you up through your grandmother and it was my decision only to assure your financial needs. I never married nor had other children in my life and was happy to accept that responsibility.

Gugga puzzled over the veracity of this man. He knew too much about her and her grandmother not to be her father, and he was certainly keeping a dispassionate distance between them even now.

"How do I know what you are telling me is the truth? What proof, other than your story, can you produce to verify that you are my father?'

The Captain sat back in his chair and reached into his inner jacket pocket producing a photo and carefully handed it to Gugga.

"I gave a photo such as this to your mother one day and perhaps she kept it in her things. I can only hope that you will recognize it. I understand why you would be cautious."

He handed her a photo of himself and her mother embracing together in front of a familiar landmark in Iceland. It was definitely her mother, and the man beside her exhibited a striking resemblance to the man said to be her father in the photograph given to her so long ago by her mother. Gugga felt her heart open to the possibility that this man before her was indeed her father.

Gugga's thoughts shifted to her mother and Garrett. Gugga still did not know her fate and she wondered whether her alleged father truly looked for her mother or knew her fate. And who was this man in reality? He may be her father, she would concede, but somehow she felt a mistrust that emanated from a place in her heart she could not herself understand. Part of the mistrust stemmed from the wild proposal by her father to entice Garrett to follow him into some mystical fate, an adventure that would separate her from her new husband. Gugga's mixed emotions disturbed her in ways she could not easily reconcile.

The Captain felt comfortable that Gugga accepted the photograph as proof. He knew, however, he would have to keep their relationship as neutral as possible. The mission with Garrett was his prime duty and nothing could be allowed to distract him from what he referred to as his *journey*. One day, perhaps, he could be more open with her, but now his meeting with her served as a necessity as she would have a strong influence over Garrett's decision to join him.

Gugga felt that she and her new family would need time to assimilate all that had happened. They were planning to leave for California in a few days and that could give them time to reflect on all the events which had occurred during this beautiful and strange week.

As she left the hotel and entered her car to drive home, Gugga paused and worried whether Garrett could fall under the spell of this very charismatic man. She knew that she would have to convince Garrett to forget all the grandiose promises made to him by her newly revealed father. She didn't know whether she had the strength and power to persuade Garrett that he should not follow Wermoutt to Germany to engage in what she imagined to be a life-threatening and frightening journey. Gugga decided that she needed support and would appeal to Garrett's father for help.

Ollie was busily making preparations for their return journey to California when Gugga approached him. Garrett was over at the airport taking one last flight with Bjorn and Thora with him. She had shown the family propensity for flight and Garrett and Bjorn had already begun flight instruction for the young girl. Thora enthusiastically took to the task with great interest and capability. She hoped to be fully certified soon.

"Dad," Gugga addressed her new father-in-law in a reluctant voice, "I need your help with Garrett."

Ollie took off his glasses and instantly acknowledged his daughter-in-law and replied, "With Garrett? Of course my dear, you know I would do anything for either of you. How can I be of help?"

"I'm frightened for him. I'm afraid that the Captain, my father, has convinced him to go to Germany with him to see what this Holy Lance episode is all about. Deep down, I don't trust him and I'm not sure why."

Ollie stood up, wrapped his arms around Gugga and gazed deeply into her eyes, seeing the distress that she was feeling.

"In truth, Gugga, I also have misgivings about him. I have had the same uneasy feelings, and I too, don't know why. What do you propose we do? We're leaving in two days and we are all expecting Garrett to come with us. Do you think he has already made up his mind?"

"I don't know. I can only read his body language and tone and try to interpret his comments without alerting him to my concerns. But I feel that he is deciding to follow my father."

"Perhaps we could approach him together," Ollie suggested. "Maybe we can dissuade him from pursuing this improbable proposal."

With Ollie on her side, Gugga felt more comfortable knowing that she had an ally who understood and empathized with her concerns. They did not have much time and the Captain had several individual meetings with Garrett without any of the family knowing what transpired in those meetings. They decided to speak with Garrett that evening after he returned with Thora from the airport.

Garrett returned from the airport eager to share with the family the progress Thora had made in her flying lessons. Not only was she turning out to be a competent pilot, but she was highly interested in all aspects of the plane – its construction, flight worthiness, and how the engine functioned. He proudly exclaimed how pleased he was with the amazing progress of his young daughter.

After the hearty congratulations and attention given Thora, Thora revealed that she was tired and asked to go up to the hotel room with her new grandmother and take a nap. Jackie thought that was a marvelous idea and joined her.

The opportunity was now ideal. Gugga and Ollie were alone with Garrett and opened the conversation. Gugga approached Garrett with some trepidation but got straight to the point.

"Garrett, I'm concerned about you and I've shared that with your father. I believe we need to talk."

Garrett was somewhat surprised by the sudden shift in the tenor of the conversation and saw immediately the concern evident in Gugga's face. He glanced over at his dad as if to see if he was part of this concern but didn't detect any obvious signs. He looked tenderly at his wife and said, "What is it, my love that concerns you?"

Gugga, always direct in her communications, gazed lovingly at Garrett and related her apprehension and fears.

"I'm fearful that you have fallen under the spell of my father and are planning to go with him to Germany on this fanatical journey. I'm afraid you are deciding not to come to California with the rest of us and, instead, embark on a scary mission. I'm just afraid for you, and for us."

Garrett reflected on Gugga's thoughts and once again looked to his father for support.

"Do you share her fears, Dad?"

Ollie paused for a moment, searching for the right words. He wanted to support Gugga but he, too, was transfixed by the events of the past few days. Again he was torn between keeping his family together and admitting that the adventure had appeal for him also.

"I do share her concerns, Garrett. But I understand the allure of the adventure based on what we both know to be real. You have a family that loves you, a daughter that needs you and a wife who loves you more than any man can ask. You must make the decision yourself, weighing all the competing factors and your own conscience. Personally, I don't want to lose you again."

Garrett squirmed slightly. He was confronted with a Hobson's choice – neither choice seemed right. This couldn't be the choice between good and evil to which Thal was referring, yet it was certainly a choice that would irreversibly alter his life. He knew he had to choose.

"I don't plan on going with the Captain," Garrett finally uttered. "Leaving with my family and traveling to my other home in Berkeley makes good sense. We'll all leave together."

Relieved and reassured, Gugga kissed Garrett and Ollie on their cheeks.

"Thank you for clearing that up for me," Gugga softly answered, "Now I can focus on our trip without the distraction of useless fears."

****

The day of departure finally arrived. The family gathered at the airport waiting an hour before the flight was scheduled to leave. All were enjoying smiles of anticipation, joking with one another and exchanging last minute thoughts.

Garrett, however, was not his usual buoyant self. Since admitting to Gugga and his dad that he was committed to returning to Berkeley with the family, he was having second thoughts. Those second thoughts were brought into the present moment when the Captain suddenly appeared. This would be his last chance to convince Garrett to come with him.

"Garrett, may I speak with you for a moment? I know you are ready to leave and I want to plead once again, to have you reconsider and come with me. The *Knights of the Holy Lance* has gathered together at Wewelsburg Castle,[1] the headquarters of the Ritters, in West Germany to welcome you into the Order. This is our final opportunity. It has been in the Arianni plan for years. A real chance of world peace is at stake. You must reconsider! You are our final hope."

Garrett looked over at Gugga and the family. His daughter was clinging to her grandmother while Ollie was quizzically studying Garrett. Gugga intuitively felt that Garrett was going to leave with the Captain. She rushed over to him, ignoring her father, and hugged him tightly. Garrett looked at her tenderly and glanced over at the rest of the family.

"I have to go, Gugga. I'm sorry, but I have to go. Please understand. This will only take a couple of weeks, and I promise I will then join you all in Berkeley. I love you more than I can ever say and I give you my word I will return to you and Thora."

Tears welled up in Gugga's eyes as she resigned herself to Garrett's decision. She embraced him heartfully as Thora ran over to join the impromptu union. Ollie and Jackie hugged him and let him know that they would take care of his family until he returned. As

Ollie acknowledged the Captain, he held Garrett in a long hug and whispered, "We'll be waiting for you. If I don't hear from you in two weeks, I'm coming after you."

Garrett released from the grip of his dad, gave him a final hug, and walked off with the Captain, not looking back.

"I just don't trust this so-called father of mine," Gugga reiterated to her father-in-law as Garrett disappeared with the Captain into the streets of Reykjavik.

Chapter Notes

1. An ancient triangular shape stone-walled castle built in West Germany near the city of Paderborn and refurbished by Himmler during the 2nd world war to provide a unique headquarters for the occult events of the SS, Himmler's Special Forces. See photo p. 153.

Chapter 13

WEWELSBURG CASTLE

Iceland to Germany

*G*arrett's mind raced, bouncing back and forth between the fear of the unknown and the lure of excitement. He had not felt such conflicts of emotions since he left his home in California to flee to Sweden. It was mid-summer and he was accompanying the Captain to Germany in spite of the worried pleas of his family. The journey was fraught with unknowns and steeped in mystery. Yet, something deep inside him compelled him onward, his curiosity and innate sense of adventure battling his fear. What was it that was driving him? What was the strange power the Captain seemed to possess over his decisions? Was it wise to leave the comfort and safety of his family to embark on this wild sojourn? Each step he took away from his loved ones seemed that he was stepping away from sanity and preparing to jump from a high cliff without a vision of a safety net at the bottom. His thoughts continued to bounce and swing precariously like monkeys darting from tree to tree.

Suddenly, however, those thoughts were jolted into the moment when the Captain addressed him.

"You have just made the most important decision that one can make in a lifetime," the Captain solemnly stated. "In the name of the Arianni and the Ritters of the Holy Order, we commend you for your foresight, your courage, and your commitment. My plane is ready for flight at the other end of the field. It will take us directly to Wewelsburg Castle, in Northwestern Germany, where we will land nearby and drive up a hill to the entrance."

Garrett was impressed with the private jet that the Captain had provided for their travel. He had assumed that any trip to the continent would be by commercial airline. It was a small six passenger luxury jet plane of a Swiss design put in private service by the Lear Jet Aircraft Corporation just a few years prior.

"Is this yours?" Garrett asked, impressed with the sleek lines and interior décor of the plane.

"Not exactly," chuckled the Captain. "It belongs to the Order of the Teutonic Knights. The Ritters have access to it whenever they choose, as long as it doesn't conflict with priority missions, such as this one. Besides, this will give us a chance to fly over the Castle so you can get a good look at it before we land. Our pilot is a trusted helper of the Order and knows exactly the procedures to follow. Please, make yourself comfortable. We will arrive in just a few short hours."

Garrett settled into the well-appointed craft and noted the luxury of the interior décor. He had never before been inside a private jet, although he and Bjorn had seen one at the airport where Bjorn kept his small craft.

The small jet quickly powered up and almost immediately was airborne. It wasn't but a few moments in flight that the Captain offered Garrett a drink. Garrett politely declined. The Captain nodded at Garrett and poured himself a small glass of a clear beverage and drank down the Kirschwasser with a satisfied grimace.

"Ahh," the Captain softly belched, "there is nothing like a brim of Kirsch to open one's eyes and relax the body."

He adeptly put down his glass, settled his seat into a reclining position and immediately fell asleep. Garrett vainly tried to fall asleep himself, but lay awake with his eyelids bobbing open and closed regularly. There was no way he could relax, he thought, for some time. They were flying over the Atlantic and would not see land for an hour, so there was nothing of interest to see out of the small window next to his seat. Garrett closed his eyes and attempted to drift into a meditative state that often had calmed him in the past. His meditation attempts, however, were regularly interrupted as the aircraft bounced through some turbulent air pockets. Garrett resigned himself to continually focus on his meditative practice, even if it was not completely successful.

Garrett's first glimpse of the European Continent was from several thousand feet up and he could not make out any landmarks. They had been in the air for a few hours, the Captain still, apparently, asleep. The pilot gave no attention to his youthful passenger.

Emerging out of a light sleep, Wermoutt opened his eyes wide and said something in German to the pilot that Garrett could not quite make out. With his modest grasp of German, Garrett surmised that the Captain was giving the pilot some specific instructions.

"We are over Germany, Mr. Hill. I have asked the pilot to descend to a lower altitude when we reach the area of the castle so we can get a good aerial view. Please pay close attention to what you can see."

Wewelsburg Castle is situated in the center of a rolling, green valley, perched on a hillock overlooking a small village. It had been Heinrich Himmler's dream to convert the historic stone monolith into an occult headquarters for his SS generals and staff. Himmler viewed Wewelsburg as the Grail Castle. He believed that when the Nazis ruled the world, the artifacts stored in the castle would radiate magical power. Himmler was one of the architects of the Holocaust and it was here that he developed the plan to eliminate any persons not considered Aryan and began collecting items that contributed to his grand dreams. He spent an enormous amount of money redecorating the castle to reflect his ideals, embracing many ancient and occult artifacts, carvings, and stonework that coincided with his Nazi/ Occult leanings. Because the castle was built as a triangle, with the point of the triangle pointing north, Himmler explored the occult meanings the shape implied; including the *spear of destiny* that Hitler himself had claimed showed him his future. The history of the castle enticed Himmler to utilize this unique structure as a product of ancient wisdom and harbinger of a new age. Wewelsburg Castle in that historical time became the center of Nazi occult activities. Today, as the headquarters for the Teutonic Knights, the castle had become the ideal repository for the Holy Lance.

As he viewed the castle from the air, especially with its triangular configuration pointing decidedly north, he listened with rapt attention to the Captain's narration about why the Ritters chose this location as their home and the site for their own elaborate rituals.

"Yes, we are aware that this was once Himmler's dream palace, where he practiced his dark arts and mystical rituals based on flawed logic. When we obtained it, we realized that he had knowledge of the Holy Lance by the overall design of the countryside leading to the castle. If you will look closely, you will notice that the triangular castle, seen from the air, can be seen to be the point of a large spear whose shaft is incorporated into the surrounding countryside. The design itself represents the Holy Lance. Himmler was one of the Nazi leaders who had some control over the possession of the Lance, but he did not know its true power. Today, the castle is owned and protected by the Holy Order of Knights and is the safe repository of the Holy Lance."

"Are you saying that the Holy Lance is here, in this castle?" Garrett inquired anxiously.

"Yes, when it was retrieved from Antarctica by a party of Teutonic Ritters recently, it was brought here for safe keeping."

Wewelsburg Castle

Ritter Wermoutt paused for a moment, put his hand on Garrett's right shoulder and said, "That is where you come in, Mr. Hill. When you have been properly prepared, the Ritters will invite you to partake in an initiation ritual before the viewing of the Lance. After the ritual, you will be presented to the Holy Lance which will then officially proclaim you a fellow Ritter and you will precede in learning the power of the Lance from the Arianni. You will meet twelve Ritters who have previously held the Lance in their hands and acknowledged the power within. After you have viewed the Lance and received instruction from the Arianni, you will begin from that moment to put your knowledge of the Lance to bear and inaugurate missions of world peace and prosperity, with the help and following of the Holy Order of the Knights, of course."

A short time later the small plane landed on an airstrip nearby the castle. As they exited the plane, Garrett noticed a black sedan parked nearby with its back doors open and a driver standing by. Captain Wermoutt gestured to Garrett to follow him as the pilot ferried his luggage to the awaiting sedan. Within a few minutes they had navigated their way over a single lane stone bridge leading to the southwestern arched entrance of the castle. Two medieval garbed guards greeted them and guided them into the courtyard where they were directed to park their car. Garrett watched each movement with curiosity and awe.

The courtyard itself was fairly narrow at the north end and widened into a triangle at the south. Three-story stone walls laden with numerous multi-paned windows comprised the three sides of the structure with the roofs pitched at a steep angle. On the north end was a large circular four-story tower with a flat roof, shaped with four cutouts that could serve as observation lookouts or defense positions. Two narrower five-story towers with conical roofs completed the triangle at the South end.

Garrett and the Captain were escorted into an upper sleeping room near the southern entrance. The room was decorated with renaissance paintings on the walls with fresh flowers on the tables. On the far side of the room, framed by a large curtained window, was a large wooden ornate bed with tall dark oak bedposts and protected by a sheer canopy giving an elegant feeling of royalty to the surroundings. It had an exquisite view to the south overlooking the small village that surrounded the castle. The Captain, who obviously had been here before, directed the escorts to place Garrett's bag in the room and said, "For now, you may rest and recover from the flight and the frantic moments before. I will stop by in three hours and take you down to dinner. I'm sure you will be comfortable. There is a restroom adjoining your room where you may refresh yourself. If you need anything, simply ring this bell and a caretaker will assist you. We want you to be comfortable. Is there anything else you require as of this moment?"

Garrett thought for a moment and shook his head. "No, it looks as if you have thought of everything," he suggested. "I look forward to a couple of hours alone and the rest will be welcome."

"Oh, by the way," the Captain directed, "in the closet next to your bed are some fresh clothes for you to wear. When you meet the Ritters, you will want to present yourself as appropriately as possible."

The Captain bid him goodbye and closed the sleeping room door. Garrett immediately pulled back the canopy surrounding the bed and flopped unceremoniously on the feather-stuffed bed. He was too excited to fall asleep as his thoughts bounced from missing his family, the events that led him here, to the energy of the castle that opened him to images of the history that the Captain related. It seemed to feel right for him to be here.

****

It was 7:00 sharp when a knock came at the door. The punctual Captain appeared fresh and rested and took Garrett by the arm as they strolled to the ornate dining hall where a host of finely prepared German cuisine selections were offered. They were soon joined by three well-dressed gentlemen with vested suits and mysterious medallions around their necks, each sporting a closely cropped white beard and mustache. As they entered, they approached Garrett and were formally introduced by the Captain. All three regarded Garrett curiously and with obvious respect. Garrett was so taken by the circumstances that he promptly forgot their formal titles.

"You may address each of them simply as Ritter," the Captain suggested.

Garrett gratefully acknowledged the Captain's advice as they all seated themselves around the table.

"We have been waiting a long time for this moment, Mr. Hill," the tall host on Garrett's immediate right offered while extending his hand. "The Order has been looking forward to this for years and it is a distinct pleasure to finally meet you in person."

"Thank you," replied Garrett, firmly grasping the extended hand of his host. "I must say that this is both a great mystery and a greater honor to be here with you."

The Ritters each smiled at Garrett and at one another, feeling Garrett had made the proper response. Honoring them was a sign of a promising future relationship. The evening gathering lasted little more than an hour. The Ritters asked Garrett many personal questions about his family, his political philosophy, his wife and daughter, and a myriad of questions regarding Garrett's personal values. Garrett attempted to answer them all with integrity and frankness. After all, he determined that he was going to be who he was, not some twisted automaton feigning to please his hosts.

By the end of the dinner, the Ritters seemed to be satisfied with their conversation with Garrett. Throughout the meal they were exceedingly polite and spoke eagerly to him even as they were scrutinizing his responses and body language closely.

The Captain suggested that he and Garrett go for a walk around the grounds so Garrett could ask any other questions he may have and to give the Captain a chance to brief him on future events. Garrett readily agreed and bid good evening to his hosts as he shook hands with them, each grasping Garrett's hand firmly in parting salutation.

The evening was bright with a full moon that cascaded light throughout the castle and onto the courtyard. Most of the castle lights were dimly lit as they strolled slowly about. Garrett looked at the Captain and asked, "Well, what do you think? Do you think I was what they expected?"

"The Ritters knew exactly what to expect as they have been following your activities for several years. They do not like surprises and take every opportunity to mitigate any peculiar circumstances. Yes, you are what they expected. They know you are ready and we will begin the initiation rituals tomorrow evening at midnight. Do you have any more questions?"

"Of course I do. But it seems my questions have to be answered by me. I am looking forward to meeting the other Ritters. How many of them are there?"

Wermoutt mulled over Garrett's response and question. He realized that Garrett was struggling with shock and perhaps some misgivings, but felt certain the initiation ceremony would allay any reticence when Garrett was present in the power of the Knights. Garrett would then realize the import of his destiny.

"You will be in the presence of twelve Ritters, each of whom have held the power of the Lance and have the collective power to enlist you as a comrade and fellow Ritter. There are, however, over two-thousand of us world-wide; each will be pledged to serve you in your mission with the Arianni. In time you will meet them all."

As the Captain and Garrett strolled slowly around the castle grounds, Garrett was able to get a general understanding of how the castle was laid out. He mused about the absurd thought that he might be the new "king" of this magnificent and foreboding castle, while at the same time laughing inwardly at the crazy proposal of his destiny.

The two of them exchanged final evening salutations and went to their separate sleeping rooms with Wermoutt suggesting breakfast in the early morning.

Garrett's head spun as he continued to acknowledge that this was not a dream.

Chapter 14

HOME IN BERKELEY, CALIFORNIA

*T*he bright California sun angled its brilliant rays and created a multitude of prisms through the collection of rocks and gemstones neatly arranged on the backyard table. Thora had been attracted to stones and other *power objects* since she was a child and treasured them all. Her fascination with rocks, gems and various colorful artifacts led her to study the lineage and power that she equated with their spirits. She and her father had studied the power in stones from a stone healer while in Iceland. She became very sensitive to healing power utilizing the mystery of the stones and continued her attraction while living in California.

The natural sunshine, abundant in the Northern California town of Berkeley, filtered through the succulent garden plants in the garden of her grandparent's home – her home away from home – until her father would join them as he had promised. As she examined each of her precious gems resting on the large, round, mosaic table in her grandparents garden, her eyes transfixed upon each individual variation as she tuned into their esoteric meanings. None of her friends back in Iceland with the exception of Meda, collected stones. She became enamored with the proximity of the Sierra Nevada Mountains which promised the discovery of more specimens for her growing obsession. She had promised Meda to gather some for her too.

"Which one is your favorite?" asked her Grandmother who had stepped into the yard to join Thora.

"They're all my favorites, Gramma," Thora proudly proclaimed. "Each of these stones is my friend and has a story to tell and I want to hear what each one has to say. I have to talk to them so they can talk to me. I think that they feel comfortable with me and want me to hear their tales."

"How wonderful for you and for them," Jackie affectionately responded, always ready to support the joys and fancies of her grandchild. "Every object, every being, has a vibration that calls for nurturing, doesn't it?

Thora smiled at her grandmother's words, nodding appreciatively. She had truly accepted and cherished the role of granddaughter and knew how much her long absent grandparents loved her. It was easy to love them, she thought to herself.

"Thora? Mom?" Gugga's voice echoed from within the house as she called out to them in the yard, "What are you two sweethearts doing?"

"We're out here, Mom," Thora shouted out to Gugga. "I'm showing my stone collection to Gramma."

As Gugga joined them in the backyard, Ollie heard their voices from his study and decided to see what the commotion was about. As Thora was gently caressing each of her precious collectables, Ollie came outside to sit with them to enjoy the sun – and to examine Thora's collection. Next to her collection was a small ornate wooden jewel box, lined in purple velvet, where she sequestered her very special stones, along with a velveteen sack where the bulk of the rest were kept.

"What an interesting collection," Ollie remarked, gently resting his hand on Thora's shoulder, "You must be very proud of such a wonderful selection of beautiful minerals."

"I am," Thora triumphantly replied, "These stones are my most valued possessions. I truly love to feel their vibrations in my hands – that's how they talk to me."

Gugga was smiling, yet she was preoccupied with a growing concern for Garrett. He had assured her that he would be in contact with them within two weeks and would be joining them in Berkeley shortly thereafter.

She finally blurted out to her new family, "I'm worried. Garrett said he would contact us by now. It's been over two weeks and we have heard nothing from him. Are any of you feeling nervous the way I am?"

Ollie sighed, "I've become more and more concerned over the past few days, but then I keep letting it go, thinking we will hear from Garrett soon. I, too, am worried."

"Why hasn't Daddy contacted us?" Thora added with a tinge of fear evident in her voice.

Jackie was relieved that the subject was finally broached. She shared the same feelings expressed by her family.

"Ollie, is there something we can do?"

Ollie quickly responded to his family's concerns, as all their eyes had turned to him. "I told Garrett that if we didn't hear from him within two weeks that I would come after him. I think that's what I need to do."

"I must go with you," asserted Gugga. "He is with my father and I don't trust him. I don't think he would keep me away from Garrett and I don't think he has Garrett's best interest in his heart."

Jackie paused, agreeing with Ollie and Gugga, and turned to Thora, saying, "How about if you and I remain here together so your mom and granddad won't have to worry about us? It'll be great for the two of us to spend more time together and we can be available for them in case they need us for something."

"I would rather go with Mom to find Dad," Thora countered, "But I realize that they'll probably have an easier time finding Dad if there were just the two of them. I know Mom would worry about me all the time. Of course I'll stay with you Gramma. We'll be here and we can get them help if they need us."

Gugga hugged Thora, held her for a long moment, and looked at her with loving, admiring eyes. All three were impressed with the maturity and wisdom exhibited by the young girl as their minds collectively raced, contemplating what the future might hold for all of them.

Having made the decision to take action, Ollie responded to the urgency of the situation with haste, not knowing the current status of Garrett or whether he was in trouble.

"We're going to assume that he needs us now and plan accordingly," Ollie said, "I'll use my navy contacts to fly us to Germany immediately. We can rent a car there and drive to the outskirts of Wewelsburg Castle. From there we'll have to play it by ear, depending on the situation. There's always the possibility that he won't want our assistance and will be upset that we're there. We'll have to take that chance."

Gugga quickly agreed and blurted out the plan for a rescue she had been developing for the last week based on her worried assumptions that Garrett was in need of help. She was more than grateful to Ollie, whose leadership and wisdom she had come to greatly admire and respect, for his willingness to act now.

"I could arrive at the castle in a cab and could insist upon seeing my father and husband under the pretense that I wanted to help him and Garrett complete the mission with the Arianni. They would probably trust me as I would produce for them the curious pebble to assure them of my knowledge and willingness to work with them. Perhaps you could wait nearby in the village. I could lead Garrett out to safety. You could arrange a plane to meet us nearby and we could complete our escape."

"Well," Ollie reasoned, impressed with his daughter-in-law's strategic mind, "that's probably as good a preliminary plan as we can have. It, hopefully, will get you into the castle. However, getting you both out safely will be the biggest challenge. We'll have to give it some real thought. We'll more than likely only get one chance. You'll have to be a convincing actress because if not, you could be in serious danger."

Gugga paused to recollect the meetings she and Garrett had with the Prophet over the past few years. She remembered the stories of the Holy Lance and the Prophet's belief of beings that live in the center of the earth. She remembered explicitly the plaque on the Prophet's wall that had the runic symbols arranged in a triangle with a spot for an *energizer* stone in the center. She recalled vividly the narration by the Prophet that the symbols were a key to the hollow earth mystery. She and Garrett had mused often about the symbols ability to remove barriers to the entrance to the hollow earth as well as any other blocked entrance a believer might encounter. Garrett had said recently that the curious pebble given to him by Thal could possibly be the energizer stone, but admitted that it might simply be his fascination with the story. Gugga now was more inclined toward this speculation and began to think that the pebble could be something very special. She would gather the runic symbols and the pebble and take them with her and Ollie, just in case. She didn't know why, but her instinct led her to do this not really knowing why. Her psychic feelings were in full control and she would carry all the runes as well as the pebble with her and keep it with her at all times.

While gathering her necessary clothing for the journey, Ollie appeared to check on what she was bringing, as he knew they needed to travel lightly.

"I have all the items we might need: a compass, binoculars, sharp knife and a first aid kit. I wanted to tell you that I am also bringing the pebble that your father gave me when we met with him. He called it a curious little pebble and somehow I think it could be significant. If nothing else, maybe it will bring us good luck."

Gugga chuckled, a bit embarrassed, she grinned and produced the runic symbols and the similar pebble that Garrett had received from Thal.

"We are thinking alike, Dad. I recalled the time when Garrett and I met with the Prophet and he explained to us the runic triangle and the energizer pebble. Garrett and I thought it might be a key, so I am bringing it along, just in case."

Ollie took a deep breath and let out a small sigh.

"Gugga, you are an amazing woman. I'm so glad that we are doing this together. We do understand one another, don't we?"

They both engaged in an impromptu hug and continued with their packing. If they needed other supplies, they would get them from the navy exchange in Germany.

Ollie had arranged a flight from Alameda Naval Air Station near San Francisco. He and Gugga would be passengers aboard an Air Force Stratotanker to New York and subsequently on to Ramstein U.S. Air Force base in Southwestern Germany. From there they would procure a car and drive to the village of Wewelsburg, a 200 plus kilometers trip to the northeastern quadrant of the German state of Westphalia, the location of the old renaissance castle, where they would attempt to retrieve or rescue Garrett.

Jackie was having recurring thoughts of the possibility of losing her youngest son, compounded with the fear of perhaps losing her husband and daughter-in-law in the process. She presented a brave front, but deep inside she realized that this was no ordinary trip to Germany. Both her husband and daughter-in-law were at risk. She convinced herself that keeping Thora with her would somehow ease the fear and provide comfort to the youngster. She helped Ollie with his packing while continuingly reminding him to keep in touch with her. Ollie knew this was hard on Jackie and promised her several times that he would contact her to keep her informed.

Thora was concerned, of course, about her mom and dad, as well as for her grandfather. She wished she was a few years older and could contribute to the potential rescue, but resolved to stay with her grandmother to provide a life-line for them, if needed. The next couple of weeks could be a major turning point in her life, and she knew it. Thora understood well the legend of the Holy Lance and certainly was aware of the pebble that was given to Garrett by the mysterious Thal and the one given to Ollie and Garrett by her newly discovered blood grandfather. Her understanding of the inner earth was part of local legend and she was convinced that it all was true. Her propensity to talk to the stones in her collection was known by her family, but they did not know that Thora had psychic conversations with the stones and the stones had revealed to her insights that defied logic. Thora knew those privileged communications from the energies within the stones were meant for her alone.

Commander Oliver K. Hill used his considerable military and personal influence to procure passage for both he and Gugga on a U.S. Air Force K-135 Stratotanker, a refueling aircraft used to service fighter jets while still in the air. Based on the design of the Boeing

707 commercial jet liner, the Stratotanker would take them to New York, refuel and subsequently fly them directly to Germany. While providing limited, but not luxurious accommodations, the trip would be relatively comfortable and would guarantee their personal safety and security in case any of the mysterious MIB or others attempted to follow them. The U.S military did its best to provide transportation for their officers' personal needs and often accepted limited family members as well when space was available. The well-respected Commander Hill received high priority attention for his request.

Ollie and Gugga left early in the morning just two days after their backyard conversation. They bid Jackie and Thora a tearful good-bye amidst hopeful hugs and boarded the Air Force jet without incident. Within a few minutes of their being seated securely for takeoff, the huge plane lumbered down the runway picking up rapid speed as it slowly lifted easily into the morning sky. They would be in Germany by late evening of the same day.

Chapter 15

Intrigue

Germany
September, 1980

The slightly audible squeak of the large wooden door to his spacious and ornate bedroom in the early morning brought Garrett back from his disjointed dreams. His now familiar man servant, Hermann's, entry was a welcome respite from a fitful and sleepless night. Garrett, having been very apprehensive when he first arrived at the castle, had calmed down a bit from his initial concerns that were laden with a host of unidentifiable fears. Hermann quietly entered the room and immediately opened the darkened curtains to reveal the morning sun just rising, sending muted streams of light into the room cascading as light crystals over the foot of his bed. Garrett was relieved to witness the new day and his on again, off again, angst-filled slumber.

He had been pondering the dinner conversation with the three Ritters the night before, and felt conflicting emotions regarding the adequacy of his demeanor and whether or not he had made a positive impression. His answers to the myriad questions asked by each man somehow seemed inadequate when directed to such cultured gentlemen. He was impressed by the striking dress, carefully trimmed beards, precise speech and seemingly august presence that each of the three Ritters exhibited. As he reflected on his brief experience here at this ornate castle, he wondered how he could possibly measure up to the expectations that were being laid out for him in this Camelot-like destiny.

Hermann allowed Garrett to slowly bring himself out of his muted sleep-state and poured him a cup of hot tea to soothe his awakening. His smile assured Garrett that all was well and told Garrett he would be summoned for breakfast shortly.

Unbeknownst to Garrett, the Ritters and Captain Wermoutt had met long into the night to prepare for Garrett's initiation into the Teutonic Knight's Royal Order. This was no small endeavor, as the Order had been anticipating this moment for many years and wanted to impress upon Garrett the magnitude of his role and participation. They met secretly in the lower crypt of the castle's North Tower under dimly-lit candles that were placed in small alcoves throughout the oval room. There was an air of solemnity to their discussion as they realized that they were very close to the completion of their, as they termed it, *journey*.

The gathering involved a number of Ritters residing at the castle. They were dressed in their ceremonial garb and began their meeting with summary prayers and incantations, a ritual that was passed down from many centuries of the Order's traditions. Captain Wermoutt also had donned his Ritter ceremonial robes and joined the others in the circle.

The Grand Master, Ritter von Zant was the first to speak.

"I should like to hear first the impressions of the Ritters who interviewed the young man at dinner. Did he fulfill the expectations for the ritual? Will he be able to act as the liaison between the Holy Order and the Arianni? This is crucial to our journey as we must be assured that the Arianni will trust us. Young Garrett will have to be unimpeachable for them to accept him."

Ritter Wermoutt leaned forward from his pillowed alcove chair and took the liberty of explaining the long and complicated trek undertaken to lure Garrett to the castle and said, "This has been a precise and thoroughly orchestrated plan unfolding for many years. We know the risks we have taken and can assure the Ritters that Garrett has been apprised only of what he needs to know. What has been an elaborate ruse to entice him here has taken many twists and turns in order for him to believe why he is here. It was fortunate that Thal befriended Admiral Byrd and Garrett's father which allowed us to build a believable story for the son that encompasses many years and connections. Without that foundation, the mission would have been far more difficult, if not impossible. The Arianni's MIBs have been in constant surveillance of both Garrett and his father over the years and have reported directly to the Arianni and to the Holy Order to keep us all apprised of the progress."

Ritter Frederick responded that he, too, met with Garrett the evening before.

"He is a very naïve young man, yet bright and articulate. I believe he can be the emissary that we need. He believes that he is destined to lead the world to peace. His encounter with Thal has convinced him of the gravity of his mission. I don't believe he suspects anything more than that.

The Grand Master nodded his head as if to agree with Ritter Frederick, and then went on to say, "It is incumbent upon our mission that he is treated with as much honor, respect and hospitality as we can muster. His role will define our relationship with the Arianni and allow us to gain their absolute trust, well beyond the strained relationship that we now have. They have to believe that he is the savior they are looking for. After all, it was our recommendation that we focus on Garrett rather than the original plan for his father. As their liaisons on the surface world, the Arianni need to know that we are comfortable with their designate while maintaining our control over him. We have to realize that he is only useful to us as long as our friends exclusively hold the power of the Holy Lance. It is our destiny to complete the journey for the glorious establishment of the new thousand-year Fourth Reich!"

"And once everything is in place and the Arianni share with us the secret to secure the power that is the culmination of our journey," a third Ritter questioned, "What do we do with the young man?"

Ritter von Zant softly replied, "We will face that after we unleash the power of the Lance and assert control over the unenlightened masses. His presence after that point will be superfluous and, perhaps, dangerous to us."

Each Ritter dutifully nodded his head in agreement.

"The midnight induction ceremony will require all of us to perform our parts with honor, dignity and reverence and to follow the initiate procedures that are sacred to the Order. When Garrett views the Lance, we will bestow all the rights and responsibilities of the Order upon him. He will not, however, receive the sacred ring which would seal his entrance into the Order. After he views the Lance, we must be sure that the magical powers of the rituals and the power of the Lance do not elevate him into a super-conscious state wherein he sees through our gambit and discerns who we really are and what we are doing. For this to happen would be disastrous to our journey. We must be aware of any changes in his understandings. Is that agreed?"

Each Ritter nodded in the affirmative as the Grand Master led them in meditation and chanting practices to conclude their meeting.

"We will gather again at midnight here in the crypt in two days," said von Zant as the Ritters exited and returned to their respective quarters.

****

Hermann dutifully laid out a new set of garments for Garrett to wear for his initiation ritual. He was very particular as to how the clothes should be assembled, assuring Garrett that each layer had a special significance in the ceremony. Garrett took his time dressing under the watchful eye of his man-servant.

Each of the articles of clothing that was given to Garrett had a special array of colors all within the hues of cardinal red, black and various shades of white. Several Teutonic and Runic symbols were emblazoned on the tunic and breastplate medallion while sleeves with ornate lace cuffs were wrapped around the end of each arm.

"Quite impressive," Garrett thought to himself as he admired his personal transformation in the mirror.

"These ceremonial garments make me feel like a king," he spoke aloud to himself as Hermann was admiring his clothing handiwork. They were even more royal-appearing, Garrett thought, than the robes the Ritters were wearing the other night at dinner. He was prepared for the ceremony, at least prepared in what he believed would be appropriate dress for the ritual. His thoughts, however, were still racing and his anxiety surfaced regularly. His fear occasionally captured his mind as chills would go up and down his spine in anticipation of a mysterious future. He recalled his "dream" about Thal and his cosmic elevator ride to his flugelrad. He pondered the significance of the pebble that Thal had given him and the prediction that he would one day have to choose between good and evil. He wondered what that meant. It was a thought he could not shake from his consciousness.

He had almost put out of his mind his family, his adoring spouse and daughter, as well as his father and mother. The time had passed so rapidly with so much wonder and activity that he hardly had a chance to think or even care about whether they were worrying or not. He had, in fact, lost track of the days.

It was later in the afternoon, after a sumptuous lunch, that there was a loud banging on the door of his room. It was the Captain in his full-dress Kreigsmarine blues. He appeared with an uncharacteristically puzzled face, seemingly bordering on panic. This was not at all the accustomed demeanor of the Captain that Garrett had previously witnessed.

"We have to talk," The Captain said forcefully.

"Of course," said Garrett, sensing the urgency in the captain's demeanor. "Please come in. What is it?"

The Captain came into the room, his anxious demeanor revealing some obvious discomfort as Garrett invited him to sit down. The Captain was somewhat out of breath. It was apparent that he had dashed some distance to get to Garrett's room. He then blurted out his news.

"It's your wife," he said. "She's here!"

"Gugga here?" Garrett retorted in disbelief, "Here at the castle?"

"Yes, she arrived here just a short time ago and demanded to see the two of us. The guard summoned me and told me a young woman was here to see her father and husband. The guard suggested that I come immediately to resolve the situation. I went to the entrance and was at a loss for words when I met her as she firmly demanded to see you. I calmly greeted her and led her to our entry room and made her as comfortable as possible, reassuring her that you were safe and in preparation for the initiation and that you could not be disturbed. I don't think she was satisfied with that response. She said she is concerned about your safety as it has been over two weeks and you have not contacted her as promised. She is apparently alone, but I can't be sure. I suggest that you see her and assure her that you are safe and will be home soon. It is critical that she doesn't stay here."

Garrett was stunned. Fearful thoughts for the safety of his wife now preempted his grandiose adventure thoughts. He remembered that Gugga did not trust this man who claimed to be her father. The Captain, however, had never once exhibited any behavior or said anything to Garrett that would cause him to distrust him. Garrett, of course, would certainly see Gugga and, hopefully, assure her of his safety and make her aware of the pending initiation that would take place that evening at midnight.

"Show her to my room and leave us alone for awhile and I'll resolve the issue," he said to the Captain, while at the same time sensing an impending concern for both himself and Gugga.

****

At the sight of his worried wife, Garrett gathered her into his arms and held her tightly. Gugga's response to their touch reminded him of the bliss that they shared with one another. Her presence triggered a longing in him to just leave with his beloved and forget all this promise of world peace through his initiation into the Royal Order.

After a few moments of affectionate greetings, both Gugga and Garrett settled into their tender companionship. Gugga was relieved to see Garrett safe and healthy and, for the moment, happy and relieved that she had come to Wewelsburg Castle to find him. As she looked at Garrett in his resplendent royal regalia, she has a momentary doubt as to the worth of her mission. He looked like royalty.

But, after a brief moment of admiration, she regained her demeanor and said, "Garrett, my love, you must leave this place and forget this wild dream of my father's. I don't trust him and you should not either."

"But, the ceremony is tonight, I cannot leave now – just as we are about to fulfill our destiny."

"Yes, I know your dream, but it is a fantasy. I don't know why, but I sense a real danger for you and my father is complicit in something that is frightening and dangerous. I know it! I had a premonition and saw us running for our lives to escape a horrible menace. It was a real experience, not a dream – something I haven't experienced since I was a little girl. You've got to listen to me!"

Garrett knew of Gugga's clairvoyant abilities. She had shared many instances where her premonitions had become reality. He never understood how she knew things, but both Gugga and Thora shared that gift so he usually listened to her when she relayed her thoughts.

"My dearest Gugga, I think this time you're having a bad dream, not a premonition. Your father, the Captain, has been nothing but kind and considerate to me and he and the other Ritters have treated me with honor and respect. I do understand your feelings and I apologize for not keeping you up to date on my welfare, but you have come here for no reason. The ceremony is tonight. I know you cannot attend the ritual, but I will insist that you are able to stay here with me tonight and wait for me to return from the proceedings."

"I have always known how stubborn you can be, I knew it from the first day we met. But believe me, this is not a delusion I am having. It's a real premonition and we must pay attention to it," she pleaded.

"I love you Gugga, but this is something I must see through. We can talk again after the ceremony. I promise you that."

Gugga sighed in resignation, her eyes darting as she searched for words to convince him, but it was no use, he was committed, much to her chagrin.

"By the way, how are Mom, Dad and Thora, are they doing well?" Garrett asked, trying to change the subject.

"Your mom and Thora are worried about you. Thora asks when her father is coming home and your mother worries that she may have lost her son to some cult. Your dad, however, is with me and is waiting for me, or us, nearby . . . just in case. He enthusiastically agreed to come all this way with me. He remembered telling you that if you didn't appear in Berkeley in two weeks, he would come looking for you. He used his naval rank and influence to get us an immediate flight to Europe. It would be wise, however, not to alert anyone here of your father's whereabouts."

It was less than an hour after Gugga arrived when the Captain's knock on the door alerted both Gugga and Garrett that their time alone was at an end.

As the Captain entered, it was apparent he had regained his composure and become his usual charming self again.

"We'll I'm glad you both had a chance to see one another and for Gugga to see that we are all safe and healthy. I will be happy to escort you to the airport," he said to Gugga, "So you may begin your journey home. As soon as Garrett is initiated and spends just a few more days with us, he will join you at your home back in Berkeley."

"It's true that Garrett is committed to going through with the initiation," Gugga said in resignation to her father, "But, I would like to stay here a couple of days to assure myself that Garrett emerges from this process as healthy as he is now. I know that probably is not in your wishes, but he is my husband and, as my father, I implore you to accede to my need to know that my husband is safe. You must surely understand how I feel."

The Captain was not pleased with this turn of events, but he knew that Gugga could disrupt the ceremony plans if she were forced to leave. There was too much at stake to risk having her depart, with the possibility that unwanted visitors would then come back. He deduced that the plan could still be carried out with Gugga at the castle. She would then have to be dealt with later, along with Garrett.

"It is highly unusual for another to be here during the period of initiation," the Captain replied, "But under these unforeseen circumstances, you may stay in Garrett's quarters until after the ceremony."

Gugga breathed a measured sigh of relief. She still, however, held out the hope that she could convince her reluctant husband to flee the dark drama of this castle.

****

Ollie waited in his car for Gugga to return. Their contingency plan was to have Gugga insist on staying with Garrett if he was safe. If she did not return, Ollie was to wait until he somehow heard from Gugga or Garrett to dictate their next move. Ollie was uncomfortable with this lack of clarity as his military background always demanded a complete plan with any potential contingencies examined in advance. But they didn't have the information or time they needed to develop a more stable plan for rescue. They were playing it by ear.

The Commander, however, realized that one contingency that needed to be addressed would be their ability to fly out of Germany. With the possibility of an emergency escape looming, Ollie had made arrangements at the local naval base to utilize a small plane to fly to a safe location. Fortunately, his flight status was up-to-date and he had the rank and commission to access an available small-engine craft. His foresight in this circumstance was to prove invaluable.

Ollie had brought with him, drawing from his own intuition – a sense that he would find useful – the Byrd Diary, the map, and the crystalline pebble sent to him by Admiral Byrd so many years ago. Byrd had passed away in 1956, but Ollie had treasured his keepsakes and kept them close to him all these years. His inclusion of these artifacts on the trip seemed a natural addition to his necessary items for travel. The haunting memory of the final meeting with his beloved Admiral was etched in his mind as well as the hurried introduction and greeting from the strange individual who was with Byrd. That image of Sven Olafsson, with his striking Nordic features distinguished by a large and prominent silver front tooth, enthusiastically grasping his hand, suggested that a knowing connection existed between them and, as such, continually intrigued him over the years. Even more mysterious, at the time, was the hand-drawn map given to Ollie by the Admiral in the package he received years later by mail. Now, with the saga of his son and the distinct memory of Byrd's experiences, this map made more sense inasmuch as Ollie's or Garrett's escape into the hollow earth had been apparently foreseen and planned many years ago. The mysterious pieces of the puzzle were starting to fall into place.

The map revealed Byrd's flight plan in 1947 to a small hamlet called Spitzbergen in the Norwegian archipelago of Svalbard, about 500 miles from the North Pole. The map gave not only directions, but included a cryptic message that added, "at 88 degrees due North, the crystalline rock," the so-called *curious little pebble*, "would begin pulsating" and "to stay on course, despite the predictable gyrations of the compass, as this stone will guide you into the center of the earth and safety." It became clear to Ollie that Admiral Byrd knew the possible parameters of all this intrigue from the start.

****

Garrett's thoughts began to surface again regarding his rendezvous with Thal and the flugelrad. It seemed that, as he got closer to the ceremony, his thoughts were becoming more discerning. The Captain had indicated to him briefly that the Arianni needed to confirm the choice of Garrett so as to complete the circuit of initiation. However, the Captain had not once mentioned that Thal or the Arianni would be part of the ceremony. Wouldn't it be prudent to let him know what role the Arianni would play in this initiation to the Holy Order? Why hadn't the Captain mentioned them more than just in passing if they were so critical to the initiation? He reasoned that the Arianni would somehow be involved, especially since he had a prior encounter with the aliens. It seemed at the time that Thal had already approved Garrett as their representative of peace on the surface world and that the Arianni had insisted upon and were prepping him for the kind of situations that would challenge him. Garrett began to wonder what he was missing from this equation, or was this just fear and paranoia creeping into his mental menagerie? What did Gugga's premonition have to do with this whole scenario? His gut feeling was bringing up some aspects of inner distrust which he could not classify or sort out. In his mind's logical conversations, he vowed to be alert to any kind of patterns before and during the initiation that would suggest or cause him discomfort. He must keep his spiritual eye open to any miscreant activities that would trigger his latent mistrust and be ready to react – or so he told himself.

****

Gugga was not allowed to be present for the completion of the ritual dressing of her husband. Instead, she was ushered into a companion room which looked out and away from the North Tower and the Crypt where the ceremony would be held. The Ritters placed a watchman at the room to assure that she would stay in her new quarters, as they did not want some unanticipated outbreak of emotion or demands at the ceremony.

The dutiful man-servant, Hermann, was assigned the task of assuring that the final and complete ceremonial attire was properly fitted and ready for the traditional rites of the Teutonic Royal Order. He had done his job well as Garrett once again marveled at the vision of himself as the royalty for which he was, apparently, destined. At the knock on the door, Hermann opened it to reveal the Captain flanked by four guards.

He was escorted by these palace guards in their full ceremonial regalia, led by Ritter Wermhoutt who walked three paces in front of Garrett. Garrett was accompanied by two of the guards in front and two behind. They slowly and ritualistically marched in high-kick and measured steps down the hallway, passing dozens of banners, shields, icons, and paintings on the wall commemorating past Ritters and their exploits, until they reached the entrance to the North Tower and the Crypt below where the ceremony would be held.

****

Wewelsburg North Tower is fifteen meters in diameter with four major levels. Garrett observed that the top level was an outside observation platform with the second level consisting of a holding room. The third level was the great, main circular hall, decorated in a style reminiscent of the court legends of King Arthur of mythical Camelot. In the center of the great hall stood a massive round table of solid oak carved with ancient runic symbols and designs. The table was partially covered by a red velvet cloth and draped with a large white cloth on which would be placed the Holy Lance, enclosed in its protective glass case. Around the table were thirteen ornate and regal throne-like wooden chairs fashioned with runic carvings, polished and finished to shining perfection. Each chair was upholstered with boar skin, hunted and gathered by each member as part of an initiation ritual for new recruits. The name of each knight was engraved on a highly polished silver plate attached to the back of each chair. During the Nazi days only the chairs of Himmler and Reinhold Heydrich were permanently labeled. Heydrich was so accorded the honor because he was the one man who fully understood the power of the Holy Lance. Himmler had Heydrich sit on the left side of his heart suggesting that he, Himmler, was the power, life and vitality of the order. On Himmler's right was the individual to be initiated or honored.

The lower level of the North Tower, known as the Crypt, featured a fixed concentric circle with twelve individual accommodation stations having large stones as seats, one for each of the initiates of the Order. The floor is hewed with stone slabs and the walls constructed with perfectly placed stone blocks. In the center of the floor was a circular space about 4 meters wide that was lower than the rest of the floor. Garrett descended to this lower level center by three steps. The center was surrounded and protected by a polished stone ring creating a larger circle that rose a few centimeters above the level of the rest of the floor. In this polished stone ring that surrounded the center, there were three rectangles which indicated the positions of West, East, and North. The steps that descend to the depression of the center of the room were in the Southern position.

In the exact center of the floor of the Crypt there is a tactically important point approximately a meter in diameter around which spins all the supernatural projections of the Order. Located therein is an empty space on which the members of the Order project the strength of the *Sonnenrad* [1] *(Sunwheel)*.

Looking upward, in the center of the ceiling of the Crypt, gathering and channeling the strength projected in the interior, there is a *swastika*. According to the principle of the swastika, the center of the field of strength created by the Sun Wheel inside the Crypt causes a spiral movement that generates a rotation in the material reality.

The Crypt design, created by the Order, promotes an expansion of its radiation energy and projects the creation of a magical fortification – a magical circle whose psychic center is the Northern tower of the castle. The Sun Wheel generated in the magical enclosure projects its *extraterrestrial* strength – that is, another universe – collaborating with the Royal Order.

The Sun Wheel

From the room of the *Sun Wheel*, one descends down into the interior of the Crypt through a narrow flight of stairs that connects the two levels.

The Crypt was illuminated by thirteen resin-filled torches that burn behind each one of the seats that surround the room. This was the only illumination in the dark and mysterious room.

The knights, reunited in this interior, know from previous ceremonies what is about to take place. Their prior experience gave reason to anticipate the ceremony that begins once each of the participants has occupied his place.

There is a hushed silence as the knights, according to the principles of the Order, begin the metaphysical rites in the crypt to stop the flow of the world's activities accessing a space out of time to commune with their spiritual nature. Slowly, one by one, the Ritters enter into the metaphysical astral world while projecting their collective power of the Order to the center of the Crypt.

As each Ritter synchronized the strength of the Order, the work on the astral plane begins. At this juncture, they project the sacred runic ring to take the form identical to the physical adornment that each Ritter wears on his ring finger of the right hand. The astral ring, maintained by the will of the thirteen Ritters, then begins to take a visible form in the astral, acquiring consistency and "solidifying itself," while being concurrently recorded in the astral.

In the course of the ritual, the ring projection acquires real consistency and form because it is no longer the projection of one, but a unification of all thirteen minds. In that stopped time, each Ritter is immersed in spirit and maintains only one mind in a unification of strength that create enormous power, affecting and acting on the reality of space-time.

The ring projection adopts a position in mid-air above the stone circle that surrounds the central depression of the Crypt. In this magical space the ring projection grows to a size far larger than its actual physical size. In the astral the dimensions of the material world are distorted and they are relativized in size. Therefore, the object on which works the will and the attention increases in size, while the rest of the scene remains in a secondary plane. Due to its lack of importance in the third dimension, the secondary plane remains smaller.

The action on the magical world of the astral is the task of the Royal Order of the Ritters: to maintain a mystical communion that sustains the work of the Order. From these rituals, a power from the astral plane gives concurrent power to the Order so that it can impose its own "realities" upon the material world and space-time.

The Ritters of the Order realize that this power can be effective only in the material third dimension world only, and after consorting with the Arianni, they concluded that in order to mobilize the unknown power of the Holy Lance, which could be used to keep order in the material world and bring about world peace, they decided that they would need to be in league with their inner earth neighbors, whose extraterrestrial and *intraterrestrial* knowledge and advanced technology was far superior to their own. The plans of the Royal Order would only be compatible with the Arianni if the Order could reach an agreement with them. They would assure then their version of world peace which to them meant their own complete control of the surface population. The Arianni, with their sense of values and survival, simply want the end of the destructive energy being developed by mankind and believe that the Order would be the ones to assist them. The plan was for the Arianni to grant Garrett the power of the Holy Lance as to all appearances, as they were certain he was committed to peaceful world habitation and would therefore assure the safety of the Hollow Earth inhabitants.

The Order was not aware that the Arianni were keeping close tabs on their activities and were very much cognizant of the heightened apprehensions of Garrett as he approached entry and acceptance into the Teutonic Order. The Arianni had been suspicious that the Order's true intentions were not honorable and recently had become acutely watchful for the Order's potential insincerity based on the detailed observations and reports of their loyal surface observers, the Men in Black.

****

As they entered the Crypt Room, Garrett was amazed by the simple elegance of the room and its occupants. The initiation of Garrett Oliver Hill was about to begin with Garrett still unaware that he is viewed as a pawn in an international conspiracy to trick the Arianni and establish a one-thousand year Fourth Reich.

The lead Grand Master invited both the Captain and Garrett to stand strategically near the circle in front of two high-backed wooden carved chairs. He began an incantation calling in the spirits of the Lance to accept a glorious new member into their Order. He then bade each Ritter to bow from the waist to the new inductee to show their respect and honor to their newest member. He invited them to sit down and began his ritual sermon.

> *We invite the spirits of the Holy Order of Teutonic Knights and the past holders of the Sacred Lance, the Spear of Destiny, to witness and approve the actions of this Order. We honor Garrett Oliver Hill and salute him as the, holder of the power, who we will serve and follow as we assure that the power of the Lance will always and only be used as an end to wars and assure an era of cooperation and harmony amongst all people in the pursuit of a peaceful world.*

He then looked around at the convocation and asked, "Do any of the holy Ritters wish to ask further questions of the initiate?"

After a hallowed and seemingly long pause, Ritter Frederick asked, "Honored Initiate, have you forever decided to join the Royal Order of Teutonic Knights without reservation and do you pledge your full allegiance to our cause of a peaceful world?"

Garrett's mind was in alignment with the words for he certainly felt the allegiance to a ideal of a peaceful world and could, indeed, pledge his honor to such a cause. He took a deep breath and spoke the required words.

"Yes, with the guidance of the spirits, I accept your honored invitation to become a Knight in the Holy Order of Teutonic Knights and to pledge full allegiance to the cause of a peaceful world."

With that statement, the Captain, standing beside Garrett, breathed a measured sigh of relief. He could rest assured that he had fulfilled his part of the journey to obtain the power of the Lance. The rest of the Ritters paused with the satisfied relief knowing they had brought to the Order the one man who the Arianni would accept. The secret to the Lance was close at hand and the Order would now consolidate their long dreamed *journey*.

Ritter von Zant then acknowledged the tacit agreement of the attending Ritters and declared,

> *"I now, with the power granted to me by the Holy Order of Teutonic Knights, do affirm and declare that Garrett Oliver Hill will heretofore be known and addressed as Ritter Hill, according to this writ of the Holy Order of Teutonic Knights. Welcome, Ritter Hill!"*

Garrett was virtually speechless. He managed a weak-voiced *thank you* and waited for the next step.

The presiding Grand Master, Ritter von Zant, then declared the revealing of the Spear of Destiny, the actual Holy Lance which was kept secreted behind a hidden vault door on the north wall of the crypt. Now because of this special occasion, the Holy Lance was to be brought from the vault by the Grand Master for viewing by the new Ritter.

The Grand Master manipulated three runic symbols and another small stone in front of the vault. After a moment's delay the vault opened, as if by magic, to reveal the Lance. The Grand Master carried the Lance, wrapped in its case, gracefully and reverently. He stood in front of Garrett, gazed deeply into his eyes and echoed the following words:

"With the revealing of the Holy Lance to Ritter Hill," Ritter von Zant declared, "the final initiate journey will be activated and the power of the astral will reveal to him the eternal presence of the historical knights and their illuminating presence here in this holy crypt.

Open the viewing vault and reveal the Holy Lance!"

At the end of the invocation, Ritter von Zant opened the red velvet lined case and placed the Lance in the hands of Garrett, the newest Ritter of the Holy Order of Teutonic Knights of the Holy Lance.

Chapter Notes

1. **Sunwheel:** The term *Black Sun*, also referred to as the *Sonnenrad* (German for "Sun Wheel"), is a symbol of esoteric and occult significance. Its design is based on a sun wheel mosaic incorporated into a floor of Wewelsburg Castle during the Nazi era.

Chapter 16

THE HOLY LANCE

*a*s Ritter Von Zant placed the Lance in Garrett's outstretched palms, the impact on the young man's body and consciousness was profound. An inner awareness, ignited by the ancient mystic power of the Holy Lance, sent waves of supernatural vibrations throughout his entire being. Garrett had felt the sensation of being transported to another world, one of images and understandings of another dimension, a dimension uncluttered by thought or relativity. He entered a sphere of clarity and universal knowledge far beyond that which he had ever countenanced. His mind transcended the time and space of his physical existence and took him to the dimension of creation, the same mystical time-space reality that the Holy Order had invoked. Garrett's last conscious vision was the fixed gaze from the piercing, deep blue eyes of the Grand Master as Garrett accepted the Holy Lance into his hands. At that moment he knew his life would never be the same.

Garrett was transported into a mystical journey and he moved effortlessly into this different vibrational consciousness, one that was revealing and shocking to his Soul. His vision began to change; his perspective took on a new discernment as the crypt assumed the semblance of a metamorphic journey back through time.

Garrett's awareness allowed him to see through the present time reality, producing a past apparition of each person in the room. The Ritters of the Holy Order surrounding him seemed to change into their authentic historical persona, replete with period clothing, weapons, and robes of their respective times and station. His attention was focused on the facial transformation of each of the individuals. As they renewed their karmic bodies, their faces morphed into various known personages affiliated with the Holy Lance as far back as the days of the crucifixion.

As the changes manifested in Garrett' vision, he began to recognize the merging images and personalities arising from the individual Ritters surrounding him, giving him an immediate and uncanny knowledge of each. He was witnessing an unveiling of the past holders of the Holy Lance, most of whom met their demise after the misuse of the power available to them through their possession of the Lance.

With his newly acquired vision and understanding, Garrett was suddenly able to identify each historical luminary that circled him. They were a fearsome group of past influential leaders. Garrett's vision of them made a deep connection between his conscious awareness and his enlightened apparition.

Garrett immediately noted the presence of the famed *Frederick I Barbarossa, (1123 – 1190)* with his distinctive red beard from the House of Hohenstaufen. He was a legendary hero and a symbol of unity to the German people who carried the Holy Lance as his emblem of faith and Christian dedication. Next to him stood *Otto III* who was emperor of the Holy Roman Empire in 996 A.D. and who regarded himself as the leader of world Christianity. It was during his reign that a nail from the cross of Jesus was inserted into the holy spear. Garrett's visuals brought to him a wide array of historical figures that peopled his vision, such as *Emperor Constantine the Great, Charles (the Hammer) Martel, Charlemagne the Great* and several others. It was a remarkable array of past lords of power.[1]

As his gaze swept the room, Garrett's eyes rested on the final figure in front of him. To his chagrin and shock, the face of Ritter Von Zant slowly, but unquestionably, began transitioning to the sardonic, smiling face of Adolf Hitler. As he finally broke his fixation upon the Hitler countenance, he abruptly turned his head to his left, as if to seek an explanation from his ethereal mentor, the Captain. In the same transcendental moment, the Captain, in whom he had placed his trust and safety, morphed into the vaguely recognizable face of a Roman Centurian. The scene changed once again, and he and his companion Centurian were at the base of the cross of crucifixion, looking up at the limp body of the Christian savior, Jesus Christ, hanging by his nailed hands and feet on the cross.

Garrett reeled backwards at this revelation, staring at the fellow Centurian in disbelief. Then it hit him. It was he, Garrett, who was at the cross. It was he who was piercing the ribs of Jesus to assure that he was alive or dead. The truth was dramatically revealed. The date was April 5th, 33 AD. He was Longinus. The Holy Lance was in his possession. *He was the beginning of the legend of the Holy Lance.*

Garrett slowly returned to his conscious mind as each of the Ritters reassumed their present day appearance and the physical setting of the castle environs was restored to the present time. He had experienced an epiphany of his soul-mind-body and it triggered an intense moral reexamination. Now, in his conscious thoughts, he realized that he had seen the faces of those who had been corrupted by the use of indiscriminate power and understood his destined role as the protector of the Lance. As he gathered his spinning thoughts, the words of the Arianni pilot, Thal, echoed in his brain.

I am an emissary from Asgarth, the Citadel near the inner Sun . . . Garrett Hill, and it is from this place that we call upon you. You must choose between good and evil. You will be shown the vehicle of that power. . . I present you with your key. Keep it with you at all times . . . You are trusted to choose to act for earth's salvation. You must always reject the path to evil. You will have that choice.

Garrett now understood the meaning of those words for the first time. He knew intuitively what he had to do.

The Ritters, however, were convinced that Garrett – upon witnessing the Lance and experiencing the power the Lance invoked within him – was one of them. The Holy Order believed that they could now execute the last phase of their *journey* and use Garrett to win final favor with the Arianni.

They did not have any idea that the revelation Garrett experienced was a complete reassessment and rejection of his decision to join the Order. In his new state of mind, he dismissed the plan to work with the Order, as he clearly saw the misuse of power of those past abusers who held the Lance. The vision of the Grand Master of the Holy Order as Adolf Hitler and the startling realization that he was the historical Longinus, the initial holder of the Holy Lance, convinced him that his destiny was to rescue the Lance from the Holy Order and return it to the Arianni.

The Grand Master was convinced, as were the others, that the ceremony had cemented an unbreakable bond between their newest Ritter and the Holy Order. He proceeded to end the ceremonial proceedings with a series of traditional chants and prayers. Garrett was royally escorted back to his quarters by the same guards who brought him. Captain Wermhoutt accompanied him to the entrance of his room, but did not enter as he was aware that Gugga was awaiting him. Wermhoutt was fully convinced that Gugga could have no influence upon Garrett's new identity, as she would never be able to comprehend the gravity and depth of the initiation. Garrett was fully indoctrinated.

****

Gugga had been anxiously pacing the room in anticipation of Garrett's return. Her mind was racing with various scenarios depending on what effect the ceremony and initiation would have on him. She tried to focus on her next steps if Garrett had enthusiastically become part of the Holy Order, how it might change him, how it might change their relationship and that of their daughter with her father. What would she do? What would she tell Ollie, who was waiting for her and Garrett camped in a car just across the bridge and down the road from the gate of the castle? And what if he decided to escape with her? What kinds of perils would they face? It had been almost three hours since the guards and her father came to escort Garrett to the Crypt. How much longer would it be? The dilemmas racing through her thoughts were excruciatingly difficult to contemplate. Her biggest frustration, however, was the seemingly interminable wait. Her anxiety was reaching a peak.

When she heard the lock on the door open and saw Garrett standing there in his Ritter clothing of red, black and white, her heart dropped. He looked the part of a Ritter, a stranger to the man she knew and loved.

The old wooden door closed behind him and he looked lovingly into Gugga's eyes and simply said, "I'm back!" With that, Gugga ran to him, threw her arms around his waiting gestures, and hugged him as she had never hugged him before.

"Garrett, is it you?" as she gazed deeply into his eyes.

"Yes, but I'm another person," he said with conviction. "Another person who now realizes what a fool I've allowed myself to be. Gugga, we have to get out of this place . . . as soon as we can. We have to take the Lance from these men and return it to the Arianni. I need your help."

"Oh Garrett," Gugga responded with great relief, "I will do anything you want to do to get out of here, to leave this frightening place. And I know how we can do it."

Garrett once again took Gugga into his arms, stared into her eyes and said, "But there is one crucial task we must do before we leave . . . recover the Lance and take it to the Arianni – in the center of the earth. Are you willing to do that with me?"

Gugga barely paused in her response, she was so happy to have her husband sane and wanting to be with her.

"I'm more than willing, my love; your dad and I have been planning such an escape and have a plane ready for us at a moment's notice. We will get the Lance, slip out of the gate at the precise moment when the guards change and hurry down the hill to meet your dad with the car. He will drive us just a few kilometers to the waiting airplane and fly us to where we need to go. Your dad has some information from the diary of Admiral Byrd that tells us the route and where we can take the Lance."

"Then we must plan how to get the Lance in our hands without arousing any immediate suspicion," Garrett excitedly responded. "I know where it is kept and I observed the Grand Master manipulate some runic symbols to open the door of the vault. I kept remembering how the Prophet had shown us the Icelandic runic symbols on the wall, referring to it as the runic triangle. Remember? You made a detailed sketch of it!"

"Of course I remember," said Gugga. "And your father figured out that the stone, that curious pebble that you both have, is the activator of the triangle. I have the sketch with me; somehow I knew that it was important. I'm sure that must be the key to the vault."

"It's not just the key to the vault," Garrett enthusiastically agreed, "but the key to the entrance at the polar cap. That's what Thal was telling me when he brought me to his spaceship . . . and I thought it was a dream. That pebble has been the key all along!"

Garrett and Gugga hastily made plans to find the Lance and spirit it away with them in their escape. They studied the drawing of the runic triangle that Gugga had created at the Prophet's home some years ago and kept with her in her notebook. Gugga replicated a makeshift triangle in her unfolded palms as it corresponded to the drawing, using the precisely placed runic symbols in their designated positions.

Garrett reached into his sheltered pocket and produced the activator, the crystalline stone, given to him by Thal.

"And this is the final piece to the puzzle," Garrett mused, as he placed it in the middle of the newly formed triangle of runes. They would carry it with them to the vault entrance knowing the talisman would perform as expected. If they were wrong . . . well, they affirmed to one another, "We can't be wrong."

It was less than an hour later when they began executing their plan. They reasoned that any possible escape attempt would not be anticipated by the Order, evidenced by the lack of guards at the door to their quarters so soon after the ceremony that had pledged Garrett to the Order. They were correct in that assumption as, indeed, the guards had been dismissed. Garrett knew the most efficient way to the Crypt vault as he had been escorted there on occasion and he had determined to keep on his Ritter garb in case they were met or detained by anyone. They found their way to the eerie room.

Gugga nervously manipulated the runes for the triangle as she fashioned it on the palms of her hand while Garrett, with measured anticipation, placed the crystalline stone in the middle of the triangle.

The effect was instantaneous! The vault swung open, revealing the glass encased Spear of Destiny. Both were mesmerized momentarily by the gravity of their accomplishment but immediately realized that the caper was not over. They still had to get out through the gate undetected long enough to find Ollie and the car and get to the makeshift air strip to get away. Garrett reverently took the Lance out of the case, closed the vault door, and slipped the Lance securely under his ample multi-colored Ritter garments. They followed a small stairway down to the courtyard and walked gingerly and calmly towards the gate in a drizzle of rain, following in the shadows of the stone walls of the great castle and hoping that no one would see them. Upon reaching the gate, a single guard emerged from the shadows and challenged the couple as they approached. Seeing Garrett in his Ritter outfit, the guard immediately came to attention as Garrett explained that they were going for a walk across the bridge and would be back in a half hour or so. The guard did not want to offend a Ritter's desire and obligingly opened a single door next to the main gate and let them pass.

Garrett's decision to wear his Ritter outfit and robes proved to be a fortuitous and fortunate act. Their exit from the castle completed, they hurried down the hill searching desperately for Ollie and the car.

Less than a few kilometers down the winding road snuggled between two sparsely leaved trees and hidden by some local vegetation, the two escapees spotted the car. Ollie, who had kept a sleepless vigil, became alert when he heard a commotion on the road and sprang to attention when he saw Gugga and Garrett, both breathing heavily, dashing in front of him. He called quietly out to them and they hurriedly got into the car. Without hesitation, Ollie began driving, picking up speed as they motored as fast as they could, occasionally challenged by harrowing turns that tested the vehicle's roadworthiness.

Fortunately, Ollie was a good driver and the rented Mercedes-Benz handled well. In less than twenty minutes, they reached the airstrip with hardly a word spoken between them, reflecting the solemn gravity of the moment.

A Cessna 180 4-passenger plane, a slightly smaller version of Bjorn's aircraft, was parked and fueled as planned by Ollie, and ready to fly. The navy often kept on hand some private non-military aircraft for the use of officers or retired personnel for privileged purposes. The three family members quickly stowed their gear on board. Garrett, during the car ride, had removed his Ritter threads and donned a pair of jeans and shirt that befitted his personality and situation. He carefully placed the Lance on the vacant back seat of the plane as Ollie taxied the Cessna down the rough runway strip and took flight.

A collective sigh of relief engulfed the anxious passengers as the plane reached an appropriate altitude and leveled off. They were on their way. But to where?

****

Meanwhile, the guard, somewhat concerned about the Ritter walking outside the castle, decided that he should report the exit of Garrett and Gugga to the Grand Master. His phone call roused the secretary to Ritter von Zant who hesitatingly wakened the Master and informed him of what he surmised was unusual activity. The Grand Master, somewhat groggy from being awakened from a satisfying slumber, rose immediately and sounded an alarm for the guards to give chase and return the two to the castle. Three of the sitting Ritters were also alerted to accompany the guards on a possibly crucial mission. The recent late afternoon rains left a marked trail of the car on the road and directed the pursuers to the abandoned air strip just a few kilometers southwest of the castle. They hurriedly returned to their own airstrip and made immediate arrangements for pursuit. The Order's private jet, the very one Garrett had flown in, was commissioned to give chase as the sophisticated radar on the modern jet could trace the flight of any plane the escaping pair could commandeer. Each guard was already fully armed and the plane had ample supplies of weapons and ammunition to meet any necessity.

****

The droning sound of the single engine Cessna seemed to affect a calming influence on its occupants. They became more relaxed and began to settle in after their harrowing escape, apparently done without alarming the occupants of the castle. But how long would it be before the guard relayed to the Ritters that they had left the castle? Each knew that there would be a pursuit after them, and could not be sure of how long a lead they had.

Ollie was the first to speak. "Tell me what happened. How did you get away?"

Gugga, after catching her anxious breath and reflecting on their escape, excitedly gave Ollie an overview of what had occurred and how the escape went. Garrett followed up with the story of the purloining of the Lance from the Crypt vault and briefly telling the story of his experiences.

"Dad, do you know where we are going?" asked Garrett.

"We're flying to Spitzbergen, a small town in a Norwegian archipelago to meet up with an old acquaintance of mine, a man by the name of Sven. I was able to contact him from information that I had received years ago from Admiral Byrd. This information is in his diary. It is likely Sven will be expecting us as he has lived there for years in the service of the Arianni. According to Byrd, he has maintained the old German vintage Fokker that Admiral Byrd flew in 1947 into the center of the earth to make contact with the Arianni. The Arianni, from information gleaned from the MIBs, will alert him that we are in flight and when we are expected to arrive. From there, you will fly the plane to specified coordinates that will allow you to enter the earth's center civilization. Your arrival in the center civilization will be welcomed as you bring with you the Holy Lance."

"Wow, Dad! That's quite a flight plan. Are you coming with us?"

"Are you kidding? Of course not! Who will take care of Thora and Jackie if all of us simply disappear? You may not be able to return right away. Besides, I owe it to our family to come back and let them know what is happening. Jackie and Thora would be devastated if I left them without explanation."

Garrett stared at Gugga. "Are you sure you can do this? We could never be sure when we would see Thora again."

The thought of not seeing her daughter again weighed heavily on Gugga's mind. What kind of sacrifice would she be making? Give up her family? And for what?

"Gugga, this is not just for us, or for that matter, Thora. This journey can protect the world from certain tyranny. The consequences of our choice are monumental."

Garrett selected his words carefully. He was faced with a seemingly impossible choice and his halting thoughts troubled him enormously.

His own misgivings were evident in his emotionally charged voice as he looked at Gugga's tearful face.

"But what about Thora?" Gugga tearfully responded. "She's our daughter who loves us and deserves to have her parents with her. She is just a young teenager. How can I possibly leave her?"

"Dad, help us out here. What shall we do? What can we do?" Garrett pleaded.

Ollie certainly felt the pressure that his son and his new daughter-in-law, with whom he had developed a deep love and respect, were under. His response would profoundly change his life too. Having them disappear into the center of the earth was not an option with which he felt comfortable and certainly not a satisfying decision when neither Thora nor Jackie would have a say. But he knew the import of the mission and, reaching into his reservoir of military discipline, knew there was only one answer.

"It has to be your collective decision," Ollie began haltingly. "I can't make it for you. Giving up your family for a cause such as this might seem unquestionable to some, but the price of that sacrifice is more than profound. Just know that I understand and empathize with your decision and pledge to you that, if either or both of you choose to go and are not able to return right away, your mother and I will raise Thora with the love and devotion that only grandparents can give. I will reassure Thora that you will find a way to contact her and let her know that you are safe. Whatever you choose, I will support you and her with my love and my life. You know how much I love you both."

"Well, when you put it that way, I guess we really don't have a choice, do we, Gugga?" Garrett reasoned, "I could go alone and have you stay. But I know I have to do this and it's shattering my heart."

Choking back her tears, Gugga hesitantly paused in her thoughts as she abruptly perceived an accustomed telepathic message from

Thora. Gugga envisioned an apparition urging her to go with Garrett and that Thora understood. Both Gugga and Thora had experienced such connections on many occasions even as Garrett would always be stunned at their spiritual communication techniques.

With Thora's timely urging, Gugga reaffirmed to herself that she chose a life with Garrett and would stay with him, no matter the consequences. As painful as the choice is, she reasoned, there could be no comparison between their personal sacrifice and the specter of a peaceful world. Thora was a capable young woman, thoroughly grounded in telepathic transmission and spiritual understanding. Her relationship with her grandfather and grandmother would assure a wonderfully supported life. Gugga reasoned that this sacrifice was one that had no superior option, yet offered one that now sounded more compelling to her fevered mind. She convinced herself, somewhat wishfully, that it would only be for a short time.

"Yes," she announced, holding back her mushrooming emotions, "we will, together, return the Lance to the Arianni and pray that we can return home soon. We can do this. I know we must do this."

Chapter Notes:
1. For an historical list of the holders of the Holy Lance, refer to Appendix 1.

Chapter 17

SPITZBERGEN

Norway

S ven Olafsson was an unusual man by anyone's standard. He towered over most folks with his nearly 7-foot frame. His large body was accented by square shoulders that jutted out from his neck like two powerful platforms of steel. His wind-swept, red cheeks blossomed on his face, highlighting his Nordic fair skin. Long arms, a sturdy upper body and long legs, portrayed him to most as a giant among men. As he was affable to his neighbors, no one seemed especially intimidated by his size. Sven generally kept to himself at his private airplane hangar where he kept an older Fokker tri-motor plane in perfect running order as evidenced by the roar of the engines as he regularly tested the integrity of the motors. Why he was so focused on the old plane was a puzzle to most, but others just attributed it to a personal eccentricity, a common social trait among many of the local residents.

Plummeting down from his amply-proportioned head were long, curly locks of blonde straggly hair, which he tied behind to prevent from falling over his eyes. He projected a perpetual smile which displayed an array of craggy teeth, and while noticeably large, did not protrude prominently from his square jaw. His smile was almost disconcerting as a large silver front tooth dominated his unique appearance.

Perhaps the foremost reason why people did not interact much with Sven was his constant companion, a fully grown male polar bear named Loki, which he had nursed to health after rescuing it from its dead mother. Sven became the bear's surrogate parent and Loki developed into more than just a pet – but the huge animal seemed to be a friend and companion. Folks would wander by on occasion to find Sven and the bear snuggling together, with Sven sipping on an unknown beverage from an old German beer stein, holding one-way intimate conversations with Loki. The two went on walks together, ate together, and Loki seemed to enjoy lounging in the hanger with his human friend while Sven performed his daily tasks maintaining the older plane. Loki was well trained and incredibly loyal to Sven. He would fetch as a dog would when his master threw an object for the bear to retrieve. When Sven whistled, the bear would come and would initiate an impromptu wresting match as a greeting. Loki seemed to love the interaction and had an obviously special relationship with his surrogate parent. They were quite a sight to behold. The townsfolk, because of their respect for one another's choices, simply ignored Sven's many idiosyncrasies.

The howl of a small engine plane shattered the silence of the sleepy hamlet of Spitzbergen. Only occasionally would a craft enter the air space, usually to deliver mail or supplies to the residents. This plane, however, was not attempting to land on the municipal airstrip to the east, but appeared to be landing on Sven Olafsson's makeshift landing field, which only he used, and then only when he would take the tri-motor up for an occasional maintenance spin.

Ollie decided to fly over the coordinates listed on his map before attempting the landing. He circled the strip once and began his approach after checking the primitive wind sock that showed the direction of the wind. His landing was a bit bumpy, not because of Ollie's skill as a pilot, but because of the unevenness of the landing field. The plane, with its weary passengers aboard, taxied up to the hanger as Sven waved them closer.

With the motor shut down, the three escaping neo-fugitives from the castle disembarked with Sven shouting directions as to where to bring their gear.

The temperature was nearing zero degrees and frost was quickly gathering on the wings in the cold night air. All three winced in the biting cold, so different from what they experienced in Germany and hurried inside to the relative warmth of the hangar. The travelers huddled around the wood stove that the burly Norwegian kept burning twenty-fours a day to keep the interior of the hangar temperate, predominantly for the safe-keeping of his beloved Tri-motor. Sven, after stowing his new guests' meager gear near his plane, joined them around the emanating heat.

"Welcome to Spitzbergen," Sven bellowed, as he greeted each with an appropriately encompassing bear-hug. He immediately turned to Ollie and reminded him of the time they met so many years ago outside the navy briefing room with Admiral Byrd.

"The admiral told me that one day you would be here. I know you didn't realize it at the time," he said in perfect English belying his rough appearance, "But I knew you would be here today, as my benefactors within the earth informed me of your imminent arrival. And here you are!"

"Yes, we are here," Ollie affirmed, "But now what?"

Sven pointed to the immaculate Fokker Tri-Motor just a few feet in front of them. It was pointing north from the hangar seemingly ready for take-off.

"That's what," Sven retorted. "This is your ticket to the polar entrance. After you get something to eat and a little rest, we will load the plane and prepare to bid you well on your historic journey."

The group was visibly nervous when the huge presence of Loki lumbered into the hangar, peacefully and quietly lying down nearby without acknowledging the presence of the new arrivals.

"Oh, this is Loki," Sven said as if he were casually introducing another person. "He is my friend, companion, and protector. You needn't be afraid of him as he knows by my reaction to you that you are not a threat. He wanders in and out of the hangar at his leisure. He generally likes to spend his time outside near the ice flows, but tonight he is curious about the three of you."

Loki suddenly stood up on his hind legs and met Sven head to head, the massive animal still towering above his master. The three newcomers gawked with amazement as the huge male polar bear stretched upward to greet Sven.

With Sven's unique introduction of his bear friend, Loki snorted, rose from his position, and trotted unceremoniously back outside.

"Were you followed?" Sven inquired of his amazed guests.

"We're not sure," Garrett responded. "One of their guards saw us leave and I'm sure he reported it to his superiors."

"Well, my young friend, you can be sure that you have been followed. It's just a matter of time as to when they will arrive. We will not take the chance that you were not. Let's load the plane now to be ready to leave at first light. We are nearly 20 degrees north of the Arctic Circle at about 80 degrees North Latitude and first light does not mean the same as it does where you come from. Where is the Lance?"

Garrett reached into the small plane's rear compartment and produced the Holy artifact as Sven examined it thoroughly.

"Yes, this is the original," he concurred softly. "I will keep it safe and load it into the plane just before you take-off. In the meantime, let me give you a quick lesson in flying this wonderful old masterpiece."

Garrett was an experienced pilot, but had never flown a Fokker

Tri-motor. Surprisingly, the controls were fairly simple, displaying a far less complicated instrument panel than the more modern aircraft he had flown. Ollie listened intently as Sven explained the idiosyncrasies of the vintage Fokker to Garrett. In the limited time available, Gugga attempted to catch some sleep before their anticipated departure in just a short hour or so.

****

The three Ritters, including Captain Wermhoutt, managed to trace the flight path of the Cessna. That part was fairly easy. The difficult part was to catch them before they had a chance to refuel and depart again. Their sleek jet, however, flew considerably faster that the escapee's plane, giving the Ritters confidence that they would catch up and retrieve the Lance before they lost their trail. They assumed that the distance of the runaway's lead would be overcome by the speed of their modern jet. Wermhoutt was uncharacteristically anxious for it had been his reassurances that led to the Ritter's acceptance of Garrett as the proper initiate to appease the Arianni. If Garrett had turned against the Ritters, the former Captain would be certainly disgraced and possibly removed from the order. This caused him great angst.

It was getting a bit lighter and ground visibility had greatly improved. They were approaching Spitzbergen flying as low as possible so not to arouse any undue suspicion. They observed a small single engine plane, in apparent isolation, sitting on a tiny makeshift airstrip near a small hangar.

"Ah, that must be them," the Captain exclaimed. "That's the radar signature we have been following."

The small landing strip, however, was clearly not adequate to receive the modern jet, so the Captain directed the pilot to land at the city landing field that was much larger and could accommodate their landing. After setting the jet down, the Ritters and the guards quickly exited the plane, gathered their weapons, and commandeered an old U.S Army 4x4 utility vehicle from the airport. They proceeded speedily across the tiny hamlet to the small landing strip envisioning a surprise arrival at the strip and an immediate seizing of the undefended hangar. Victory was in sight. The ire and anxiety of the Captain was palpable. Yes, it was his daughter he was chasing, along with Garrett, but he felt little blood allegiance to her with this betrayal. The mission was paramount and no amount of risk or danger would keep him from his duty and the recovery of the Holy Lance. He would deal with Garrett and Gugga in some appropriate manner later.

Sven had detected the jet and assumed it meant pending trouble. He quickly loaded survival gear into the Tri-Motor and hastened his guests to get on board. He climbed aboard to start the engines and get them prepared for take-off. Time was of the essence and it was fleeting.

The Norseman was preparing to load the Lance into the plane when a hail of gunfire blasted the hangar side door open and three armed men burst in and demanded their surrender. It was over. The Ritters had caught up with them and now held them captive.

The Captain, displaying a fresh and arrogant satisfaction, entered the hangar.

"You are fools," the Captain admonished with a disdainful voice, "You could have had everything and you threw it all away . . . and for what? Now there is no way out for you. You have forfeited your legacy and abandoned your exalted position.

Garrett looked over to his loving wife and said apologetically, "I'm sorry Gugga, this is my fault. I made a poor decision thinking we could get away with the Lance."

"You did what you thought was right," Gugga whimpered, "and I agreed with you. It's nobody's fault. I love you."

"And," her father voiced to Gugga with a military-toned finality, "I had hoped it would not end this way. But you have left me with no choice."

At that moment, Sven let out a piercing whistle that surprised and puzzled everyone. Suddenly without warning, the tense moment was deafeningly interrupted by the growling and charging of a giant polar bear. It was Loki, bursting into the hangar through the open door and charging into the stunned crowd. He snatched the Holy Lance from the outstretched arms of Sven, and in the disorienting commotion and scattering of all those in the hangar, charged out the door with the Holy Lance gripped firmly within his powerful jaws. The entire entourage was struck dumb by the surrealistic scene. The frightening tension shattered and everyone was thrown into a disoriented panic.

Wermoutt couldn't believe his eyes as he watched Loki charge out the door with the Lance in his mouth. His immediate instinct compelled him to chase after the bear, yelling desperately at his men to shoot the animal before it got to the ice flow. He couldn't just let the bear steal the prize when he almost had it back in his hands! The guards and Ritters, abandoning their captives, chased after the bear, shooting randomly and frantically at the creature without success. As the bear leaped onto the islands around the ice flow, the men clumsily followed. Loki, however, could easily outrun them and dipped underwater, eluding his pursuers and scampering from one broken ice island to another, regularly reentering the freezing waters and confounding his pursuers.

During the commotion perpetrated by Loki, Garrett and Gugga took immediate advantage of the wild events and ran to the lumbering Fokker, climbing in and guiding the plane outside. They taxied

Loki, with the Holy Lance replica

onto the strip to take off. They reached the airstrip just outside the hangar and launched the Tri-motor slowly but surely into the early morning sky.

Due to Sven's foresight, they carried with them the original Lance, as Sven had painstakingly fashioned a reasonable copy over the years that Loki had carried out to the icy waters. He had anticipated and covered every contingency – even waiting until the last moment to load the duplicate Lance.

Gugga and Garrett observed the bizarre, unfolding drama below as they flew over the hamlet of Spitzbergen and turned the plane northward to rendezvous with the coordinates of the northern polar opening that Byrd had provided in the packet sent to Ollie some years ago. What would happen when they reached the prescribed co-ordinates was still an exercise in faith

Watching the historic Tri-Motor fly over the ice flows where the Ritters and the guards were now stranded, Ollie and Sven recognized the absurdity of the outrageous events that they were witnessing. With difficulty containing their joy in seeing the pursuers bobbing up and down helplessly on the separating ice islands, they glanced over at one another and doubled up with laughter at the bizarre scene. Sven, with an unhurried gait, nonchalantly walked back into the hangar and telephoned the local naval base notifying them that some armed marauders had shot up his hangar and were stranded on an ice flow just outside his personal air strip.

Standing in the moment of realization with a grateful sense of relief and accomplishment, both men embraced one another and stared at the clear northern sky watching the dimming lights of the Fokker Tri-Motor disappear into the night.

Loki was safe. He avoided any gunfire and later came back to Sven, without the fake lance. It had served its purpose even beyond Sven's imagination when he created it. Ollie would refuel his Cessna, return it to the navy base, and begin his trek home to his wife and granddaughter. What a story he would have to tell!

His heart ached as he whispered a goodbye and paused to send a silent blessing to his son and daughter-in-law he had come to cherish. It was a day comingling the highest joy with a deep sorrow.

Chapter 18

ARE WE THERE YET?

*T*he droning three-engine antique that Garrett and Gugga had trusted their well-being and safety to was so noisy that intimate conversation between them was very difficult. Both sojourners had to speak forcefully to be heard above the engine's reverberations. An added problem with cockpit communication was the need to wear sound-muting ear muffs. Nonetheless, both were relieved that they were free from their pursuers, somehow having avoided a potential fate of almost certain death.

As Garrett paid close attention to his piloting and navigation, Gugga was studying over a map of the region that Sven had provided them displaying the appropriate headings and coordinates for the flight.

Somewhat startled by the markings on the map, she pulled off her sound muffs and shouted to Garrett, "Garrett, we are going to be entering a U.S military no-fly zone very soon. It says on the map that anyone in this area will be shot down. What do you think that means? Are we going to be a potential target for the United States Air Force?"

"I hope not," he shouted back to his worried passenger. "Perhaps they won't pick up this old relic or will not view us as a threat. Just in case, let's get the runic triangle and the activator stone ready."

Gugga, acknowledging his suggestion, reached into her storage bag that contained the runes and glanced once again at her old drawings of the magic triangle. She fashioned the runic arrangement in the palm of her hand, mimicking how the vault was opened in the Crypt. Meanwhile Garrett struggled in his makeshift flight suit and searched his pockets until he felt the presence of the stone with his fingers. Clasping it in his hand he pulled it out and stared at the now familiar pebble.

"I guess this is the moment of truth, isn't it?" he spoke forcefully while gazing into the eyes of his courageous spouse, feeling the stone's unique texture for the last time before passing it over to her waiting hands.

"I was told to anticipate the activation of the pebble and be prepared to observe it pulsating, which will tell us when we are about to enter the vortex of the inner earth. Go ahead and place it in the center of the Runic Triangle and let's see what happens."

Gugga anxiously placed the *curious little pebble* at the appropriate position in the center of the Triangle and stared at the objects, poised for something magical to happen.

"It's not working," she shouted in an uneasy voice.

"Well, we still have a few minutes to go before we reach the coordinates," Garrett assured her.

The minutes dragged on in what seemed like an eternity to the young couple. They felt suspended in air, the only orchestration being of struggling engines in the background, without any sense of actual movement.

Their silent anxiety was suddenly shattered by the crackling sound of the aircraft's ancient radio, still operable after all these years. "This is U.S Air Force Pachyderm One, Major Tomas J. Hecker. You have entered restricted air space and are directed to turn around immediately!"

The voice was ominous and very earnest. Garrett was frozen, facing a dilemma that he could not ignore. He knew that a disciplined air force pilot would follow the necessary protocol if he did not get a response. As Garrett pondered his next move, he noted that they had reached the position shown on the map coordinates.

Almost immediately he heard Gugga scream, "The stone is pulsating! The stone is pulsating!"

The U.S. jet fighter, a Phantom F4, accompanied by a similar companion jet, cruised easily aside the lumbering Fokker as once again the pilot issued his dire warning.

"If you do not turn around immediately you will be shot down. This is your final warning."

With that direct command, the pilot banked hard to starboard and circled into position to open fire. Garrett did not know what to do. The pulsating stone took on an eerie glow, but they still had no confirmation from anyone or anywhere as to the next step. Garrett watched in horror as the two F4's circled into an attack formation, knowing that the pilot meant business and that their lives were in immediate peril.

"Are you guys crazy?" the pilot shouted disbelievingly over the radio. "I'm making my final approach. Turn back NOW!"

Garrett continued to not respond, mostly out of indecision, but also focusing his gaze on the pulsating stone waiting for some mysterious miracle to occur.

Major Hecker moved into his attack position, assuming he had no choice. The old aircraft was deliberately ignoring his directions. Reluctantly he targeted the Fokker with an air-to-air missile and paused until he could wait no longer. He fired his missile.

A substantial explosion appeared before the two air force pilots and they assumed the old plane was blown out of the sky. However, what appeared before them at the same instant was a distinctively different type of craft, a craft that they had never seen before.

Darting before them, displaying unheard of speed and maneuverability, was a saucer-shaped craft occupying the airspace of the vintage bi-plane they had just destroyed. The two pilots veered sharply away from the direction of the explosion and circled to regroup.

"What the hell was that?" Major Hecker shouted excitedly into his intercom to his companion who had also broken formation to avoid the strange craft.

"I don't know, Tom. Let's get out of here. I don't want to engage that thing."

"Roger on that. Returning to base," he declared. "What are we going to say in our briefing report? Who's going to believe us? They'll think we're nuts!"

"I think we report that we destroyed the target as ordered and that we encountered a foreign craft with which we chose to avoid engagement. All I know is, whatever it was, it was beyond our combat capabilities. I'll buy you a drink when we get back. I think we both can use one."

"Roger on that. Make mine a double!"

****

Garrett and Gugga were jolted into a new reality as they found themselves somehow attached to the alien craft and being guided towards the earth's opening. It seemed they had crossed a dimensional barrier into a calming white zone. The engines of the Tri-motor continued to hum.

"Are we dead?" Gugga whispered in a bewildered voice.

Glancing upward they witnessed an unbelievable sight. They were attached to a whirling circular aircraft by a tunnel of light which acted as a tractor beam that held and guided them towards the surface. It had complete control of their plane. The alien craft maneuvered to a position wherein the pilot was clearly visible. The pilot displayed a wide grin and waved to the young visitors. Garrett's jaw dropped as he suddenly realized that the alien pilot was intimately familiar.

"My God," he shouted out . . . "It's Jared! It's Jared! . . . Gugga, it's my brother Jared. It's him! He's alive! He's alive!"

The next thing they experienced was a sense of dropping slowly through what appeared to be an unseen elevator shaft until reaching the apparent entrance to a hollow earth civilization below. Their descent brought them into the view of a landscape much like the temperate regions of the outer globe, yet with an unusual muted glow to the scene. They could make out beings on the surface as they were gently landed by the circular aircraft and detached from the mysterious beam of light. As their hearts pounded they were approached and greeted by a host of individuals. They were reassured to see that their welcoming committee strongly resembled the general appearance and affable manner of their friend, Sven.

"We are gratified that you reached us safely," said the first alien. "We have been expecting you."

The bewildered couple stood dumbfounded and speechless. All they could muster was a weak "thank you" in response to such a welcoming. Garrett was absolutely perplexed over seeing his brother once again.

They hugged one another, Garrett still in disbelief at the whole scenario.

Jared, still grasping his younger brother, gushed, "You have a lot to learn my young brother, and I will be here to teach and guide you. Welcome to a new world!"

Most of the inner earth dwellers greeting them had human form, yet were taller and generally thinner than surface dwellers, with long limbs, ocean blue eyes and wide dolphin-like smiles. As Garrett and Gugga disembarked from their still intact airplane, they were led through a glimmering city pulsating with rainbow hues of color. It felt as if they had descended into paradise.

Garrett and Gugga were offered a delicious cool beverage which they readily accepted. They were led down a long corridor of a gleaming white building lit by rose colored hues that seemed to be emanating from within the walls. One of the beings motioned for them to stop before a great door. The door slid quietly open and they were beckoned inside by a kind, rich voice.

"I bid you welcome to our domain."

The two travelers stepped closer to the welcoming being. He was a large Nordic male who seemed to have a vague familiarity to Garrett. His features were prominent with the etching of years dominating his face.

"Garrett, do you remember long ago when I delivered you to my craft and gave you guidance for the future and I told you we would meet again?"? I see that you heeded my advice and have made the proper choice between the relative values of good and evil. And you have returned to us the Holy Lance which holds the power to bring peace to the surface world. Now you are ready for more lessons before we return you to your world with the power to implement such peace. By doing so, you can help us preserve both worlds, yours on the surface, and ours in the interior. We welcome you to Asgarth, the Citadel of the Inner Kingdom."

Garrett and Gugga stood awestruck in the gravity of the moment. Of course Garrett recognized the master in front of him. It was Thal, the being he encountered after he was drawn up on what Garrett now concluded to be a cosmic elevator from the hospital ward after the Viet Nam war protest in 1968. It must have been a similar device that captured their airplane and brought it to the center of the earth. He bowed his head to Thal, paying homage to the majesty of the moment.

Thal went on to explain that they, like Admiral Byrd, were summoned to the Inner Earth for a purpose. They were commissioned to bring a message and lesson of peace, respect, and humility to the surface world. They would become ambassadors of the Truth. According to Thal, they would remain here in the inner world until they were trained to become powerful emissaries.

The Ritters would be informed that the Lance had a new master. Their families would be notified that they and Jared were safe by an Arianni telepathic message and that their safety would be heralded by the appearance of the Holy Lance.

Chapter 19

A HARBINGER OF HOPE

Berkeley, California

*I*n Berkeley, California, several years after the disappearance of
Garrett and Gugga – thought by most to have perished in an
improbable venture towards the North Pole – Ollie, Jackie, and Thora
had gone on with their lives. They remained stoic in the face of the
seeming loss of their loved ones knowing that Garrett and Gugga
were safe and, one day would return to them.

It was early spring. Thora sat on the amply covered front porch of
Ollie's and Jackie's home on a peaceful tree-lined street in Berkeley,
California. She had made her home with her grandparents. Spread
in front of her on a mosaic inlaid table, Thora was having unique
conversations with her ample collection of gems and rocks, her most
treasured piece among the glittering stones was the curious little
pebble given to her by her grandfather after his return from his Arctic
adventure. She cherished it as a memorial stone in remembrance of
her father and mother. She often held vigil like this in front of the
house in patient anticipation of the return of her beloved parents.

Thora had matured greatly as she grew older. Her young age belied
her intuitive and classical knowledge as she had immersed herself into
the study of subjects that stimulated her gift of her understanding of
the many spiritual dimensions. At nearly eighteen, she had blossomed
into a physical beauty resembling her mother and reflecting the inner

strength, courage and inquisitiveness of her father. She looked forward to the day when they would be reunited and share their mutual destiny as peace ambassadors for a new earth.

As the sun crossed the horizon of the spring sky and the shadows from the numerous oak and birch trees that lined the streets began to shade the bright sunlight, a reminiscent postal truck rumbled down the street. It did not make any stops until it pulled up in front of the Hill residence. The driver exited the truck with a package in his hand and proceeded to the porch where Thora was sitting.

The man had an odd gait to his walk and was not dressed in a normal postal uniform. Instead, he was attired in a dark black suit with a matching black fedora and dark sunglasses. He approached the porch and looked at Thora directly, taking off his sunglasses to reveal his strange cat-like eyes with their vertical pupils as he smiled a sardonic smile.

He addressed her in a halting, deep voice and said, "I have a package for a Miss Thora Garrettsdottir Hill."

Thora smiled knowingly at the strange man, recalling the description that her grandfather had relayed to her when he received the mysterious package from Admiral Byrd many years ago. She was not alarmed by his demeanor or appearance, but was bemused by the odd antics of the black-clad messenger.

"I am Thora," she replied, as she nodded her head appreciatively to the man.

The MIB produced an artificial smile in reply, looked at her intensely and finally concluded, "Of course you are. This is a special delivery for you. Handle it with care please."

As he departed and returned to his truck, Thora knew intuitively what the package would contain. She had been anticipating it for some time. She hastily went inside, abandoning her precious stone collection for just a moment, to alert Ollie and Jackie. The two, now retired, set aside their activities as they hugged Thora and bade her to open the package. With deliberate motions, Thora unwrapped the silk covering that she recognized from her mother's collections and carefully placed it to her lips and nose while inhaling the fragrance of her mother's signature perfume.

The velvet wrapping inside covered the metal relic and protected the Holy Lance with its delicate softness and reverence. There was no note, but one wasn't needed. In the same delivery, wrapped in a silver linen cloth was a set of metal military dog tags. The name and number on the tags was, *Jared Pendergast Hill, Lt; AF19468411.* Jackie quickly snatched up the tags and held them to her heart.

"Is it true? Do I have both of my sons again?" she cried through her halting and stammering. "Jared is with Garrett? My prayers have been answered!"

The family gasped as one, knowing instantly the significance of the moment as tears of joy readily flowed freely from each. It was the confirmation from Garrett and Gugga for which they had all been waiting for such a long time. And Jared was alive!

Thora reverently brought the package to her room and proceeded to mount the Lance on her wall of memorabilia in a hallowed area that she had previously prepared and reserved. She stared deeply at her new heirloom for a moment, recalling and vicariously living the adventure that brought it to her. Her knowing and smiling face reflected the wonder of the moment. After the impromptu ceremony, she walked alone back to the front porch just in time to join her parents to witness the sun dropping behind the trees. Her sparkling and contented blue eyes gazed upward, reflecting a deep understanding beyond her youthful years. As she fixed her gaze upon the rapidly disappearing sun, she pondered a life-long promise she had made to herself – a promise that her life's purpose would, from this day forward, radiate a new meaning.

Appendix I

HOLDERS OF THE HOLY LANCE IN HISTORY

1. The first was **Longinus** who on Friday, April 5th, 33 AD pierced the side of Jesus with the spear to confirm his death. Longinus received the spear from his antecedents and it was passed along through his descendants. The legend of the lance has persisted for over 2000 years.

2. The importance of the Lance was reaffirmed in 286 AD when it was in the possession of **St. Maurice**, also known as **Mauritius.** He was a direct descendant of Longinus as the spear passed from generation to generation. He carried the spear not as a weapon, but as a symbol of his faith. Mauritius became commander of the Theban Legion sent to crush a revolt in Switzerland. When he found out that the enemies were Christians, he refused. The Emperor instructed him to destroy the Lance, denounce Christianity and embrace the Roman gods. The Emperor Maximian told them that one of 10 would be beheaded if the edict was not obeyed. The first was Mauritius, holding the lance above his head. After that, one in ten were decapitated. The rest stepped forward and 6666 legionnaires volunteered to be beheaded. Every man met a martyr's death.

3. Although **Maximian** was a bitter enemy of the Christians, he along with co-emperor **Diocletion**, ordered the burning of the scriptures but could not carry out his own order to destroy the Lance. He carried it away believing that it was indeed the spear of gods who had brought about the voluntary deaths of the over 6000 legionnaires.

4. In 308 AD, Fausta, daughter of Maximian, married **Emperor Constantine the Great** (280-337) in 313 AD. The Lance was given to Constantine as a wedding present. Constantine initiated the evolution of the Roman Empire as a Christian state.

5. With some improbability, history shows the Holy Lance next appeared in the hands of **Atilla the Hun.** The Lance was relinquished by Roman emperor **Theodosius II** in exchange for not sacking Constantinople. Atilla was invincible before receiving the Lance but began to collapse and afterwards, in frustration, he galloped his horse to the gates of Rome and hurled the Lance at the feet of officers who had been sent out to surrender the city. Thus, the Lance saved the city because Atilla did not understand the use of its power.

6. The spear then passed through a series of Roman Emperors without attracting much attention. It then appeared in Gaul in the possession of Frankish general, **Charles Martel (Charles the Hammer),** when he defeated invaders that saved Christian France from the forces of Islam. The year was 732 AD.

7. The Holy Lance then passed into the hands of **Charlemagne the Great** (742-814 AD) who used it as a force of unification in consolidating nearly all Christian lands of Western Europe. He carried the Lance during 47 successful campaigns, never slept without it, and believed it was the source of his clairvoyance.

8. In due time the Lance came into the possession of **Heinrich I, Duke of Saxony and King of Germany** (876 – 936). Heinrich (also known as Henry the Fowler) used the Lance to bring a nine year truce with the Magyars of Hungary.

9. At some point in his reign, Henry is believed to have presented the Lance to the **English King, Athelstan.** Athelstan wrote six codes of law designed to suppress theft and corruption, mitigate punishment of young offenders and provide comfort for the destitute. Athelstan returned the Lance to Germany when his sister, Eadgita (Edith) married **Otto the Great,** son of Henry. The Lance was part of her dowry.

10. **Otto the Great (912-973)** German king and Holy Roman Emperor, carried the spear during the consolidation of the First Reich (empire). He solidified relations between the Eastern and Western empires by marrying his son, Otto II to the Byzantine princess, Theophano. **Otto II (955- 983)** inherited the Lance from his father and passed it on to his son, **Otto III (980 – 1002).**

11. After being crowned King of Germany, Otto III managed to have his cousin elected as Gregory V, the first German Pope. Gregory, in turn, appointed **Otto III as emperor of the Holy Roman Empire in 996 AD.** Otto III proceeded to make Rome his headquarters and planned to recreate the glory of the Caesars. He regarded himself as the leader of world Christianity. During his reign, a nail from the cross was inserted into the holy spear. The metal was weakened and a fracture occurred. The two parts were fitted with an iron clamp designed to hold them together. (The imitation Lance of Krakow was also created at about this time).

12. **Henry II, the Saint (973 – 1024)** seized the land and the insignia of the German Kings and Holy Roman Emperors on the occasion of the death of Otto III. By this time the insignia included a crown, globe, scepter, sword, cross, gauntlet, and other symbolic items.

13. The Lance was then passed on to **Henry III (1017 - 1056)** who in turn left it to his son, **Henry IV (1050 – 1106).** Henry IV had the lance fitted with a silver sleeve bearing a Latin inscription. A golden sleeve was added at a later date *(the silver was replaced with gold during the reign of Charles IV of Bohemia (1316 – 1378).* Both attachments bore the Latin words "Clavus Dominicus," (the nail of our Lord).

14. One of the more interesting chapters of this history took place after the Lance came into the possession of **Frederick I Barbarossa (Redbeard) in 1123 – 1190).** He was the King of Germany and Holy Roman Emperor. Barbarossa was the son of Frederick, Duke of Swabia, of the House of Hohenstaufen. His long career was closely entwined with that of *Duke Henry the Lion of Saxony*. Frederick became a legendary hero and a symbol of unity to the German people. In the spring of 1189, Frederick answered the call to the Third Crusade to free Jerusalem from occupation by Saladin's army and to recover the "true cross." He formed, along with *Duke of Swabia and Duke Leopold of Austria (1159 – 1194),* the largest Crusade army to that date and set out for the Holy Lands by an overland route. **Barbarossa** carried the Holy Lance as his emblem of faith and Christian dedication. The Lance failed to protect him as he drowned (1190) while trying to cross the Saleph River in what is now Turkey. Under the other two Dukes, they reached Palestine which returned the Lance back to its original point – over 1000 years later.

15. After the siege and capture of the city of Acre in 1191, **Leopold** quarreled with the powerful *King Richard of England* and decided that the Lance should be hidden in some secret place. In that year, a secret organization of crusaders formed the Teutonic Knights, or *Knights of the Teutonic Order*. Leopold placed the Lance in their custody. Richard of England forced Leopold to quit the Crusade and come home.

16. The Teutonic Knights assumed a military character in 1198 under their grand master, **Hermann von Salza (1210 – 1239).** The Lance went with them and served as their banner of faith during the conquest and Christianization of Prussia. During the reign of **Frederick the II (1194 – 1250),** *grandson of Frederick Barbarrosa*, the *Mongols* threatened Europe from the East under the successors of *Genghis Khan*. The Teutonic Knights felt that the Lance would be safer if removed to western Germany. They returned it along with other sacred artifacts of the Holy Roman Empire.

17. *Nothing very dramatic appeared in the history of the Lance for the next 550 years.* By 1806, Napoleon had overrun most of Europe and *brought the first Reich to an end*, after it had endured for over 1000 years. He dissolved the order of the Teutonic Knights, but did not fall heir to the insignia of the German Kings and Holy Roman Emperors. The Lance and its companion pieces were hidden in an ancient tunnel beneath the ramparts of Nuremburg Castle. However, there was still concern that the treasure might be found by Napoleon, and so it was sent to *Vienna, Austria* for safe keeping.

18. The Lance was received by **Francis II**, who had been forced to abdicate as *the last of the Holy Roman Emperors*, but was still **Emperor of Austria**. Thus it was passed into possession of the lords of the House of Hapsburg and placed in the treasure room of the ancestral palace, The Hofburg, in Vienna. After Napoleon lost power in 1814, German authorities requested that the treasure be returned. They met with considerable resistance, although the Austrian Empire did reinstitute the order of the Teutonic Knights in 1834. In Vienna, the Lance rested after its long journey through the first Reich.

19. More to this journey. By 1795 the shaft of the Lance was detached and left behind. The shaft was later transferred to the Vatican where it can presently be viewed.

20. Adolf Hitler first encountered the Lance of Longinus in 1907. It was his source of mystic inspiration for the rest of his life. It passed from his hands in 1945 and was secreted in an ice cave in Deutsche Antarctica. It was subsequently brought back to Germany by a contingent of Teutonic Knights in 1978 and is held in a secret location by the Order of the Teutonic Knights.[1]

I AM THE POWER

The name of my angel is Gabriel, whose name means the power of God. When you call on Me in the name of my Son nothing is impossible. I will send my angel to you and with his help you will rise above all others for good, but he will slay you for evil. I am the power, I am the power, I am the power. There is no power in the Lance, except through Me. I am from all ages, from all times, from all places and to all men. There is no god before Me. I am the power.

The Secret of the Lance[2]

1. Adolf Hitler and the Secrets of the Holy Lance, Bernhart, Wilhelm. Thunderbird Press Inc., Metairie, Louisiana USA. 1988 pp. 49-60.

2. Ibid.